the

Sisters We Were

A NOVEL

WENDY WILLIS BALDWIN

sourcebooks
landmark

Published by Sourcebooks Landmark, an imprint of Sourcebooks
P.O. Box 4410, Naperville, Illinois 60567-4410
(630) 961-3900
sourcebooks.com

Library of Congress Cataloging-in-Publication Data

Names: Willis Baldwin, Wendy, author.
Title: The sisters we were : a novel / Wendy Willis Baldwin.
Description: Naperville, Illinois : Sourcebooks Landmark, [2023]
Identifiers: LCCN 2022027848 (print) | LCCN 2022027849
(ebook) | (trade paperback) | (epub)
Subjects: LCGFT: Domestic fiction. | Novels.
Classification: LCC PS3623.I57749 S57 2023 (print) | LCC PS3623.I57749
(ebook) | DDC 813/.6--dc23/eng/20220613
LC record available at https://lccn.loc.gov/2022027848
LC ebook record available at https://lccn.loc.gov/2022027849

Printed and bound in the United States of America.
VP 10 9 8 7 6 5 4 3 2 1

This story is dedicated to Tiffany Anne Willis and her truly remarkable triumph over our shared childhood trauma

"'Help one another' is part of the religion of sisterhood."

Louisa May Alcott

Author's Note

What you're about to read is a work of fiction, inspired by some actual events and circumstances. At its root, this is a story about sisterhood and the way our most intimate relationships expand and contract in direct relationship to the secrets we keep. For too many years, my own sister and I kept dark family secrets hidden from each other and the rest of the world. But childhood trauma and shame have a sneaky way of surfacing in our lives, in our relationships, and yes, even in our bodies. Just like the two sisters in this story, my own sister and I had very different, yet often equally destructive, coping strategies for what we endured growing up. It has taken many years to arrive at a place where I could write with the benefit of so much hindsight and create authentic, flawed characters (much like ourselves) who manage to evolve, one step forward and two steps back, well into adulthood.

At her heaviest, my younger sister, Tiffany, weighed 531

pounds. I chose this same weight for my protagonist, Pearl Crenshaw, because I could easily use my own sister's real-life, astonishing 349-pound weight loss as an authentic point of reference. I also chose this because, despite the global obesity epidemic (which is rooted in everything from depression and disordered eating to insulin resistance, high-fructose corn syrup, systemic racism, poverty, processed foods, institutionally driven reductions in physical activity, and genetics), most people can't even begin to comprehend what it would be like to weigh that much: the implications of it—practical, logistical, professional, physical, and personal. Although I've never struggled with obesity, I have loved my little sister ever since we were still small enough to fit in the same bathtub and make long beards out of bubbles.

Prologue

Even with training wheels, Pearl Crenshaw fears she might, at any moment, fall over smack-dab in the middle of Cherry Lane. Still slick from an overnight storm and splattered with squishy earthworms, this seemingly never-ending steep stretch of asphalt offers the predictably rude awakening Pearl dreads. But today she simply has no choice in the matter; this is the only way she'll get to school before the bell rings. So, as best she can, she pushes on, dodging wigglers left and right. One labored breath at a time, she marvels at the sheer number of them, each totally blind to the dangers of their own little West Austin ecosystem. The mass tire tread carnage is everywhere, and Pearl wonders why they don't seem to know better than to get stranded this way in the middle of the road.

The uphill climb to the top of the block feels like it's happening in slow motion, each pedal stroke requiring more effort than the last. Lumbering past one lawn at a time, Pearl tries not to huff and puff as much as she tries to ignore the approaching chorus of bike chains. Zipping by on both sides, the other neighborhood kids pass her, like always, their legs pumping in two-wheeled, out-of-the-saddle smugness. Just like the worms, out here on the street like this, it's survival of the fittest.

Up ahead at the intersection of Exposition Boulevard her big sister, Ruby, dutifully waits, shrouded in morning mist, for Pearl to make it up and over the big hump on this leg of their mile and a quarter journey. From a blanket of bluebonnets at the corner, Ruby's already straddling her bike, not even winded, looking down at the rest of them. Ruby is the fastest fourth grader this side of Town Lake, and this fact alone makes Pearl sometimes wonder if maybe, just maybe, she was adopted.

"Come on, Pearl," Ruby megaphones, cupping her hands to her mouth. "You can do it!"

Pearl does not share her sister's certainty, speed, or enthusiasm for all this pedal pushing. Frankly, Pearl prefers the carpool.

But on this sticky spring morning, the air-conditioned back seat of their mother's navy-blue Suburban is not an option. Well before Ruby and Pearl even rolled out of their matching four-poster beds, Birdie Crenshaw was already up, out, and off to cater yet another working breakfast at Dell Computers. As much as Pearl wished her mom had been available to give them a ride, on days like these, there was some consolation in the form of the all-you-can-eat breakfast buffet Birdie left waiting for them on the bar in the kitchen. Treating her girls and their father, Teddy, to surplus fresh-squeezed orange juice, homemade frittatas, and baked banana muffins, still warm and buttery, was Birdie's way of nesting—especially when duty called. If she couldn't be there in person to feed her family, she made sure they had plenty of her fancy catering creations to savor and sample—one of which is secretly tucked into the New Kids on the Block lunch box dangling from Pearl's handlebars.

As she tugs on one of the too-tight straps of her too-small, hand-me-down denim overalls, Pearl thinks about the extra muffin she packed—imagines how later in the cafeteria, she'll stress the importance of it. How this very muffin was made especially for Michael Dell himself. And by any measure of second-grade deductive reasoning, in a school filled with nothing but Dell computers, this fact alone makes Pearl practically famous.

"Last one there's a rotten egg!" Autry Atwood yells, zigzagging his way through some of the more prepubescent peloton. A social climber from birth, he's always the one to declare their collective morning commute to the front steps of Casis Elementary a competition. And Pearl knows all too well that losing this hilly, high-stakes race to school would be flat-out embarrassing.

She's certain Ruby knows this, too—not from personal experience but vicariously. Ruby has seen this all play out before; Pearl, still using training wheels even though she's nearly eight, not because she can't balance on two wheels but because Autry Atwood once said "pudgy Pearl" would probably pop the tires if she didn't have all four to support her weight. So far, Pearl does not feel comfortable testing his theory. In Pearl's estimation, the only thing more humiliating than still using training wheels in second grade would be causing flat tires on your Schwinn on account of how fat you are.

Seeing her struggling sister, Ruby coasts back down the block, past a blur of leftover Ann Richards for governor yard signs, and pedals alongside Pearl.

"You can't look down," Ruby says, coaching. "You have to keep your eyes up. If you keep your eyes up, you only see where you're going instead of where you are."

"Not true," Pearl says, trying hard to keep pushing ahead. "If I look up, I see that I'm dead last."

Ruby shakes her head in frustration and scans the street, sizing up their competition. It's not that Pearl wants to be the rotten egg, but considering how many times she's earned this distinction before, she's just more or less used to it. Ruby's efforts to reason with her simply don't square with what Pearl has already learned in her young life—that nobody even expects someone like her to be one of the fastest kids on the block. And back at home, Pearl has a drawer full of green participation ribbons to prove it. Even so, something about her sister riding beside her does give Pearl a boost so, for the sake of Ruby's blue-ribbon pride, she tries to pick up the pace. But suddenly, Ruby drops back behind her, bringing up the rear.

"Where are you going?" Pearl mutters, trying to conserve what little energy she has.

"Pearl, whatever you do, don't look back now!"

"What? Why?"

"Remember the chupacabra we saw on Discovery Channel?"

Upon hearing the word *chupacabra*, Pearl does not dare look back. Instead, she readily calls to mind the hairless, hideous, bloodsucking creature purported to roam the Texas hill country. Everyone knows about the chupacabra, and the very last thing Pearl wants to see up close and personal is a chupacabra.

"Pedal like your ass is on fire, Pearl," Ruby says, insisting. "Goooo!"

Pearl's heart practically skips a beat. Hearing her sister use such forbidden profanity can only mean they are in extreme and very imminent danger. She musters all her might to spin her chubby little legs as a sly grin emerges on Ruby's face.

"Pearl, I see three of 'em running through the Mayfields' front yard," Ruby adds, gauging her sister's improved pace. "Hurry! They're gaining on us!"

As if the Discovery Channel's Shark Week hadn't already scarred her enough, now she had to worry about some four-legged land mammal whose name she could hardly pronounce as yet another existential threat to her very survival.

"That's it, Pearl! Keep going. The chupacabras are on our tails, and if we don't move fast, they're gonna suck our blood right here and now!"

If she lets that happen, Pearl knows good and well Ruby will probably kill her, so she powers on while Ruby incessantly presses her high-pitched bike bell to sound the alarm, cattle prodding her sister in a frantic frenzy toward the top of their block. Pearl lets out a shriek, which distracts some of the other kids, causing all but a couple to look back. Their confusion about the look of sheer terror on Pearl's now rapidly approaching face, causes many of them to lag, parting the way for Ruby and Pearl.

Together, they accelerate, Ruby flanking her younger sister, still goading Pearl to make it to the top where, presumably, these vicious animals won't dare venture into oncoming traffic.

"Faster, Pearl, faster! We slow down, we die. Do you hear me?"

The sight of Ruby and Pearl Crenshaw moving at the same clip, the actual same high rate of speed, takes the other kids by surprise. Together, the girls use this distraction to their advantage, astonishing even themselves with their rapid ascent. Neck and neck they cross just beyond the swath of bluebonnets along the corner of Exposition.

At the crest, where the road begins to flatten, Pearl is finally able to catch her breath. Only then, as they turn, does she dare to look back. Much to her surprise, she is not the rotten egg, and the only wild beasts trying to catch her are the Autry Atwoods of the world—the kind her mom says are all bark and no bite.

As she and Ruby wait for the signal change, Pearl wipes the sweat from her forehead with the back of her hand, savoring the view from the top of the block.

"See," Ruby says, leaning over the handlebars for a high five. "You did it."

Although they have not yet beaten the first tardy bell, in this fleeting moment, Pearl relishes her rare victory. Ultimately, her harrowing uphill haul may have been little more than a fat girl's race to save face, but Pearl Crenshaw had managed to triumph over adversity, real or imagined, training wheels and all. Even if her sister is full of shit, at least she's always on her side. And for Pearl, that's a way bigger win.

"Come on," Ruby says, nodding at the light. "We gotta go."

Together, she and Ruby pedal tandem into the lifting fog, off toward school.

Once again, Pearl is doing her best to keep up.

"You lied about the chupacabra," Pearl shouts. It's the closest she gets to thanking her.

"You're welcome," Ruby yells over her shoulder. "Don't you get it, Pearl? If you're scared enough, you can do anything."

PART ONE

Heaviness

Chapter 1

Numbers don't lie. Of this much, Pearl Crenshaw is certain. The scale's red digital display is now seared into her memory, along with so many other disappointments. She tries blinking the digits away, but what has been seen cannot be unseen. Slowly, as she lumbers self-consciously toward the exit, her battered black rubber flip-flops slapping against her calloused heels, Pearl almost can't bear the shame she feels.

Despite it being January, she wore these shoes to her surgical consultation to avoid the struggle of trying to bend over and take them off. Now outside, in the chilly central Texas air, she admits the truth: only fat people wear flip-flops in forty-two-degree weather.

Just shy of her Altima, she tries looking down at her feet, but she can no longer see them when she's standing. Shaking her head in disgust, Pearl unlocks the door and glances around, hoping no one is watching, before she awkwardly maneuvers all 531 pounds of herself into the driver's seat. It's not until she's tugged the door shut and wrestled into her seat belt that she allows herself to cry.

Through watery eyes, she stares up at the sign on the glass doors: Austin Weight Loss Specialists. She lets the block letters blur along with the humiliation of the entire appointment. Pearl tries recalling the last time she actually stepped on a scale, let alone looked at the numbers. There was that unpleasant visit to the gynecologist a few years ago; it was her twenty-sixth birthday, a day she spent trying to forget about her doctor's cautionary concerns for her escalating BMI. She recalls how vulnerable she felt with her feet in those exam stirrups, wearing a one-size-fits-all gown that, even back then, only covered half of her torso. The thought of it makes Pearl shift a little in her creaking bucket seat. At that appointment, the scale in the clinic only went up to 350.

"We'll just have to make an educated guess." She remembers the short, plump nurse saying those words, remembers her sympathetic winking, how politely she refrained from stating the obvious—that if you're over the maximum reading on a scale made for humans, you're definitely way overweight. But even if she had been a little more than 350 then, how, in just three years, had she ballooned all the way up to 531 pounds?

The vibrating buzz of her cell phone prevents her from answering this question. Pearl rummages through the deep, cavernous innards of her handbag, sifting through a couple months' worth of wadded-up receipts and crinkled straw wrappers until she finds it, recognizes the all-too-familiar 254 area code from Gatesville, Texas.

"Hello," Pearl says, wiping her tears with the back of her hand, waiting for the recording.

"This is a call from inmate Elizabeth Crenshaw Benzer at the Mountain View Prison Unit. Press one to accept."

Every time her mother is referred to as anything but Birdie, Pearl bristles at the formality of hearing her full, legal name. Yet dutifully, just as she's done for the past twelve years, she hits the number 1 on the keypad.

"Mom? Can you hear me?"

"How's my Pearl? I'm dyin' to hear what all the weight loss doctor had to say."

Although it comes from inside an all-female prison, the sound of her mother's voice provides Pearl with a small morsel of normalcy—proof that anything (including obesity and incarceration) can become ordinary if you live with it long enough, and her mother's raspy twang is as comforting to Pearl as the seclusion of her car.

"First of all, he's not a weight loss doctor. He's a bariatric surgeon. But he says the same thing every other doctor has ever told me—if I don't lose a substantial amount of weight soon, I may not live to see forty."

Pearl swallows the emerging lump in her throat. She knows better than to waste their timed calls on tears.

"Anyway, he says I'm a good candidate for the sleeve surgery."

"Oh, honey, it's times like this I hate being in here the most."

The comment guts Pearl and makes her wish they really could time travel their way back to 1994 or some other alternate reality where she doesn't actually weigh a quarter ton and her mom isn't serving a twenty-year prison sentence for manslaughter.

"You know, I've been reading up on those brochures you sent about the various procedures. They tell you everything you need to know except the actual price tag. So how much are we talking about for the sleeve?"

"Fourteen thousand," Pearl says. Again, the numbers start to add up. One-fourth of her annual salary is what it will take to even begin to tip the scales back in her favor. "It's like being disqualified before the game even starts," she adds, defeated. "And even if I could afford it, I just don't think I can do it, Mom."

"Oh, honey…"

Pearl's tears turn into sobs. She can't help it. None of this is what she expected, and all the numbers swirl in her head, quantifying the colossal fucked-up-ness of her whole life: Twenty-nine years old, five foot ten, 531 pounds, a body mass index of 79.18. A normal BMI for a person her age and height is 26. Dr. George had referenced these off-the-charts figures to make a convincing scientific argument for her perilous descent toward, among other things, diabetes, heart disease, stroke, joint problems, at least seven different types of cancer, and, sadly, depression. On balance, spending fourteen thousand dollars to save her own life seemed like an investment she should seriously consider. He told her she was worth it, and Pearl hated herself for the way she rolled her eyes when he said that. With his plastic anatomical model, he had walked her through the surgical procedure, lifting the normal size stomach up and off, revealing the smaller one he planned to create for Pearl. Sitting there in his office, with all the plastic parts spread out on the exam table, he made the whole process look as simple as a set of shrinking Russian dolls. But given the complexity of everything she will have to do before she can even secure a slot on his surgery schedule, Pearl can't help but feel like the odds are stacked against her. For her, everything, the cost of the surgery, the time away from work, the solo recovery, and most especially, such mammoth weight loss, seems totally out of reach. And why did Dr. George, the only man to ever see her at her worst, have to be so good-looking? It was yet another cruel reality she wished she didn't have to face.

"If you keep going like this, it will kill you."

Those were his exact words—a death sentence. In fact, if she continues to gain weight at this rate, he said she would likely be bedbound within another year or two. Pearl doesn't share this detail with her mother. Checking the time, she reaches for one of the used tissues crumpled in her purse and blows her nose. Time, it seems, is never going to be on Pearl's side: since 2005, when Birdie was initially incarcerated at Mountain View, their all-important mother-daughter talks have been crammed into closely monitored, fifteen-minute increments. She doesn't have time to waste.

"I'll figure it out," Pearl says, not really believing herself.

"Like I've said before, sell my old Rolex watches. Between those and both of my wedding rings, you'll have more than enough to pay for it. No sense hanging on to that stuff. Might as well put 'em to good use."

"If I sell off your valuables, what are you supposed to do for money when you get out? I mean besides the house, you won't have much of a cushion."

"Don't you worry about me. I still know how to cook. Besides, we'll deal with the future later on, but right now is here. Promise me you'll take this step. I one-hundred percent agree with what he said about you being worth it, Pearl. You deserve to be happy, and we both know you haven't been for a long time. So you listen to me—I want you to do whatever it takes to get healthy today. Tomorrow will take care of itself."

To Pearl, it all sounds so utterly implausible. Just as she can't see her feet when she's standing, she can't visualize a healthier, slimmer version of herself. In fact, it's hard for her to visualize anything but that god-awful number: 531.

"Have you talked to Ruby?" her mom asks. "Did you tell her you're considering this surgery?"

"Not yet." Pearl cringes. The notion of using her own personal health crisis as a reason for rekindling any kind of meaningful relationship with her older sister seems futile. Plus, it reeks of desperation, and Pearl has made it her life's mission to present herself as cheerful at all times—especially to Ruby. Besides, Ruby is probably too busy being actually healthy and happy to be bothered with painful reminders of their past.

"Keep reaching out. She'll come around."

Pearl rolls her eyes, doubting. There is nothing to suggest that Ruby will ever come around. And the fact that their mom maintains this false sense of hope sends Pearl back to the greasy Whataburger bag still open on the passenger seat of her car. Despite being cold, the French fries she willed herself not to eat before the appointment are still sickly satisfying. She sucks the salt off each one, considering more numbers: the 560 calories in a single serving of fries, the 195 miles between Austin and Dallas. But the distance between Pearl and Ruby can't be measured in miles.

"Mom, in twelve years, Ruby hasn't been to see you once, not at Christmas, not on Mother's Day, not once. And other than Facebook, since the day she moved into her dorm at SMU, I've only seen her about twelve times myself. And for the record, each of those times involved me getting in my car, driving up I-35 to be on her turf—not the other way around. I mean, it's not like she lives on the moon. She lives in Uptown. So the fact that we almost never see her sort of suggests Ruby just doesn't want to see us."

The one-minute warning beeps, reminding both of them their time together is almost up.

"Pearl, reach out to your sister. I raised you girls to stick together. Her pain didn't get turned into extra pounds the way yours did, but it's there just the same. At the end of the day, she's the only sister you've got and, besides me, your only blood. For all you know, Ruby probably needs you just as much as you need her. I'm sure she'd be delighted to offer some support."

Pearl licks the salt off her fingertips, wondering how many prisoners actually use the word *delighted* and how her mother can be so optimistic from behind bars in the first place.

"Ruby runs away from trouble, Mom. She's not exactly one to come finding it."

"Right, but, Pearl—"

But before her mom can finish her thought, their fifteen minutes are up.

In her mind, Pearl tries finishing Birdie's sentence, but she gets distracted by a man approaching the glass doors of the clinic. Like her, he's definitely a pre-op candidate, she guesses, and looks roughly her age. Even though he's wearing what she estimates is the largest cotton T-shirt money will buy, it's still not enough to cover the paunch protruding over his baggy black pants. But it's the aluminum tripod cane he's carrying that really gets her attention. So young yet so disabled. Joint problems, she figures. Maybe even diabetic neuropathy. Pearl guesses his weight, studies him top to bottom, flip-flops and all. As he makes his way inside, she considers walking over to his F-150, peeking through the window to see how many wadded-up fast-food bags he's collected on his floorboard.

But she really doesn't have to go looking to know.

Chapter 2

During the three days since her surgical consultation with Dr. George, Pearl has woken up, without setting an alarm, at exactly 5:31 a.m. On the first morning, she thought it was mere coincidence. On the second, it spooked her, prompting her to turn up the volume on the TV, a device she leaves on at all times for company. But when it happens again today, Pearl heaves herself up from her worn-out mattress and lets her feet find their footing on the rug beneath the bed before slowly rising. Moving 531 pounds of anything from a horizontal position to standing is no small feat, and the metal bolts in the bed frame grate with relief as the weight of Pearl is transferred from her remarkably resilient four-poster to the floor. By the time she makes her way to the bathroom, she checks the time on her phone again: 5:33. But she knows what she saw when her eyes opened: 5:31. It's a sign, she thinks. Surely, this is a sign. It's as though her internal biological clock has suddenly synched with the universe and there is simply no more time, no other number to see but 531— her sheer poundage the mother of all wake-up calls.

But even if her eyes hadn't popped open at exactly 5:31, yet again, the pinch of the broken porcelain toilet seat on her backside is a more undeniable sign of the state of Pearl's life. This is what she's thinking when she turns to flush. Standing there, examining the unsightly crack in the oval ring, she makes a mental note of the number of toilet seats she's had to replace since her mom went to prison. This is the fourth. Before she turns to face herself in the mirror, she vows it will be the last.

At the sink, she studies her complexion, noting the dark circles under her eyes. She looks every bit as sleep-deprived as she feels. But instead of starting her day with so much negative self-appraisal, Pearl leans into the mirror for closer inspection, searching for something, anything, positive. In spite of the bags, she gives silent thanks for her totally zit-free face. Growing up, unlike Ruby's, Pearl's face was never pocked with pimples. To this day, it's the one aesthetic asset between them where Pearl continues to have the upper hand. But as a geriatric case manager at Glenwood Manor, an assisted living center in East Austin, her income doesn't leave any room for spa facials, microneedling, or any of the other high-maintenance indulgences her sister's job affords.

As the senior brand manager for DALLUX, an online magazine catering to the upscale, upwardly mobile, uppity class of

Dallas society, Ruby's very job not only necessitates the sampling of injectables like Botox and fillers, it's actually considered a cost of doing business. Just two years older yet light-years apart, Ruby lives in a world where there are clear and infinitely debatable distinctions between things like collagen brands, thread counts, and fruit-scented seltzer waters. Hers is a special kind of Uptown utopia filled with twice-weekly appointments at blowout bars and valets who park all the cars.

As she stands there looking at her reflection, Pearl can't help but contrast. It's always been this way, the stark polarity between Ruby and Pearl Crenshaw—two sisters raised in the same nest, their mother, Birdie, now caged in the middle. Go figure, Pearl thinks, hating what she's become, hating the way her very fatness is the first thing she sees in the mirror. And she detests the way she takes up so much space as much as she deplores the very space she still occupies. After all these years, she's still living in her childhood home—like a hermit crab that refuses to leave its shell. Her bathroom, the Jack-and-Jill she once shared with Ruby, is a '90s throwback complete with never-been-updated hunter-green-and-white-striped wallpaper, the edges of which have long since started to peel away from the drywall, as if the paper itself is sick of being here, too.

From the bedroom, she can hear Chip and Joanna Gaines bantering about a remodel on some ranch-style home in Waco. *Fixer Upper* is Pearl's absolute favorite show. Five years ago, before it debuted, Pearl used to think that if she could be anyone else, she would be Ruby. But once she got hooked on Chip and JoJo, and especially since the Magnolia Market opened in 2015, Pearl no longer looks to Ruby as a role model. Instead, she's become fascinated, in truth fixated, on all things Joanna Gaines, even going so far as to grow out her thick brown hair and wear a dramatic center part to emulate her.

After she washes her hands, Pearl throws her long hair over one shoulder and subconsciously twists it into a side braid, like the one favored by her *Fixer Upper* fantasy icon. Impulsively, and perhaps partly fueled by the remodeling underway on TV, she tugs at an annoying piece of wallpaper, a piece that's been sticking out for way too long. With one swift yank, Pearl peels off a strip that reaches all the way to the ceiling, leaving a torn, glued edge, crudely exposed.

"You guys ready to see your fixer-upper?"

She hears the familiar question and moves toward the screen just in time to see Chip and Joanna Gaines pull back both sides of the giant barricade—the one that once concealed the diamond-in-the-rough home, the "before" disaster, which they've lovingly and efficiently renovated in record time. It's this, the big reveal, she lives for, the part where all the wishes come true and everyone is hugging and crying tears of joy at the miraculous transformation. It's so gratifying to watch even the most hideous of shitholes, the most run-down dumpiest of houses evolve into something beautiful. And this is when it really hits her: just like the old ranch-style house that now looks like a midcentury dream come true, Pearl is also a fixer-upper. With this bariatric surgery, she could be just like that big, sprawling house on TV, the one that's making this particular episode's homeowners, two Black professors from Baylor, burst out crying. As JoJo guides them through their fancy new kitchen, complete with farm sink and floating shelves, Pearl sees her reflection on the screen, notices the outline of the tented T-shirt stretched to maximum capacity, and the sight of her own form superimposed on that of Joanna Gaines brings tears of another kind. Just like the couple on TV, Pearl yearns for an improved, updated, reimagined version of life. Let the demo begin, she thinks.

In the kitchen, a room still drenched in wall-to-wall faux-finished mauve with the same stenciled green ivy her mom added circa 1992—before their father died—Pearl opens the fridge. Aside from a case of canned Diet Dr Pepper and a small, bright yellow box of Arm & Hammer baking soda, it's virtually empty. On the door, there is an assortment of leftover bottles of Hidden Valley ranch-style dressing, ketchup, pickles, and half-eaten jars of Cheez Whiz. Pearl doesn't cook. Never has. Most of her meals come from the drive-thru, and mostly, she eats in her car. She reaches for a Dr Pepper and shuts the door.

Above the island, a ceiling-mounted rack full of stainless-steel All-Clads hangs just overhead like a vintage prop, an ever-present reminder of Birdie's badass cooking and the boutique catering business she ran before the shooting. Pearl pops the top on her can and flips through the stack of brochures from

Dr. George's office. Going into the appointment, she knew bariatric surgery was expensive. This was verified by the protocols in the office, the way they whisked Pearl from the exam room to another less clinical but well-appointed consultation lounge. To Pearl, it looked like the waiting room of some day spa she couldn't afford—nice enough to further justify the hefty surgical price tag. It reminded her of her first trip to the orthodontist, back in the mid-1990s. Once the X-rays and exams were out of the way, a treatment-plan specialist sat Pearl and Birdie side by side on a love seat next to a giant aquarium. As the specialist droned on about spacers, retainers, and braces, the chubby, then bucktoothed, nine-year-old Pearl sat watching neon tetras and guppies shit out their fish food in long, black, skinny strings. At Dr. George's office, there was no aquarium. Instead, his lounge was equipped with wall-mounted flat-screens that showed animated depictions of flesh-toned stomachs being laparoscopically sliced and stapled. It wasn't fish poop, but it was equally mesmerizing.

Of course, Pearl is no fool. She knew the cartoon depictions made it look like the whole surgery takes place in about ten minutes, without any mess or a single drop of blood. The really mind-blowing part was how the sleeve procedure pared down the stomach into something compact, about the size and shape of a small banana. One banana. And this, even beyond the price of the surgery, is the part Pearl still can't wrap her brain around. As she leans against the bar, her belly partly resting on the countertop, she tries to imagine her stomach being reduced to something so small. Sifting through the documents, she scans the lengthy questionnaire. The section called Weight Loss History catches her eye; there, she scans a graphic that includes words like *Atkins, Weight Watchers, keto,* and even *Xenadrine.* Pearl cringes, remembering all those unwanted trips she took to Jenny Craig in Westlake Hills after her mom married Skip. Even then, as a freshman in high school, her size had been a source of conflict.

On another page titled Patient Sleep Screen, the instructions say to check the box of each that may pertain to you.

- ☐ Do you snore?
- ☐ Have you been told your breathing stops or pauses at night?

Although she hasn't slept in the same house with anyone since her weekend trip to Ruby's three summers ago, Pearl knows the answer to these questions; she recalls how she struggled to avoid snoring so as not to disturb Ruby's beauty rest.

"Oh my God, Pearl! You've really got to do something about your weight. You do realize you snore even louder than Skip did, right?"

Those words had pierced her, had made Pearl feel a sense of profound shame about something as simple and universally human as sleeping. But Ruby's very Rubyness has always had a way of making Pearl feel less than. Her sister, in all her five-foot-seven, 128-pound flawless wisdom, was full of a whole litany of how-to-be-skinny tips. During that same visit, when Ruby came back into her condo after a five-mile run to find Pearl splayed on the tufted leather sofa flipping through the latest issue of *InStyle* magazine, Pearl recalls her sister had been exceptionally generous with the weight loss suggestions.

"You simply have to burn more calories than you consume, Pearl. And sitting around like you do isn't going to do the trick."

Easy for a size four to say, Pearl thought. Size fours like Ruby are always so good at pointing out the obvious.

Pearl takes a swig of her Diet Dr Pepper, checks the time on her phone, considers calling Ruby with an update on her big news, but thinks better of it. Telling Ruby she plans to go through with bariatric weight loss surgery means there is no turning back. Sharing news with her sister is tantamount to signing on the dotted line, and Ruby isn't someone who understands ambiguity. So for now, the phone call to Ruby, the one her mom encouraged her to make, can wait. And since she doesn't have to be at work until 8:00 a.m., Pearl still has plenty of time to kill sifting through the informational brochures and the annoying but necessary questions about sleep apnea.

☐ Do you fall asleep if you sit in a quiet place too long?

☐ Are you sleepy during the day even though you slept that night?

Pearl knows there will also be the pre-op sleep study, to determine whether her obesity is compromising her health— even while she sleeps. The idea of trying to sleep in front of strangers is too much to contemplate, so she moves on to the Written Agreement to Comply with Therapy, a letter she's expected to sign and date.

I, Pearl Crenshaw, have reviewed all the information includ- ing the bariatric manual and the information provided to me by Dr. Henry George about my upcoming surgery. I understand the Roux-en-Y bypass/sleeve gastrectomy procedure and the need to follow a strict postoperative dietary program. My success will be based on several life- style modifications including but not limited to increased exercise. I also understand that post-op clinical visits are an important aspect of care to avoid potential complica- tions. To ensure optimal weight loss, I agree to comply to the best of my ability with all the therapeutic recommen- dations made by my physician, including:

Taking vitamins and supplements as directed for the rest of my life.
Following the guidelines of the pre-op and post-op diet.
Exercising on a regular basis after surgery.
Not becoming pregnant for at least two years after surgery.

Remaining tobacco free for two months prior to surgery and remaining tobacco free for the rest of
my life.

Attending recommended follow-up appointments
at two weeks, three months, six months, twelve
months, and at least every year thereafter.

The reference to *the rest of her life* and the phrase *every year thereafter* pack a particularly permanent punch. These words require such commitment, she thinks. But on the bright side, if she's going to be stuck having to see one doctor for the remainder of her living days, at least Dr. George is a hot one.

She shuffles the papers and tucks them back into the glossy Austin Weight Loss Specialists folder, noticing some words highlighted in yellow: *surgery date to be booked at time of payment.* There it is—the weighty matter of how she is going to fund this life-changing, perhaps life-saving procedure. She thinks about her mom's jewelry, so well hidden for so long, buried, like treasure, under some old family quilts in the cedar trunk at the end of the hall.

Alone, in the same kitchen where her dad, Teddy Crenshaw, once taught her to waltz, letting her little girl feet rest atop his own, Pearl contemplates her family's complicated past, which is crammed into these twenty-nine hundred square feet: the good, the bad, and the ugly. Staring over toward the only other TV in the house, the one in the living room, she notices the inaugural preparations underway in Washington, DC, and remembers what day it is. Just like the weather in the nation's capital and the mood of the country as a whole, CNN is muted. Images of Donald Trump appear all over the screen, and she doesn't have to hear anything to know what's being said. This is history in the making, she thinks. Just as our elections have consequences, this kind of elective bariatric surgery is a monumental decision from which there is no turning back. The stakes are high, and Pearl knows this. And as she embarks on this inaugural year of self-improvement, she hopes and prays that maybe, just maybe, her fixer-upper fantasies will come true.

Chapter 3

The Glenwood Manor Assisted Living Center is nestled just off Lady Bird Lake, east of I-35, where a couple of decades of gentrification have erased any trace of Austin's oldest slums. The center is, ironically, in the hipster part of town, and its developers artfully positioned the complex among the ancient live oaks that line the river basin so that it looks like an enormous, contemporary, Frank Lloyd Wright tree house instead of an eldercare unit. For the near decade she's been working here, Pearl has always appreciated the cleverness of a multicampus facility where residents can move from assisted living to the skilled nursing unit without ever leaving the lush old-growth canopy of Austin's original downtown.

These days, everything in Austin seems to be under construction. Even Tarrytown, the once-quiet neighborhood where she grew up, is now a noisy litany of nail guns and backhoes.

With Austin's population boom, this mostly well-to-do web of old-world wooded lots is now peppered with an eclectic mix of new-world architectural makeovers. In fact, Pearl's childhood home is one of the few in this zip code not being transformed into a midcentury modern mansion. Instead, the old Crenshaw house is vintage 78703—a modest, once inviting, hidden-gem craftsman whose original beauty is no longer visible from the curb because of all the overgrown Alamo vine and Texas sage. Despite the long list of improvements that need to be made, the house does have one very attractive feature: it's paid for. And for as long as her mom remains in prison, Pearl gets to live there for free. Plus, by Austin standards, her commute is an easy one. It only takes her about half an hour to get to work, and as she winds her way up the long Glenwood Manor driveway, Pearl slows a bit, trying to catch the final minutes of her favorite new podcast—*This Happened to Me*. Each episode features individuals purging previously untold secrets of their past from some lofty vantage point of personal growth, and she craves every sordid detail just as much as she's still craving that third breakfast burrito sitting on the passenger seat. There's still a half hour to kill before she has to go inside. Pearl likes to give herself plenty of time in the mornings. She's not one to be late. In fact, to a large degree, she overcompensates; arriving early is little more than an effort to quash the number one assumption so many make about fat people—that they are all slow and lazy. And since the walk from the employee parking lot to the memory care unit is easily the length of an entire football field, she doesn't like to have to rush to get to her desk on time.

Once parked, Pearl turns up the volume, listening to some woman talk about being nearly fatally drugged just days after testifying against an abusive boyfriend. Pearl finds herself glued to the sordid drama and finds satisfaction in learning that the boyfriend did indeed get his legal comeuppance. Mostly, though, she relates to the victim, who, by the time she was drugged, weighed 310 pounds.

"Some of us bury our secrets," the victim says. "And that's exactly what I did. I buried my shame and self-loathing under all the extra pounds. Secrets are heavy."

Pearl turns off the ignition and sits quietly in her car, watching some of her coworkers beeline for the employee entrance. Alone with that last burrito, she hides behind the wheel for just a little while longer. When it's all gone, she wads up the embarrassing evidence of her private feast and crams all the greasy wrappers back into the sack before shoving the sack into her huge handbag. Who is she trying to fool? As she digs through the tangle of straw wrappers and faded fast-food receipts, searching for her one tube of lipstick, it would be obvious to anyone how even the very contents of her purse mirror the mess of her life. She swipes the dried-out stub of Estée Lauder across her greasy lips and checks herself in the rearview.

"Lipstick on a pig," she murmurs.

A familiar postbinge shame comes over her, sending her

straight back to her senior year at Austin High and Skip's evil rant that Halloween night. The memory of it still haunts her, probably always will. The evening had been one Pearl was dreading, mostly because both of her friends, who decided they would dress up as hollaback girls, went all out, wearing black beanies, tight white tank tops that exposed their toned midriffs, and cargo pants slung low, hip-hop style, à la Gwen Stefani. Then a size fourteen, Pearl had done her best to rock a more plus-sized version of the outfit, pairing a modest, baggy white Beefy-T with a pair of her stepdad's black joggers. The only part of the ensemble in which she took any pride was strictly from the neck up: the stacked silver chokers and chains, the one-size-fits-all beanie, her perfectly flat-ironed long brown hair, and the makeup—most especially those Gwen Stefani red lips. She'd been home from the party, snacking on Skittles when Skip came staggering out of the kitchen mouthing off. Even after all these years, she could recall his slurred speech as though he were still lurching toward her.

"Well, lookee here. If it isn't Miss Porky Pearl. Back so soon?"

She hates herself for still being able to hear his words echoing in her head. She has to make a conscious effort to quiet his voice before she can leave her car. Otherwise, her workday will be launched with too much regret and remorse.

To redirect her thoughts, she mindlessly logs on to her phone and starts scrolling through Facebook. It's all a blur of puppies, unbelievably beautiful families, and predictable political ranting.

But her scrolling stops when she comes to the Austin Weight Loss Specialists page, which she'd "liked" after her meeting with Dr. George. Today's post features a startling before and after picture of a patient named Beatrice. In the before image, a Black woman is wearing a Lane Bryant top she recognizes as one she also owns. Like Pearl, Beatrice's shape is completely hidden by her girth. In the after shot, Beatrice's spectacular weight loss is revealed. Pearl actually gasps as she looks back and forth between the "Bea-fore" and "Bea-after" images. Then she reads Bea's testimonial:

> I'm more than a number on the scale.
> Before my sleeve, my weight was everything.
> Now, I'm no longer defined by my size.

Pearl thinks about her own number, 531, and wonders if the three-burrito breakfast she just inhaled may have tipped that last digit to 2. There has to be a limit; 531 will be her limit, she thinks. It will be her maximum density, the biggest Russian doll version of herself. Staring down at her phone, she mentally calculates Bea-after's metamorphosis, allows herself to dream of a post-op Pearl, wondering which before image she might use to show how radical her own transformation will be. And although, in her mind's eye, she can't quite picture the Pearl beneath all this blubber, the dream of it boosts her mood enough so that she feels ready to do it. With her meaty index finger hovering over

Ruby's contact, Pearl does one final gut check before tapping the screen.

After the third ring, it's clear that this impulse to call and share the news about her big decision is a mistake. In the time it takes to listen to her sister's sorry-to-miss-your-call message and the beep, Pearl's made a different decision.

"Hey, it's me. I guess you're probably out on a run or lifting weights or having hot sex or something really sweaty and impressive right now. Anyway, sorry to disturb. Just call me back when you can, okay? Bye."

By not telling Ruby about her decision to both pay for and schedule the surgery, Pearl is giving herself one more day's worth of wiggle room to back away from this huge decision. She throws her phone into her purse and begins the process of maneuvering herself out of her car.

As she plods along the pavement toward the employee entrance, she can't help but notice that within no time at all, she's broken a sweat. The rapid rhythm of her heartbeat so outpaces the slow cadence of her steps that, for a moment, she stops in her tracks, trying to catch her breath. She can't quite remember when the simple act of walking became so hard. Now, more than ever, she's aware that her size is an issue she can no longer avoid. Dr. George's cautionary concerns replay in her mind as she stands there huffing and puffing. She thinks back to before she landed the job at the Glenwood Manor facility, when she used to make house calls. As a geriatric consultant, she helped seniors navigate everything from the fuzzy onset of Alzheimer's to the confusing minefield of medical expenses. Offering clarity and compassion to a population so desperate for both made Pearl feel needed, even valued. But over the years, as she got bigger, it became more and more uncomfortable to visit the homes of the elderly, which were so often filled with rickety old ladder-back chairs and creaking wooden floors. After that one time where she nearly got stuck in an antique chesterfield, the springs of which had snapped underneath her, Pearl had vowed to lose more than a few pounds and seek gainful employment in a more predictable setting—one with nice, sturdy office furniture. At the time, it didn't strike her as especially odd that she would be making a career change based on the load-bearing capacity of a standard-issue office swivel chair, but then again, dysfunction is often preceded by denial.

When she makes it to her desk, which is just past the Glenwood patient cafeteria, she spots one of the licensed vocational nurses peeling a banana for Mr. Grimes. Like so many of the other residents in the memory care unit, he's in that stage of Alzheimer's where he's forgotten how to even feed himself. If only she were that lucky, Pearl thinks. It sounds twisted, but not any more than having her stomach carved into something no bigger than the banana Mr. Grimes is about to eat.

"Oh, thank God you're here, Pearl!"

She recognizes that lovely lilt before she can even turn around. Perry Goodwin is a registered nurse and the assistant supervisor over the entire memory care unit, but everyone, including Pearl, not so secretly believes he should be in charge of this whole operation. Perry is the kind of manager, that rare breed of good human, who lets ninety-two-year-old Edith Rogers believe he is her husband; the kind of manager who has been known to roll up his shirtsleeves and wipe a bare bottom when duty calls; the kind of good guy who, last year, when Pearl's ergonomic chair broke under the weight of her, quietly disposed of it and expensed a more robust version specifically rated for up to one thousand pounds. If he wasn't gay, Perry might be the kind of guy Pearl would hope to marry. Besides her dad, he's the only man she's ever known who treated her like an actual person instead of just a fat person. Pearl considers him her closest friend.

"Hey, Perry," she says, slightly winded from the walk. "Missed me that much, huh?"

"First, I have to say, your hair looks amazing."

"Thanks," Pearl says, beaming.

"And right now, I need you and your good hair to help me with Mr. Dalheimer. He's in one of his moods," he says, rolling his eyes. "You're good at calming him down. Can you give me a hand?"

Pearl snarfs down this vote of confidence like it's a platter of green chili chicken enchiladas, savoring how it feels to be needed. Perry has a way of making her feel like a mission-critical part of their motley memory care team. Inspired by the confidence he seems to have in her, she tucks a loose strand of her Joanna Gaines side pony behind her ear and does her best to keep up with him as he jaunts down the long, wide, handrailed hall to the eighty-seven-year-old former Southwest Airlines pilot's room.

Pearl dearly loves her elderly patients, sees past their absent minds. Somewhere in the fog, she spots the essence of their personalities even when there are no memories to put them into context. Of all people, Pearl knows a thing or two about dignity or lack thereof. Maybe this is why Perry relies on her so much, she thinks.

"When I got in about an hour ago, he was in a state of panic. BT-dub, nobody's been able to convince him to put his clothes on. And, Pearl, I've got two families coming for tours this morning, so I can't have any full-frontal nudity going on today, if you know what I mean. Like I'm not even kidding. I need every one of our patients painting, strolling the gardens, or doing tai chi."

"What if some of them are napping? Naps are good, right?"

"Siestas don't really sell, Pearl. Families don't want to pay for two-hundred-dollar-a-day slobbery snoozes. Action is where it's at—activities, motion," he adds.

"Bingo," Pearl says jokingly.

"Bingo," he says. "Everyone's got to look alive even while they're dying."

Pearl nods, almost too winded to walk and talk at the same time.

At Mr. Dalheimer's partially open door, Perry knocks politely, announcing their presence, but gets no reply. He tries again.

"Yoo-hoo, Mr. Dalheimer. May we come in, sir?" Then he turns to Pearl. "Prepare yourself," he whispers, winking. "This room contains nudity that some may find disturbing. Viewer discretion advised."

Pearl suppresses a giggle. Like Perry, one of the things she appreciates about working here is how every day, there is a different story to tell: an emerging romance between octogenarians, dominoes getting flushed down the toilet, residents trying to spike their Ensure with smuggled-in Tito's. This many people gathered under one roof, with or without their faculties, and surprising stuff happens on the daily.

Gently, Perry pushes the door. Standing in the entrance to his private suite is Mr. Hurst Dalheimer III in all his buck-naked glory. Other than his black socks and dress shoes, he's totally nude. It's not a pretty picture. But being the professionals that they are, Perry and Pearl keep their gazes at eye level, addressing him as though he were wearing a three-piece suit.

"Good morning, Mr. Dalheimer," Pearl says. Casually, she reaches for his robe. "Aren't you supposed to be in the shower?"

"There is a snake in my bathroom," he says with absolute certainty. "What kind of a cheap motel is this?"

Pearl side-eyes Perry, reading his mind.

"Well, let's go ahead and get you back in your robe so you

don't catch cold while we see about this snake," she says, gently pulling his frail arms through the holes. "There you go, sir. Now, I'm going to look in your bathroom real quick while you stay right here with Perry, okay?"

Pearl scans the floors of the en suite bathroom for reptiles and immediately spots the cause of Mr. Dalheimer's alarm: the silver handheld sprayer has fallen to the tiled floor and is conspicuously coiled at the bottom of his walk-in shower. Pearl picks up the polished chrome hose and hangs it back on the clip. As she comes out of the bathroom, Mr. Dalheimer is standing there in his robe, awaiting the verdict.

"Sir, I've disposed of the snake," she says, gesturing toward the restroom. "It's perfectly safe to take a shower now."

Without hesitation, Mr. Dalheimer unties his robe and takes two steps toward the bathroom.

"Um, Mr. Dalheimer," Perry says. "Why don't we help you with those socks. Let's get those off first."

His singular objective had been to take a shower. But the snake and now the socks have interrupted his mission, broken his train of thought, and he sits on the bed, almost childlike, pouting.

Undaunted, Perry and Pearl stay on task. Gently, Pearl bends toward Mr. Dalheimer, reaching for one of his socks, but something in him snaps. Upon seeing all 531 pounds of Pearl looming over him, Mr. Dalheimer panics. Reflexively, the normally mild-mannered former pilot kicks his leg at Pearl.

"You can't fly a plane," he says matter-of-factly. "You can't even fit in the cockpit. There's a weight limit, you know?"

The sting of this unexpected insult hangs in the air like contrails. Along with the unspoken threat of whatever other cogent thoughts Mr. Dalheimer might manage to string together, his insult, however unintentional, looms overhead, circling, rendering Pearl temporarily tongue-tied.

Perry swoops in, saving Pearl from any further degradation. "Mr. Dalheimer, allow me, sir."

Swiftly, Perry peels off Mr. Dalheimer's socks and hits the call button for one of the aides to come see him through the rest of his bathing routine.

Embarrassed, Pearl retreats to the hallway. It's bad enough to have someone say something so unflattering, but why did he have to say it in front of an audience? Insults are amplified in direct proportion to the number of people who hear them, she thinks.

"Look, Pearl, before you let that little incident ruin your day, just remember the man actually mistook his handheld shower nozzle for a snake. Worse than that, he can no longer distinguish between being nude or clothed. Let that sink in, okay? He knows not what he says."

She rolls her eyes, flicks away some tears.

"Well, for a demented old man, he has pretty remarkable timing."

Perry cocks his head. "How so?"

"Of all days, today is the day I plan to schedule bariatric weight loss surgery, and it's just ironic as hell to have a resident who has lost his mind telling me something I already know about myself, that's all."

Sympathetically, Perry reaches for Pearl's hand and gives it a squeeze of understanding. He nods to the attendant entering Mr. Dalheimer's room and motions for Pearl to follow him out into the nearby courtyard.

"Look, Pearl, first of all, I'm beyond sorry he hurt your feelings in there."

"It's not your fault," Pearl says, wiping her tears with the back of her hand. "Don't worry about it."

"Well, I most certainly am worried about it. I had no idea you were considering a gastric bypass."

"Probably not a bypass," she says. "It's another procedure called the sleeve."

He nods as if he has some understanding about this subject.

"I know someone who had that," he says. "The guy I dated before James. You remember Bruce, right? We were only together for a minute, but he had a sleeve."

She scrolls her list of mental contacts and vaguely recalls the tall, not fat at all, former boyfriend.

"Wow," Pearl says. "I had no idea."

"Right," he says. "You had no idea because his surgery was a total success. He lost the weight he needed to lose. But, sadly, I learned the hard way bariatric surgery doesn't cure assholes,

Pearl. You and I only met the post-op Bruce—the one who, on the surface, looked like the very picture of health. I made the mistake of judging a book by its cover once, but never again. Remember, Pearl, I used to have a weight problem, too. You only know the Perry with the thirty-four-inch waist, but on my very first Match profile I described myself as fun and fluffy."

Pearl smiles. She wants to hug Perry for how far he's going to try to lift her spirits. Despite his efforts to relate, she can't help but feel like her 531 pounds is in a class all its own. She doesn't say this, but she's thinking it.

"Pearl, trust me, underneath this Under Armour puffer, I'm nothing but spray tan and stretch marks. No lie. You're looking at a former Teletubby."

The self-deprecation makes her giggle, helps her tears dry up a little.

"And guess what," he continues. "Being a chubby, four-eyed, gay guy growing up in the late eighties in Odessa wasn't exactly a boost for my ego."

His empathy appears to be helping Pearl stop crying, so he keeps going.

"So I was that kid in ill-fitting gym shorts, huffing and puffing my way around the track of the Odessa Permian football field. I can still hear that fatphobic coach blowing his whistle, telling me to speed up. Like, I'm forty years old, and it still gives me nightmares. I was always the last one crossing the finish line, and there he would be, pressing his stupid stopwatch. He wasn't clocking my time, Pearl. He was count-ing my shortcomings."

"Maybe we had the same coach," Pearl says.

"Right?" Perry says with emphasis.

Pearl shakes her head, rapt by such personal revelations, still trying to imagine a plumper version of her friend.

"But you know what happened," he says.

"You lost eighty-seven pounds," she says, having heard this fact before.

"That's exactly right. I lost eighty-seven pounds. Woke up one day and looked at the number on the scale and decided I never wanted to see that number again. So for me, I basically got radical about carbs and protein and water and workouts and eliminating sugar, and the weight just came off. I haven't been heavy since I was twenty-seven. So my recommendation—find your carrot."

She cocks her head to the side, confused.

"Most overweight people have a carrot, a motivator. Some of us have a dozen or more. It's that goal you dangle in front of yourself whenever you have the impulse to, say, keep digging all the way to the bottom of a pint of Ben & Jerry's or some-thing. So think about what motivates you. What's something the weight loss will do for you?"

"Well," Pearl says longingly, "it would be nice if, one day, I don't have to wear clothes that stretch."

"Goals!" Perry says enthusiastically. "That's the spirit. Fuck jersey knits! Damn them all to hell! Now that is a carrot you can really sink your teeth into. So hang onto that motivation, Pearl. If you go through with this surgery, in no time, you'll be wearing your button-fly boyfriend jeans, and the next thing you know, you'll be strutting your stuff in one of those Hérve Léger bandage dresses."

"I can only hope," Pearl says. "I just… It just…"

"What?"

"It just sucks that I've allowed myself to get to this point where I am needing actual surgery. I mean, I still have my wisdom teeth. I've never even been sedated. And it's not like I have anyone around to help me through this, you know? I mean my mom isn't exactly available to play nursemaid."

Perry knows about Birdie and why she went to prison. Their mother's incarceration isn't something Pearl hides, unlike Ruby. She can't really. Not any more than she can hide her mass.

"Three things," Perry says, holding up his fingers. "First, I pledge to be of service to you pre- and post-op, so long as your surgery date doesn't conflict with my tickets to South by Southwest." He winks and goes on. "Two, you will stop with any negative self-talk or poor-me nonsense. And three, where the eff is your sister in all this? I mean, like, what the fuck? Family is family. It's time for Ruby to get down here and sparkle."

Pearl crushes a little more on Perry; she appreciates his gallantry and can't help but think of him as her knight in shining Under Armour.

"You know my relationship with my sister is complicated.

Ruby's just always been all about Ruby. Plus, she's embarrassed our mom is in prison. I think coming back to Austin reminds her of all she's lost. I mean, all we've lost."

"I get that." Perry nods as he checks his vibrating phone.

Pearl doesn't mention what she also suspects, what deep down she really knows—that Ruby may be more embarrassed to have a sister the size of Pearl than a mom behind bars.

"Okay, I hate to cut this short, but that's one of my tours. But I just want you to feel encouraged and validated. If you believe surgery is the right choice, Pearl, don't let anything stop you."

Chapter 4

The best part about Pearl having been fat-shamed by one of her patients is that it resulted in Perry giving her the afternoon off. On any other crisp, cool January Monday, she might have gone home to binge-watch HGTV with a big bag of Chick-fil-A nuggets and waffle fries. But today is the day Pearl has decided enough is enough.

Rummaging through the old steamer trunk in the hallway at the house, Pearl feels a new sense of resolve. In her mind, a number greater than 531 simply does not exist. It cannot exist. A number bigger than that could actually kill her. The thought panics Pearl, and almost manically, she tosses aside a few moth-balled quilts and baby blankets, a stack of scrapbooks, and a shoebox of her dad's mementos. She doesn't have to open it to know what all is in there. The sealed urn containing her dad's ashes is heavier than she expected. When she was younger, she remembers being too afraid to touch it, unable to reconcile how her larger-than-life father could be reduced and contained in something no bigger than a gallon of Blue Bell. Reverently, she carries the urn to her bedroom and places it on her dresser, feeling somewhat ashamed of herself for waiting until now to resurrect it from the forgotten burial grounds at the bottom of that shabby trunk. When she returns to the hallway, she stares long and hard at the lid to the shoebox.

The masking tape label and the black Sharpie letters that say *Teddy Crenshaw* stir up feelings she would rather not face. Seeing her mom's familiar cursive calls to mind the pain the three of them shared after the car accident that killed her father. She thinks back to her dad's funeral, remembering the time she and ten-year-old Ruby spent gathering stacks of photos to take to the funeral home, the same ones she, her sister, and Birdie stared at watery-eyed in the chapel as a bittersweet video montage of the life and times of Teddy Crenshaw played to Garth Brooks's "The Dance." Pearl is tempted to take the time to open the box and find the picture of Ruby and her in the kitchen, the one with Pearl's bare feet planted atop her dad's boots, Ruby standing off to the side, watching, admiring. It's an image that flashes in her mind's eye like a lighthouse in a sea of so much darkness that followed. But she wills herself to stay on task. This is not the day to drown in any misty-eyed nostalgia. Today is about new beginnings.

She spots one of her mom's old Royal Dansk tins, the kind she would often use to store treats for her catering gigs. Popping the top, Pearl finds what she's looking for: two ladies Rolex Datejust watches, one stainless steel, the other gold with a lapis-blue face surrounded by diamonds. Pearl looks at the wedding rings: there's the one her dad gave her mom and the one from Skip. Appraising their relative value, sentimental and otherwise, she tucks the one from her dad back into the velvet box and gently returns it to the tin. With any luck, the big, flashy rock from Skip will yield enough to cover the surgery and she won't even have to sell the watches.

She's already Googled and called a high-end jeweler off Spicewood Springs Road who buys, sells, and trades. Arriving at the swanky address, she's somewhat relieved by the door buzzer and the by-appointment-only nature of the business, hoping the fancy real estate equals enough of a payoff to cover the cost of her surgery. But as she stands outside the door, clutching her purse, waiting to be buzzed in, a part of her feels like a loser. She can't shake a certain shame about not being more like Ruby, more independent and financially secure. Ruby wasn't the kind of person who would resort to hocking their mom's most valuable worldly possessions for personal gain. Pearl ruminates on this fact, thinking no wonder, no effing wonder Ruby lets Pearl's calls go to voicemail.

"Hello."

The deep baritone voice startles her.

"Oh, hi," she says, looking into the wall-mounted security screen. "I have an appointment. My name is Pearl Crenshaw."

"The Rolex watches and the diamond ring, yes?" His accent is thick and smoky, maybe Greek but just as easily Moroccan. She can't quite place it.

"Yes."

"And do you have the pieces with you?"

"Yes." She nods, holding her sagging handbag up to the camera.

"One moment."

Like a junkie about to make a drug deal, Pearl looks from side to side, making sure the coast is clear. It's intimidating carrying these valuables in her purse, and she's startled when the glass door buzzes open. A giant man in a navy suit greets her and motions her inside.

"Follow me, please."

From the look of the website, Pearl expected this place to look more like a jewelry store, but nothing about it suggests anything retail. Instead, she's escorted past a long wall of vaults to a small conference room with no windows. The man from the security camera is seated in front of a small black velvet place mat arrayed with an assortment of loupes.

"Miss Crenshaw," he says, rising to his feet, extending his hand. "Please," he adds, motioning for her to take a seat.

This simple gesture alone makes her uneasy. Swivel chairs, no matter how robust, are always a bit tricky for her, and it takes her longer than it should to lower into the seat. She feels him estimating her weight in carats.

"May I have a look at your items?" he asks, strictly business.

Pearl places all three pieces on the velvet mat.

"Let's see what we have here," he says, placing a loupe to his eye. He picks up the ring first and studies it.

Under the table, Pearl crosses her fingers while visualizing how empowering it will feel to go the bank and then directly to Austin Weight Loss Specialists to secure her surgery date. She's almost giddy at the thought of walking out of here with so much money.

"Worthless," he says, placing the ring back on the mat.

"Excuse me?" Pearl says, bewildered.

"It's fake," he says. "Not a real diamond. I assume this comes as a surprise to you?"

"Are you sure?" Pearl asks meekly.

"Yes. It's a good fake, but a fake nonetheless. The Rolexes, however, are real. So let me take a closer look at those." He bends now to the stainless watch, loupe in place.

Although it's not what she expected, the news isn't altogether shocking. Considering what a mirage of a good man her stepfather, Skip, turned out to be, Pearl's more astonished that she never suspected the diamond wedding ring was fake in the first place.

"That motherfucker," she says under her breath.

"You are not the only woman who has uttered those very words from that very spot," the jeweler replies.

Pearl shakes her head, disgusted.

"What about the watches?" she asks finally. "How much are they worth?"

He takes far more time with the Rolexes, even carries them off to another room to consult with a colleague. When he reappears, he slides what appears to be a handwritten estimate across the table for Pearl's review. The number is all Pearl sees: $3,200. Her heart sinks. She feels defeated. Tears well in her eyes.

"That is what we are willing to pay for the Datejust," he says, placing the two-tone Rolex on top of the bid. "Is a good price. These watches are in excellent condition. Very little wear. And here is what we can offer for the President."

Pearl looks at the number: $12,300.

"So if you accept these numbers, I will happily cut you a check right now."

Staring at the shiny watches, which are so symbolic of how much time she's wasted not taking care of her health, Pearl hears Birdie in her ear saying, "Promise me you'll take this step. You deserve to be happy."

And with the clock ticking on her very life, she nods and says, "Okay, sold."

In the parking lot, Pearl spots a white Lexus RX 300, the same make and model as Ruby's. For as excited as she is to be walking out of the jewelers with more than enough money, the sight of the car sends Pearl straight back to her last visit with her sister three years ago and the humiliation of not being able to buckle the fucking seat belt in her sister's car.

Ruby had insisted on driving them to get mani-pedis. It had been a day that started out with high hopes of some measure of sisterly bonding, some regular run-of-the-mill girl time, but ended before they could even back out of Ruby's driveway. Pearl can still hear that annoying beeping, the car itself reminding her to buckle up. The struggle was real.

"Seriously, Pearl?"

When it came to her weight or, for that matter, Pearl's life in general, Ruby could be so condescending. She remembers tugging, breaking a sweat to secure the seat belt, mortified she might actually bust it. But click or no click, there was no way out of the awkwardness of the situation.

"Is there, like, some kind of child setting on this strap?" Pearl's futile attempt at normalizing the abnormality of her very size did not go over well with Ruby.

"It's not the seat belt, Pearl," Ruby said, glaring up over her cat-eye sunglasses. "It's you. You're my sister—my only not-locked-up family member! Do you have any idea how hard it is for me to witness what you're doing to yourself? Who you're becoming? Do you not remember Lake Texoma? Like was that not enough?"

Pearl had cringed at the mere mention of that day, wished she could block the very public humiliation of not being able to pull herself up and onto the back of that Sea-Doo. She knew what was coming next. Pearl's ability to predict word for word what Ruby was thinking was nothing short of telepathic, no matter how torturous or twisted.

Seated here in the parking lot, holding the check from the sale of her mom's jewelry, Pearl realizes it's more money than she's ever had. Yet as emboldened as she feels about having secured the much-needed cash, even all these years later, Ruby's brutally truthful tirade still echoes in the confines of Pearl's crappy car.

"Look, there's no way to sugarcoat reality anymore, Pearl! You may call me a bitch for saying what I'm about to say, but somebody has got to level with you. If you can't buckle up, you're too fucking fat!"

To muffle the bad memories, Pearl cranks the volume on the radio, still recalling how they never quite made it to the nail salon that day. Instead, Pearl left Ruby's driveway in this very beat-up Altima where, even now, she still struggles to click the seat belt. For a moment, Pearl imagines herself and Ruby sitting side by side in white fluffy robes at an expensive spa, their hair wrapped in towels, their feet soaking in warm, swirling water. In her mind's eye, the picture of both of them laughing and mindlessly flipping through back issues of *People* magazine is as much an optical illusion as any mirage, and along with her mom's fake diamond wedding ring, Pearl stuffs these illusions into her busted glove compartment.

Alone in the driver's seat, she takes another long look at the check made out to Pearl Crenshaw in the amount of $15,500. It's exactly what she needs to pay for the surgery with enough left over to jump-start her postsurgical wardrobe. Alternatively, combined with whatever Kelley Blue Book value she might get for this beater Nissan, it's also enough to immediately upgrade her ride. For a moment or so, she weighs her options—surveys the stained upholstery, the cracks on the dash, the almost ninety-eight thousand miles on the odometer. But in the rear-view, her eyes fix on the way the seat belt bites into her fleshy neck, like a bra strap digging into her shoulder, leaving a mark. Even if Ruby's approach is wrong, her message is mostly right, she thinks. The seat belt is a sign, and in Pearl's estimation, the check in her hand is cosmic validation that maybe, just maybe, à la Dorothy and her ruby slippers, Pearl can click her heels and turn her dreams into reality. Having this much money means her goal, at least on paper, is actually attainable.

Before she can change her mind, she puts the car in reverse and races to the bank. And just as she's steering onto MoPac, with her car headed back to West Austin, Natasha Bedingfield's "Unwritten" comes on the radio. Like never before, the lyrics seem to be speaking directly to Pearl, encouraging her to put the pedal to the metal in her old yet still totally reliable Altima and stay pointed in this exact direction. Pearl cranks the radio and sings along, pounding her palms on the steering wheel to the beat of what must surely be her new personal anthem. All those lyrics about blank pages and still unwritten days ahead have her feeling, really believing, that she just might be able to release her own inhibitions and reclaim her life.

When it's over, she finds the song again on Spotify, wonders why she's never added it to her personal playlist. At least four more times, she jams to it, belting out the words with heartfelt conviction, before rolling into the drive-thru at the bank. Can a song be a drug? She wonders if it's the music or the money making her feel so buoyant. Pearl Crenshaw has officially monetized some buried treasure for a shot at a better future, and as she watches the teller shove the cashier's check into the plastic tube, she's never felt more certain of one essential truth: it's now or never.

Chapter 5

From the instant she said yes to Ruby's invitation, Pearl had a sinking feeling about boat day. But all the way to the marina, sweating like a Brahman bull, she keeps her insecurities to herself. It's bad enough she couldn't find a suitable swimsuit. No matter where she looked, the only options for someone her size were matronly, ugly, or some combination of both. Uninspired, Pearl boycotted plus-size swimwear, opting instead for a practical albeit boring outfit consisting of the most basic, loosest, drawstring knit shorts she owned, paired with the biggest, darkest T-shirt she could fish out of her closet. She had no plans of actually getting wet, but on the off chance she did, she didn't want to be caught dead wearing anything see-through, much less anything that might give her a wedgie.

In stark contrast to Pearl's big and baggy vibe, Ruby's lake look is the kind that has heads turning for totally different reasons.

Underneath a pair of loose-on-her-hips, button-fly, white denim shorts, she's rocking a navy-blue bikini. Walking side by side with her sister, Pearl can't help but feel a tinge of diffidence, because topped with her bucket hat, Ruby appears effortlessly nautical, while Pearl's getup is just plain effortless—gross, stretchy fabric suggesting she gives no shits whatsoever. Ruby hasn't said anything, and she doesn't have to. The sheer omission of eye contact tells Pearl all she needs to know about her sister's simmering disapproval.

Flip-flopping their way toward the boat slip, Pearl tries her best to keep up, all the while ignoring an irrational but very real fear that at her size, she might actually cause a pontoon to capsize. But buoyed by Ruby's rare invitation to spend an entire day boating on Lake Texoma with the steadiest boyfriend her sister has had since college, Pearl plods along, towel in tow.

"It's the ninth one down," Ruby says, pointing toward a long row of slips.

"You guys must be serious, huh?" Pearl probes, making small talk as they walk along.

"What makes you say that?" Ruby replies, tucking her sunglasses into the string strap between her boobs.

"It's just that in all these years, this is, like, the one and only time since we've been adults that you've wanted me to actually meet let alone hang out with any of your friends," Pearl says breathlessly.

Ruby furrows her brow, seems to chew on this fact while she chomps on her gum, then blows yet another big bubble before responding.

"I've already met Blake's whole family," she says. "He's been wanting to meet mine. That's all. Don't go getting your exercise jumping to conclusions, Pearl. It's not like we're getting married or anything."

With the water sloshing in the slips and their flip-flops drumming the dock, the two of them make their way toward Blake's boat. Out on the water, a young girl slaloms by, rooster tailing this side of the marina. Pearl takes note of the impressive acrobatic display, the way she very nearly lays her body almost horizontally along the surface before popping upright again.

"I just hope I don't rock the boat too much," Pearl confesses. "I'm a little nervous."

"About what?" Ruby asks, as if she has no idea.

"You know what," Pearl whispers. "My size. And even if he's not the love of your life, I don't want to be responsible for sinking you and your boyfriend."

Ruby stops in her tracks and turns to Pearl, eyes rolling.

"Pearl, c'mon! Cut the crap! If you were that worried about your size, you would have taken advantage of that CycleBar membership I gave you for Christmas."

"Ouch," Pearl says, at a complete loss for any other words.

"Ouch is not a valid response," Ruby whispers back, exasperated. "You're just being passive-aggressive. You're doing that whole thing where you don't want me to notice how much weight you've gained, but you also never seem to want to do anything about it."

Pearl does not want to open this can of worms or subject herself to Ruby's warped psychoanalysis, especially on boat day, but she hates her sister's condescending tone.

"You know, now is probably not the right time for me to try to explain the intricacies of metabolic syndrome," Pearl says, using her towel to pat the sweat off her forehead. "I mean, I realize you still believe that if I just pedaled faster and harder on a bike, I wouldn't look like this, but my weight is more complicated than that."

Ruby's lips tighten, and Pearl knows this is a potential pivot point in their emerging dockside debate. She can tell her sister wants to say so much more, almost can't help herself, but somehow, Ruby's rapid eye blinking helps her to see she's better off holding her tongue—at least for now.

"Look, we're here to have a good time," Ruby says, trying to reset. "This is, like, an opportunity for us to hang out together doing something semiactive, you know? Boats float, Pearl. So you're not going to sink a pontoon. How about we just focus on having fun, okay?"

Before Pearl can reply to Ruby's rhetoric, Blake emerges from the stern—tall, tan, and sporting a sun-bleached Colonial Golf Tournament visor. Ruby was right about his doppelgänger. At the very least, the guy standing barefoot before them could easily pass for Bradley Cooper's first cousin, maybe even his brother. Pearl feels herself blushing before she even says hello.

"Welcome aboard, ladies," Blake says, motioning toward the boat's retractable gate. Pearl recognizes the country-pop tune coming from the built-in speakers under the bench seats, a nostalgic chorus about barefoot blue jean nights—the kind Pearl has never had.

With his sunglasses on, it's hard to see the extent to which he's sizing her up, but Pearl can tell that's exactly what he is doing, appraising. It's a reaction she's all too used to. For most of their lives, on introductions like this, it always takes the new person about one beat too many to reconcile the fact that Ruby and Pearl are, in fact, blood related. Nothing—not their height, not their hair color, not their eyes—looks even remotely spawned by common DNA. In fact, the only physical similarity they share is one hardly anyone would notice and something they inherited from Birdie—identical stubby pinkie toes with almost nonexistent toenails. Pearl has always thought this a cruel yet oddly reassuring truth, because as ugly as their smallest appendages may be, without their matching stubby sister toes, both might have doubted the authenticity of their birth certificates.

"So you're the little sister?" Blake says.

Aside from the tiny pinkie toes, it's plain to see that nothing about Pearl is little, and she feels herself blush a bit more as the awkward incongruence of his question washes over all of them.

"Pearl, this is Blake Dunlap," Ruby says, redirecting.

Blake reaches over, gives Ruby a familiar peck on her forehead, and turns his attention back to Pearl.

"Nice to finally meet you in person, Pearl," he says, extending his arms for a friendly hug.

Ever so slightly, Pearl leans toward him, offering just enough of her right shoulder to call it a side hug. Even if he does look like Bradley Cooper, she's not big on being touched by anyone, let alone members of the opposite sex.

As he motions them onto the back of the pontoon, Pearl watches Ruby's runner legs seamlessly leap right off the dock and onto the plywood deck. Blake remains straddled, one foot on the dock, the other on the boat, ready to help Pearl do the same. But sensing her hesitation with this minor maneuver, he offers his hand for balance.

"Easy does it," he says, waiting on Pearl to muster the courage to move.

She can feel Ruby looking back at her, maybe even rolling her eyes in disgust at the sight of her not-so-little sister having to, so strategically, calculate her next small yet very serious steps.

"There you go. Just take it nice and slow," Blake adds, guiding Pearl as she nervously plants one foot in front of the other. It's not until she's standing in the center of the boat, hands clutching the seat backs, that she feels more confident about Ruby's earlier assertion—despite her weight, she may not sink it after all.

"All right, ladies, shall we let this little pontoon party commence?" Blake says, checking the towrope on the adjoining red-and-black Sea-Doo. While Ruby gets busy applying sunscreen, he opens a bright blue Yeti cooler, emblazoned with SMU Mustang stickers, offering up cold beers before taking the helm.

For a little while, Pearl allows herself to believe she is just like them—just another beautiful young twentysomething enjoying a day on the water. Sitting on the bench seats of this perfectly sturdy pontoon, Pearl allows herself to feel soothed by the steady throttle of the twin engines. As they skim the surface of the second-largest lake in Texas, she inhales the unfamiliar fusion of musty water, hoppy ale, and Coppertone. If boat day were a candle, this would be its perfectly pleasing scent, she thinks. With the music cranked, the sun warming her face, and the wind whipping her hair, she almost forgets about her fleshy thighs and arms and the way they jiggle each time the boat spanks a wake. To Pearl's surprise, it's shaping up to be an excellent day indeed—mostly because, at least so far, it seems like boating is the kind of activity where sitting is more or less mandatory, and conversation is more or less optional.

Two hours and two Shiner Bocks into their guided tour of Lake Texoma, Blake anchors down in a secluded cove.

"Y'all ready to have some fun?" he says, turning off the motor. "Time to break out the water toys. Pearl, you wanna ride the ski?"

"Who, me?" Pearl says.

Her eyes dart to Ruby, who is already shedding her shorts, eager to be the first one in the water. With the boat in a fixed position, it's easier to tell just how hot it is. As much as she would love to go for a swim, Pearl does not in any way trust the weight-bearing capacity of the stainless-steel ladder her sister is unfolding off the back. From one of the hidden storage areas under the bench seats, Blake produces a couple of life preservers and casually slips one on. Pearl watches him adjust the straps for a snug fit on the one he's wearing and notices, too, the way he loosens the straps on the spare.

"You first?" he says, dangling the key.

"I don't think it's such a good idea," Pearl says, shaking her head. "I can't."

"Can't never could," Ruby says, sounding just like their mom. She dives off the back and emerges, sliding slick as a seal onto the stand-up paddleboard.

Suddenly, Pearl hates being anchored down, wishes they could just cruise around happily waving at other boaters from a safe, impersonal distance. Ironically, being stationary forces Pearl to reckon with the intimidating prospect of movement.

"Hey, can you toss me my hat?" Ruby hollers, wringing out her hair.

With the boat still rocking, Pearl carefully hoists herself off the bench seats, clinging to the armrest of the captain's chair until she's sure about her sea legs. The amount of time it takes for her to do this one transfer is not lost on Ruby, who is squinting her eyes, trying to ascertain whether her sister can even manage with the sway of the boat.

"Are you okay?" Ruby says, paddling toward her.

"Yes," Pearl says, tossing the bucket hat. "I'm fine."

"Okay," Ruby says, doubting. It's the first time they've done anything together in fourteen months, the first time Ruby's seen her little sister at this size, and she has no real appreciation for just how limiting Pearl's weight has become.

"Just watch Blake. I hope you'll at least try the Sea-Doo," Ruby says. "It's fast and fun. You'll love it!"

Pearl nods, already feeling the pressure to try something new, to be more active and agile, just like Blake and Ruby. For courage, she heads over to the cooler and pops the top on her third beer.

From the opposite side of the boat, Blake offers a quick Sea-Doo tutorial, pointing out the starter button and how the key wraps around your wrist so that the power automatically shuts off in the event you get thrown off.

"That's all there is to it," he says, smiling.

"How fast does it go?" Pearl asks, acting more interested than she really is.

"This thing hauls ass," Blake says. "Up to seventy miles an hour if you want."

Pearl's eyes widen, and sensing her concern, he offers some friendly reassurance.

"But most of the time, Ruby doesn't go more than thirty-five," he says, winking.

With that, he makes a quick adjustment to his sunglasses, straddles the long saddle, revs the throttle, and gently steers away from the pontoon and Ruby, careful to avoid making a wake for the paddleboard or the boat.

With the two of them off in the distance doing their things,

Pearl picks up the life preserver meant for her. Without even trying it on, she can tell it probably won't fit. And she waits until Ruby is facing the opposite direction before confirming what she already knows. Defeated and ashamed, she sits down on the bench, nursing her beer and popping the top on a can of Pringles she stashed in her purse.

By the time Blake reappears, all that's left of the chips are the broken pieces at the bottom of the can. Pearl shoves it back into her purse and finishes the last sips of her now lukewarm beer. The three she's finished are three more than she's had in at least six months, so she's feeling uncharacteristically bold and brave. And because of all she's had to drink, she now has an urgent need to pee, which means whether she likes it or not, she's going to have to get in the water. Seeing Blake's approach, Ruby, too, heads back toward the boat.

"Who's next?" Blake asks, coasting up along the outer deck.

"Pearl, you go ahead," Ruby says from her now bent-knee position on the board. "I'll go after you."

More than anything, Pearl does not want them to remind her to put on the life preserver. Better to be swept away in some rogue current than to actually demonstrate for her skinny sister and the hot boyfriend just how small that extra-large vest really is. For obvious reasons, she hopes and prays they don't notice.

Blake gets off, sits on the deck, and lassos the Sea-Doo into position so Pearl can hop on.

"She's all yours," he says, helping Pearl steady herself.

Clumsily, she lowers herself onto her bottom along the edge of the deck. From this seated position, she attempts the transfer. With the Sea-Doo wobbling in the water, Pearl plops onto the seat, trying her best to look graceful.

"Pearl, you need a life vest," Ruby says, drying off with a towel.

"I'll be fine," Pearl replies. "Besides, fat floats, remember?"

The self-deprecation is as much beer-induced as it is fear-induced, and before her sister can insist, Pearl manages to stabilize herself on the saddle and strap on the wristlet for the starter key.

"There you go," Blake says, releasing the rope. "Now, give it some gas, Pearl! You gotta drive it like you stole it, or you'll stall."

Pearl guns the accelerator, steers away from the boat, clear of Ruby waving the stupid safety vest. Nervously, she stares at the digital display, which, at eighteen miles per hour, seems to totally contradict the fact that it feels like she's hauling ass.

"Faster, Pearl!" Blake's voice trails behind as she tests the waters, pulling down ever so gently on the throttle. Over the hum of music blaring, she hears Ruby's encouragement fading in the background.

"Yay, Pearl! You did it!"

And Pearl herself can hardly believe that she is, in fact, doing it. The farther she gets from their anchored position in the cove, the more confident she begins to feel. To her surprise and delight, the Sea-Doo is supporting all four hundred pounds of her. As she cruises out into the middle of the lake, just beyond their cove, she catches a glimpse of herself in the rearview mirrors off the handlebars—smiling! Within no time, she grows more comfortable in the saddle, waving at boaters passing by like it's not her first rodeo. Blake and Ruby were 100 percent right; the Sea-Doo is a total blast.

Now that she more or less has the hang of it, she's figured out that going slowly does, in fact, put her at greater risk of taking on water. In order to stabilize and remain afloat, she's found her twenty-eight-mile-per-hour sweet spot on the speedometer. It's not exactly driving it like she stole it, but it's plenty fast for Pearl.

However, out here in this part of the lake, she hadn't accounted for all the traffic, and she soon finds herself navigating wakes—lots of them. As Pearl does her best to dodge the strong currents, the smile on her face morphs into the pursed lips of panic. Within a few more windswept minutes, she's surrounded by a sea of swells and boats darting by in every direction. All the splashing has soaked her T-shirt and shorts as Pearl realizes she's in over her head. And just as she turns back in the direction of the mother ship she can no longer see, a long, lime-green cigarette boat, with its nose sticking way up out of the water, races by. Instinctively Pearl slows, bracing for the aftermath. And when she does, the wake wallops her watercraft, sending it and Pearl upside down into the murky, choppy surf of Lake Texoma.

After the wipeout, Pearl bobbles just above water, dog-paddling, doing her best to get her bearings. It all happened so fast, and from what she can tell, the driver of the boat either has no idea that he caused her to flip or has no intention of stopping to see about her welfare. As Pearl takes inventory of her situation, she realizes the Sea-Doo is drifting farther away. Even worse, she now regrets her poor choice about the T-shirt and shorts. Soaking wet like this, both weigh her down as she tries to stay afloat. With no choice but to swim toward the Sea-Doo, Pearl freestyles her way toward her only flotation source.

When she reaches it, sufficiently exerted from the thirty-yard swim, Pearl clings to the rubbery bumper for dear life. Just as Blake had shown her, the waterproof band holding the starter key remains on her wrist, and the Sea-Doo is safely unpowered. But at the moment, nothing about her predicament feels particularly safe. She scans the surface of the water, watching a few boats pass by with absolutely no regard for her now compromised situation. It occurs to her that from anyone else's vantage point, she probably doesn't look all that vulnerable. People jump off their Sea-Doos all the time to cool off. And then those same people, who do not weigh as much as Pearl, hop right back on again. Submerged like this, nobody passing by could even see that Pearl is especially big or that, under the circumstances, getting right back on the Sea-Doo might be an especially big problem.

Just being able to hold on to something so unsinkable gives her some initial peace of mind. At the very least, she can finally pee. But the relief from having an empty bladder is fleeting and quickly replaced by intense frustration as she wrestles with all sides of the ski in a futile attempt to remount.

"Motherfucker!" she yells, slapping the fiberglass hull.

It only takes about seven earnest efforts before Pearl fully realizes the real peril of her predicament. For another fifteen minutes or so, she hangs there, feeling alone and helpless, wondering how long it will take before Ruby and Blake get worried and pull up anchor to come find her. For a moment, she considers the fact that without this Sea-Doo to hang on to, she could very easily drown. Pearl looks toward the nearest shore, trying to estimate the distance. It's maybe a mile. There is no way, she thinks. And just as she is sure there is no way she can make it to shore and no way out of this dilemma, Pearl is sure of something else—she's mad, mad at her own body, her own Pringle-stuffed stomach, and her own colossal inability to simply help herself, to simply save herself.

But before the lump in her throat turns into sobs, Pearl notices an approaching boat, another pointy, flashy cigarette, similar to the one that nearly sank her. She wants to scream for help and wave her arms in desperation. But the shame of her circumstance, the total humiliation, prevents her from doing so. Fortunately, the boat keeps approaching anyway.

From the onboard speakers, the boaters are blasting a familiar hip-hop tune, drowning out the throaty engines. Although the midday glare forces her to squint, Pearl can't miss the occupants at the helm—three well-built guys in board shorts and ball caps—college aged, maybe. As they get closer, she bobs even more in the rough water, until she's parallel to the stern, just shy of the outboard engines, which they've apparently killed on her behalf. As a couple of them lean over the hull, Pearl swallows the lump in her throat. This is not the time for waterworks. However awkward and uncomfortable this may be, at the moment, total reliance on the kindness of strangers is her only viable option.

"Need a hand?"

They are the three most reassuring words Pearl has ever heard, and she nods earnestly. Slowly, the boat drifts into position alongside the Sea-Doo where she can easily see their faces—teenagers, all of them. Somehow their youth makes the whole situation all the more embarrassing, underlining just how much someone Pearl's age and size should have known better.

"How about we give you a lift?" one of them asks, reaching down to stabilize the ski.

"Okay, that would be great," Pearl says, scanning the boat. "Where's your ladder?"

"No ladder," the driver of the boat hollers from the bow. She watches him lasso the handlebars on the drifting Sea-Doo, wishing she could just hang on to a ski rope and let them drag her to shore.

"Here, give me your hand," the taller one says, bending toward her, as if pulling Pearl into the boat might be as simple as fishing a flyaway sun hat off the surface of the water.

With no other option, Pearl does exactly what he tells her

to do and astonishingly, amazingly, this kid manages to pull her more than halfway up before he loses his grip and she goes splashing back under. This is exactly what she was afraid of, she thinks.

"I'm so sorry," Pearl says, choking on lake water. Now, she not only fears for herself but for the potential shoulder injury she may have just caused this Good Samaritan.

"No need to apologize, ma'am," the driver says. "Tyler's just a pussy," he adds, laughing. "He's my brother, so I can say that."

As Pearl bobs next to the boat, the three of them devise a plan involving brute force and a couple of twisted towels.

"Okay, so this time, on the count of three, I'll grab your hand, and Tyler and Caleb are gonna wrap these towels around you and use them to pull you into the boat. That way, you won't slip."

Pearl has no choice but to yield to their suggestion. She hopes and, for the love of God, prays that this pulley system, with the combined strength of three beefy boys, will be enough to get the job done.

"Alrighty, here we go," he adds, leaning down with both arms. "Now give me your hands. One. Two. Three."

With a big tug, he hoists Pearl from the water as if she were a prize trophy marlin, one he wasn't about to let get away. As she's flopping next to the hull, mortified, Tyler and Caleb wrap one of the towels around her girth. With each pulling on one end, together, the three of them manage to get Pearl up and over the side of the boat, where she lands hard against the bench seat.

"Ow," she says, pushing herself up to a seated position. "I think that's gonna leave a mark," she adds, rubbing the side of her thigh.

As all four of them catch their breaths, Caleb kindly offers Pearl the other towel.

"Here you go," he says.

"Thanks," she says, wiping her face. Slumped and soggy, with matted-down lake hair, Pearl isn't just waterlogged—she looks and feels totally shipwrecked.

"Sorry to be so much trouble," she says, self-consciously tucking the towel under her armpits so that it hangs down between her legs, covering up her wet T-shirt-clad torso.

"No trouble at all, ma'am," says the one who had called Tyler a pussy. "By the way, I'm Ben."

"Thanks, Ben," she adds.

"So how long you been out here waiting on a rescue," he asks, pulling a bottle of water from the cooler. "Here ya go," he adds, unscrewing the cap for her.

Before answering, Pearl takes a long swig, surprised by her own thirst.

"Probably only twenty minutes," she says. "But it felt more like twenty hours."

"So where's your boat?" Caleb asks.

"Just over there," Pearl says, pointing off to the left. "Beyond that big house on the bluff. It's a pontoon. My sister and her friend are anchored down in the cove on the other side."

"If it's okay, maybe Tyler can ride the ski over and we'll take you?"

Pearl nods gratefully. She can't think of a better plan, and as Ben starts the engines and, once again, cranks the Wiz Khalifa, Pearl cringes at her calamity, feeling humbled beyond words by the heroics of these teenage total strangers.

"Hang on," Ben says, turning toward the cove.

Off they go, nose up—racing back to Ruby and Blake.

In less than ten minutes, they're slowing down, approaching the pontoon. Tyler trails behind on the ski as Blake and Ruby stand, mouths agape, with hands cupped to foreheads, trying to verify that the heavyset person slumped in the back of this tricked-out MasterCraft is, undeniably, Pearl.

The spectacle of the whole ordeal casts a haze on the rest of the day, and a palpable tension emerges between Ruby and Pearl. For as much as Blake tries to laugh the whole thing off to put both sisters at ease and reassure Pearl that she's not the only person to ever bum a ride on a boat in the middle of Lake Texoma, there is a pathetic truth about the whole thing that Ruby cannot ignore. Her sister is officially too big for a safety vest and too ashamed to admit it. Because of these two facts, she had come perilously close to disaster, and there isn't enough beer onboard to let either one of them forget it.

Chapter 6

Head held high, clutching the shiny folder filled with all her pre-op paperwork along with the big, fat cashier's check in the amount of exactly $14,000, Pearl walks into the Austin Weight Loss Specialists clinic to book her bariatric surgery. It's 4:45 p.m., and Ruby still hasn't called her back. But Pearl thinks it's better this way. Now, when she does actually speak with her sister, she'll be sharing a firm plan. Pearl imagines how totally mind-blown Ruby will be to hear that her can't-even-buckle-a-seat-belt, morbidly obese sister, who took seven years to finish her bachelor's in social work and who, at twenty-nine years old, still lives within the confines of their time-capsule childhood home, has not only made this life-altering decision but has also paid for it. And the thought of blowing Ruby's mind in such a delightful way produces a sly grin on Pearl's face as she approaches the reception desk.

Right away, the same cheerful Hispanic woman who greeted her last week recognizes Pearl.

"Hello, welcome back," she says, sliding open the glass partition.

"Hi. I'm Pearl Crenshaw. I had my consult last week, and I want to go ahead and schedule my surgery with Dr. George."

By the time she walks back to her car, Pearl has paid for her bariatric sleeve procedure and secured her spot on the surgery schedule: March 13. Less than eight weeks separate "before" Pearl from "after" Pearl. But between now and then, there's plenty of preparation, including a psychiatric consultation, meetings with dietitians, bloodwork, a cardiac workup, the dreaded sleep study, and yet another procedure Pearl has never even heard of and, for that matter, can't pronounce.

On Valentine's Day, she's scheduled to undergo something called an esophagogastroduodenoscopy, commonly referred to as an EGD. In this procedure, Dr. George will stick a camera down her esophagus to take a pre-op look-see, to check for things like ulcers and some dreaded infection known as *H. pylori*. With the scope, he'll also be able to map out the parts of her stomach he intends to cut away during the surgery in March. Mercifully, this is done under sedation. But the thought of a camera sliding down her throat does give Pearl pause. Placing her shiny folder (now filled with a stack of referrals) on the passenger seat, she grabs her neck, feels the breathless beginnings of a panic attack emerging. Propofol is the drug they'll use to knock her out for the EGD. But…isn't that the same drug that killed Michael Jackson? It sounds familiar, like something Skip would have taken just for fun. And before she even turns on the ignition, Pearl is fact-checking this little detail on her phone. With one keyword, propofol, a slew of headlines and morbid details appear. Biting her lips, Pearl scans enough to confirm her suspicions.

Propofol: the drug that killed Michael Jackson.

The cause of death is acute propofol intoxication, which caused the singer to stop breathing.

Propofol kills the King of Pop

"Are you kidding me?" she says to herself, still scrolling. For as certain as she was (still mostly is) about having the sleeve, she's totally freaked out by the prospect of some anesthesiologist inadvertently getting her dosage wrong. At her size, Pearl figures, this could easily happen. And although she has no idea how they do the math to come up with the propofol knockout sweet spot, she can't help but wonder if, most especially because of her weight, any of this is actually safe. And it's this yin and yang, this duality of emotions, that grips Pearl, quickens her breath. For as excited as she is at the prospect of a more fulfilling life, she's also scared shitless she might die before she even gets to have one. She types some other keywords into the search bar, words she's already entered half a dozen times since her appointment last week: chances of dying from bariatric surgery.

Her eyes land on some University of Washington study explaining how one in fifty people die within the first month post-op and how that figure jumps nearly fivefold if the surgeon is inexperienced. And as is the case when one goes down so many panic-driven internet-searching wormholes, Pearl finds herself losing all track of time. Unaware that the sun has now set and she is all alone in the dark parking lot at Austin Weight Loss Specialists, she feverishly scrolls on her phone, the light from the screen illuminating her full face.

Perhaps another review of Dr. Henry George's medical credentials might assuage her fears. Her eyes gobble up the keywords: board certified in general surgery, residency completed in 2006 at Johns Hopkins, fellowship training at Duke. For shits and giggles, she types his name into Facebook and immediately spots his profile, amazed at the more intimate granular details she can absorb about this almost perfect stranger who will soon put her under the knife. Can she trust him with her life? He's definitely not an over-poster. In fact, the most recent picture she sees is Dr. George in running shorts and a burnt-orange, long-sleeved Texas Longhorn T-shirt from the Austin Turkey Trot in November of last year. Ah. So he's a runner, just like Ruby, Pearl thinks. As she scrolls, she sees he has a thing for the famous roadside El Arroyo Tex-Mex restaurant marquee signs, whose black letters tell a new daily joke to passing Austin motorists. The signs themselves are, like so many old Austin secrets, local institutions gone viral. These days, the El Arroyo collections of witticisms are featured in everything from coffee-table books to coasters, and as Pearl reads some of the ones on Dr. George's Facebook feed, she finds herself liking him almost as much as she likes El Arroyo's chicken quesadillas—which is really saying something. Amused, she skims over some of his more current content.

Do you think Trump gets his hairpieces for free? Or does he have toupee?

Nothing moves faster than a girl untagging herself from a bad photo.

and

In dog margaritas, I only had one.

Although it's easy and not surprising at all to see he has a smart sense of humor, Pearl is stunned that Dr. George doesn't appear to be married. And from what she can glean on his social media, he also doesn't appear to have any children of his own, although as she continues to scroll through his posts, she sees a tagged picture of Dr. George standing in front of a Christmas tree flanked by twin girls in footed pajamas. The caption reads, "We love it when Uncle Henry is home for the holidays." At this point, Pearl is officially borderline stalking her surgeon, actually tapping on the highlighted name of the tagger in that family Christmas photo, when suddenly her phone rings. It's Ruby.

"Hey," Pearl says, finally starting her engine.

"Hey yourself," Ruby says flatly. "Sorry I'm just now getting back to you. It's been a total clusterfuck of a day. I've got this older woman we just hired on, a brand-new empty nester, who literally has zero clue about anything to do with technology, so I'm having to spoon-feed her all these mini crash courses on basic computer skills, stuff like how to convert JPEGs to PDFs. You wouldn't believe the digital divide that exists between us and people pushing fifty."

Before Pearl can respond, Ruby's already blabbing away about something else, as is the case for most of their conversations.

"So anyway, when I haven't been doing everyone else's jobs, I've been putting out fires with a couple of our advertisers, which is why, at this very moment, I'm running late to this thing at the Mansion."

"What thing?" Pearl asks. She's heard of this exclusive hotel on Turtle Creek, but she's never actually been there.

"Oh, Stanley Korshak is hosting a style show for the Laura Bush Foundation. DALLUX is a sponsor."

"Sounds glamorous," Pearl says.

"It might be if I'd actually had time to get a blowout or

change clothes or something. Didn't really factor all that remedial computer instruction into my busy day. Oh well, red lipstick to the rescue. What's new with you anyway?"

"Oh, just this and that," Pearl says evasively, too nervous to just spit it out.

"You okay?"

"Yep, as a matter of fact, I'm doing great. Really great."

Pearl is never doing "great," and the use of this adjective piques Ruby's interest.

"Oh yeah? Do tell."

"Well, believe it or not, I just scheduled my bariatric surgery."

"Your what?"

"I'm having weight loss surgery on March 13."

"Whoa," Ruby says. "Say that again."

"On March thirteenth, I'm having a procedure called a sleeve gastrectomy. There's a surgeon here in Austin who, by the way, happens to be both hot and, I'm almost positive, single. His name is Dr. Henry George. Anyway, he's basically going to reduce my stomach to about fifteen percent of its original size."

"Wow, that sounds drastic. Is it permanent?"

"Totally," Pearl says. "I'll basically be eating Barbie portions for the rest of my life."

"But, Pearl, are you sure you can handle that?"

The question rubs Pearl wrong, and she's not sure which she hates more: Ruby's condescension or her own self-doubt.

"Well, once the surgery is done, I won't really have a choice,"

Pearl explains crisply. "It's pretty much do or die, in terms of following all the post-op protocols."

"Well, if it's so do or die, why can't you apply the same approach and try losing weight in a more natural way? Like, say, by diet and exercise?"

Pearl anticipated this reaction but doesn't really believe someone like Ruby could possibly stomach the truth. Like how, for example, earlier today, she had devoured three bacon, egg, and cheese breakfast burritos in one sitting, or how during her lunch break, she'd consumed not one but two orders of Nachos Supreme from Taco Bell. She isn't sure Ruby can even fathom the intricacies of metabolic syndrome or the counterintuitive ways in which, even half-starving, morbidly obese people can still just keep getter fatter and fatter. No, an oral confession of Pearl's food diary is just too big a conversation to have over the phone.

"Hello?" Ruby says, prompting. "I mean, Pearl, I know so many friends who've had major success with keto."

Pearl doesn't say it out loud, but she bets not one of Ruby's friends weighs anything close to 531 pounds.

"It just seems like you should exhaust all the other options before you resort to—"

"Ruby, I have spent the better part of twenty years struggling with my weight. Don't you remember Jenny Craig? I mean, it's pretty obvious, but the natural way hasn't really worked for me," Pearl says. "Anyway, I've made up my mind, and like I said, I booked my surgery for March thirteenth."

For a few beats, there is silence. Neither of them says a word.

"How are you paying for this anyway?" Ruby asks finally.

"Mom told me to sell her jewelry and use the money to pay the surgeon."

There is more silence. As Pearl winds her way in the dark through the residential streets of Tarrytown, she imagines Ruby rolling her eyes, shaking her head with disapproval.

"So you sold her Rolexes?"

"Tried selling her wedding ring from Skip, too, but guess what?"

"What?"

"The diamond was fake."

"Hmmph, not surprised. You let Birdie know about that yet?"

"Not yet," Pearl says. "She's supposed to call me Wednesday."

"Well, won't you have plenty to report?"

"Look," Pearl says, pulling into the driveway, clicking the button for the garage door. "I called to tell you about my surgery, and I guess I just figured that you, of all people, would be happy for me."

"Oh, here we go, Pearl the martyr," Ruby says.

"I am not a martyr!"

"Yes, you are," Ruby says emphatically. "You are the same Pearl who lives in the same shell we grew up in, who has basically lived your life like it's one long, drawn-out candlelight vigil to honor all of Birdie's poor choices. And instead of grabbing the bull by the horns and doing what was in your best interest, you just let yourself go. I mean, am I really supposed to be happy that my baby sister has gained so much weight that she now has to undergo some kind of radical operation to correct for it? C'mon, Pearl. Is this where I'm supposed say yay?"

In the garage, Pearl sits there, holding the phone to her ear, staring at their twin Schwinns still hanging from hooks in the corner, cobwebbed and rusty. When they were kids, the two of them pedaled those bikes up the steep grade of Cherry Lane all the way to school, Pearl trailing behind and Ruby, athletic Ruby, always effortlessly circling back, hollering at plump little Pearl to pedal faster, harder. Tears pool in her eyes as she recalls the old tried-and-true chupacabra trick and the win-at-all-costs tactics Ruby employed to help Pearl shine, especially in competitive social settings.

What she wants to say but feels too stuck to is that she can't explain exactly why she just stopped moving, stopped living a life of forward motion.

"Look, I'm sorry, Pearl. If this is what you think you need in order to get healthy, then just do it."

"I can't do it alone," Pearl says tearfully. "Someone has to take me to the surgery and drive me home, and I'll need some help for a week or so right after that."

"And you want me to come stay at that house with you? Pearl, you know how I feel about that place. I swore when I left I would never go back."

In desperation, Pearl pleads tearfully for Ruby to make an exception.

"You think I like asking you for help? Do you seriously think this is easy for me? Could you, for once, try wearing my fat pants for a single minute and try to have some basic empathy? I mean, I realize that you have a very important job, and you've got your shit together in so many ways that I don't, but this surgery, me doing this, is my last chance at...at living. Do you have any idea how much I weigh now? No, I bet you don't. You know why? Because we hardly ever see each other. And that's because you can't stand the sight of me. You can't stand the fact that you're genetically linked to someone like me, someone who weighs what I do. Five thirty-one, Ruby! That's how much I weigh! So as much as I would love to consider natural weight loss, there's just nothing natural about my situation, okay? And although the surgery scares the shit out of me, that number scares me even more!"

The sobs come loud and hard, and it seems that hearing her sister's raw pain pulls a scab off so many old wounds the two of them share, so Ruby lets Pearl catch her breath before offering a reply.

"I'll be there," she says finally. "Just email me the dates and times and all the details, and I'll clear my calendar."

Chapter 7

At the dining room table in the cafeteria, one of Pearl's patients, Mr. Reynolds, fumbles with the buttons on his cardigan sweater. He's trying to make sense of the way the holes and the buttons articulate with one another, but since his own brain struggles to communicate with his tremulous fingers, Pearl does it for him.

"Thanks, Toots," he says. Although she's cared for him for over a year and despite the fact that her name tag clearly says Pearl Crenshaw, Mr. Reynolds has never called her anything other than Toots. But having been called so many worse names, Pearl counts it as a term of endearment and savors it just as much as she savors Wednesdays and the always-on-time, never-missed visits from Mr. Reynolds's son, Ramsay. Not only is Ramsay the kind of eye candy Pearl could totally binge on all day long, he's also, in Pearl's best estimation, a 100 percent decent human being.

A. He never misses his weekly visits with his dad.

B. He always looks Pearl directly in the eye, avoiding any impulse to size her up.

C. Without even looking at her tag, he knows Pearl's first and last name and often sends handwritten notes of appreciation to Glenwood Manor management, which Perry always tacks up on the employee bulletin board in the break room for everyone to see.

And not to be understated is the special thrill Pearl derives from seeing the letters of her name spelled out in Ramsay's manly yet elegant cursive: "Pearl's very personal approach to caring for my dad…" or "Pearl's passion for people…" and, perhaps, her favorite little morsel of all—"Pearl is the hidden gem of Glenwood Manor."

The fact is, Ramsay Reynolds is the best-looking guy to ever say anything fabulous about her, and she soaks up his thoughtful appreciation like a pancake swimming on a plate of syrup.

So although in a sixty-bed unit like Glenwood, Pearl has plenty of other residents to attend to, on Wednesdays at noon, when Ramsay is about to make his appearance, Pearl is Mr. Reynolds's shadow, a now regular occurrence that has not gone unnoticed by Perry.

And today, at exactly 11:53 a.m., the countdown is underway. With a woman from the Knights of Columbus Ladies Auxiliary pounding away on the piano, Pearl hums along in anticipation to "You Are My Sunshine." Sitting there at the cafeteria table already adorned with festive red Valentine centerpieces, she watches Mr. Reynolds pet one of the therapy spaniels while keeping one eye on the door. Perry, who tends to know where Pearl is at this time every Wednesday, does not miss a chance to razz her.

Ready for your lunch date? he texts, adding a winking emoji.

Pearl looks up from her screen, scans the cafeteria, and spots Perry over in the corner, just beyond the knitting class, winking at her in real life.

She smiles, even blushes a little, but looks down at her screen and sends Perry a middle finger emoji in return.

As if on cue, Ramsay Reynolds strolls purposefully toward Pearl. Actually, he's strolling toward his father, but sometimes Pearl allows herself to blur this distinction, fantasizing instead that he's coming for her—that she's seated at a dimly lit table for two at some swanky sushi place downtown, and instead of the little old lady from Knights of Columbus playing "You Are My Sunshine," there's an actual musician playing soft jazz on a glossy baby grand. In her mind's eye, she sees a much more exotic version of herself—a worldly, chopstick-wielding, sake-sipping food critic whose discriminating palate has earned her both fame and fortune as well as the unyielding attention of sophisticated men like, say, Ramsay—guys who think Pearl's rolls are even more dynamite than the sushi. And just about the time she starts to take this yummy little game of make-believe to the next level—imagining Ramsay's warm breath in her ear, maybe even the gentle kiss of his tongue tasting the side of her neck as he tells Pearl she's the very essence of deliciousness, that she is, in fact, his umami—she's suddenly buzzed back to reality by her cell phone. Another text from Perry:

You're seriously drooling. Am I gonna have to come chaperone?

Pearl ignores the comment and instead shifts her gaze back toward rapidly approaching Ramsay. Seeing her, he waves. Sadly, his father, Mr. Reynolds, is in the stage of dementia where he isn't aware of anyone's presence until they are right in front of him. Pearl knows that Ramsay knows this, which is why Pearl knows that Ramsay's wave is exclusively for her.

As he gets closer, she tries acting nonchalant. But she can't help but notice all six feet two of this sandy-blond hunk of a man, his disarming smile, his Patagonia fleece-vest ruggedness. There's a certain Chip Gaines quality about him that has Pearl silently swooning.

"Hey, Pearl," he says, pulling up a chair.

"Hi yourself," she says. "Buddy's been keeping your dad company," she adds, nodding toward the dog at Mr. Reynolds's feet.

"I see that," Ramsay says, reaching down to pet the pup. "How you doin', Buddy? Dad, you're looking good."

Mr. Reynolds studies his son, sees something vaguely familiar but can't quite find the words. And in watching this dynamic,

Pearl finds yet another reason to admire Ramsay—his seemingly total confidence in the most uncomfortable of moments. Like a moth drawn to a flame, Buddy gets up and plops down right on top of Ramsay's white Chuck Taylors.

"Pearl, how are you?" Ramsay asks while glancing down to check the screen on his phone.

"Oh, you know, same ol'," she says. She fights an impulse to divulge her big news—that she's less than seven weeks away from a major metamorphosis, that maybe, in time, he might not even recognize her. Ramsay is a carrot, she thinks. Mentally, she adds him to her list of post-op goals. It's within the realm of possibility, she thinks, that in another year or so, he might look forward to seeing Pearl every Wednesday in the same way she looks forward to seeing him.

"What's new with you?" Pearl asks instead.

"Well, actually, I have some pretty big news," Ramsay says, rubbing his hands together. He looks back over his shoulder toward the door. "My fiancée, Eva, is out parking her car. You and Dad will both get to meet her today."

Although Ramsay is still talking, all Pearl hears is the muffled voice of Charlie Brown's teacher and the warped wah-wah-who-wah-wah of unrequited love. As he drones on about how they met, how quickly they fell for one another, and how when you know, you know, Pearl is still processing that one word—fiancée. Feeling foolish, embarrassed, and suddenly insanely insecure, she manages a fake smile, feigns a listening ear, all the while chiding herself for her silly grade-school crush. She glances over toward the knitting class, grateful Perry has slipped off to some other duty and can't see the look on her face or the spectacle of this gut-wrenching encounter.

"There's my girl," Ramsay says, standing.

And crushing as it may be, Eva does indeed look lovely enough to be on a guy like Ramsay's arm. Pearl wants to hate her: the sleek, dark bob, her tiny, belted waist, those ridiculously long lashes she's batting at Ramsay as he leans down to give her a gentle kiss right smack on her fabulous lips.

"Dad," Ramsay says, bending down to meet his father's eye level. "This is Eva."

To their surprise, Mr. Reynolds extends his right hand up toward Eva.

"Nolan Reynolds," he says with total certainty. "Pleasure to meet you. Please, have a seat."

Ramsay and Pearl exchange a knowing glance, both amused by Mr. Reynolds's sudden, if fleeting, self-assuredness.

"You must be Pearl," Eva says with a friendly wave across the table.

"Hi," Pearl says, nodding, feeling slightly buoyed by the notion that Ramsay has actually mentioned her by name.

"Ramsay raves about you," she adds. "He says you're a natural caretaker."

And as nice a compliment as that may be, at this moment, the incongruity of this truth strikes Pearl hard, for as good as she legitimately is at caring for the residents at Glenwood Manor, why hasn't she been better at caring for herself?

"I guess I just love my job…and I'm especially fond of Mr. Reynolds," Pearl says, clumsily rising to her feet. "I'll let you all enjoy your lunch while I go check on some of the others. Nice meeting you, Eva. And congratulations."

With that, Pearl lumbers off toward the hall. It's the one day each week she sacrifices her own lunch break for a chance to be in the presence of a nice man like Ramsay. Rounding the corner, as she looks back at the three of them, Pearl suddenly feels famished.

Walking up right behind her, Perry observes the new girl in the mix and puts it all together.

"You have better hair," he says, reading her mind.

Slightly startled, Pearl just shakes her head. "Whatever," she says.

"Care to join me for lunch?" Perry says. "I'll share my roasted beet salad with you."

They eat outside on the terrace, embracing the gift of a sunny, sixty-eight-degree late-January day. Along with the sun and the salad, Perry's good company is enough to lift Pearl's spirits.

"BT-dub, I approved your request for time off next week," he says, probing. "More pre-op tests?"

She nods. Beet salad isn't something she eats regularly. And eating with someone else is out of the ordinary, too.

Self-consciously, she finds herself pacing her bites, trying to mimic Perry's own noshing.

"It's going to be a busy week of professionals prying into my innermost thoughts and dreams. Not gonna lie. I'm totally dreading the psych consult and the sleep study," she says. "There are just so many hurdles to clear before my actual surgery."

"It's all preparation for your new life to come. For the hot minute Bruce and I were together, I recall all he consumed was protein and water," he says, delicately patting his mouth.

"I guess that means no more waffle fries," Pearls says, smiling, both of them sharing a laugh.

"So are you scared shitless or what?"

She sighs, looks down at the small paper plate of kale and golden beets. Even with the big, chunky walnuts and crumbled feta, the notion of eating like this for the rest of her life seems so...so...totally undoable.

"Scared to death," she admits. "But like I told Ruby the other night on the phone, I'm at the point now where I'm more afraid of staying the way I am than anything else."

"Pearl, girl, you just have to put your double chin up," he says, winking. "You're coming into your season. It's so perfect your surgery is in March: you'll be blossoming along with all the Texas bluebonnets. You should start doing some fantasy 'Add to Cart' for motivation."

"What's 'Add to Cart'?" she asks, checking the time on her phone.

"It's where you shop online and keep filling your basket with all your heart's desires: skinny jeans, clingy cashmere sweaters, sexy silk skirts, high heels, you name it. Whatever catches your eye, whatever speaks to you, you just add it to your cart. As long as you don't go checking out and maxing out your credit cards, it's a totally healthy practice. And trust me, that digital wish list will serve as a great source of motivation. Works for me anyway. In fact, this salad we're eating is actually less about beets and more about my lust-worthy ByGeorge cart."

"I'll have to try that," Pearl says. "I never shop online," she confesses.

Perry stops chewing his huge bite of beet and looks at her in disbelief.

"I'm serious," Pearl says. "I can't ever be sure anything, including shoes, will even fit. It just comes with the territory. There's no virtual way to try on tents, Perry. That technology has not been developed yet."

"No, no, no," Perry says, shaking his finger at her. "Remember what we discussed. No negative self-talk. Tent tops are about to be a thing of your past, Pearl. So instead of looking so forlorn about Ramsay Reynolds and that pretty brunette, get excited about your future."

Pearl doesn't finish what's on her plate, not because she isn't hungry but just to sort of try on the Cinderella slipper of an "oh my gosh, I'm so stuffed" skinny girl. As she excuses herself and separates her plastic from paper at the recycling bin next to the door, she thanks Perry for sharing and heads back inside just in time to intercept Ramsay and Eva at the reception desk.

"Oh, hey, glad we caught you. Eva and I are just leaving," Ramsay says. "Listen, Pearl, I've already told the front desk, but we won't be back for a couple of weeks. Eva and I are getting married this weekend, and then we're headed down to Bali for a honeymoon."

Pearl chews on the inside of her cheeks, forcing a smile.

"Oh my gosh," Pearl manages. "You're going to have such a great time," she adds, wanting to cry.

"You've been?" Eva asks, her grin revealing a deep dimple Pearl hadn't noticed before.

And although Pearl's never even flown on a plane to Dallas, let alone the Southern Hemisphere, for reasons she can't quite explain at this moment, with the two of them standing before her, already the very picture of wedded bliss, she prefers for them to believe she has.

"All I can say is the colors of Bali are absolutely beautiful this time of year," she says emphatically. "Next to Texas, Indonesia is, like, my absolute favorite!"

Chapter 8

It's 7:00 p.m., and Pearl is sprawled out on the sofa at home digesting the Taco Bell she snarfed down during a single episode of *Fixer Upper*. By the time Chip and JoJo are making the big reveal on some historic shotgun-style house near Baylor, she's already polished off one beef nacho griller with an extra side of queso, one order of nachos BellGrande, four bean-and-cheese burritos, most of a chicken quesadilla, and every last drop of a sixty-four-ounce Diet Dr Pepper. The beet salad with Perry had done very little to hold her over, and as Pearl stares at the TV, her mind drifts. She wonders what exactly Perry ate for dinner, tries to imagine if it's truly possible to feel full eating such simple, small portions. She knows that soon enough, she will have to purge these private postwork smorgasbords on her sofa and start eating in public at an actual table, where there is actual social pressure to consume less-intoxicating servings. But for now, Pearl licks the gooey residue from her fingers, wishing she'd ordered just one extra taco.

Alone in her home, she stares at the giant plastic take-out bag on the coffee table filled with greasy wrappers, now stinking up the living room. Only moments ago, that bag had been filled with so much possibility, the promise of total fulfillment. On the way home from work, at the drive-thru, the mouthwatering warm, familiar smell of refried beans and flour tortillas had made it hard to resist busting into one of the burritos before she made it home. But now, in this postbinge aftermath, the salsa-drenched stench of shame is enough to push Pearl up and off the sofa. With trash in hand, she makes her way to the kitchen. The walk alone, especially after that little feast, is taxing. With each step, Pearl tries to justify how these are some of her last suppers. By February 26, she'll be on the eve of a two-week liquid pre-op diet, and after surgery, it'll be adios Taco Bell.

So she tells herself it's okay to live a little, to savor these waning days of morbid obesity in the company of so many calories. In the pantry, she finds the trash can too full to add these Taco Bell remnants, and the prospect of lifting all that garbage out of the container and walking it all the way out to the curb might as well be a twenty-three-mile hike to the Travis County Landfill. It's not happening, not tonight anyway. Instead, she crumples up the plastic as best she can and tosses the sack into the sink along with two empty cans of Diet Dr Pepper.

Her mom's call is right on time, but Pearl has to put a little pep in her step to get back to the living room where her cell phone is parked, as always, right next to the remote control. She mutes Chip and JoJo and instead tunes in to the prison voice recording.

"This is a call from inmate Elizabeth Crenshaw Benzer at the Mountain View Prison Unit. Press one to accept..."

"Mom," she says, fiddling with the screen. She puts Birdie on speaker. "You there? Can you hear me?"

"I'm here, sweetheart," Birdie says. "How you doin'?"

"Well, I'm just sort of kicking back and taking it easy tonight," Pearl says, lowering herself back onto the sofa.

"You watching your show?"

"I am. But I'm not loving this particular house. It's something called shotgun-style. The whole front porch isn't more than twelve feet wide. It's like a long, narrow box with a roof."

"Right," Birdie says. "That type of structure is actually very historic. The lore on that name comes from the theory that a bullet shot through the front door could exit the back without hitting anything. But really it was more about money. Used to be, you could pack more houses onto a street if they were narrow. Back in the day, property taxes used to be based on frontage, so the smaller the better. They were popular in the south because that kind of design means all the doors line up, and you could open the front and back doors and let the breeze float straight through."

Joanna Gaines pretty well explained all that at the start of this episode, but Pearl doesn't interrupt her mom's detailed explanation. After all, there is only so much wisdom a mom can impart from behind bars, and sitting there, hearing Birdie's voice fill the room from the cell phone resting atop Pearl's belly, almost makes it feel like they're together, under the same roof.

"All I know is that I wouldn't want to live in any house where the architecture has anything to do with guns," Pearl says.

"I understand that," Birdie says.

It's quiet for a moment or two, both of them silently recalling the gun and Skip, that Halloween night, and the haunting sound of that fatal shot. But they stuff the truth of that evening in a locked box from the past. The key's been missing for so long, both of them forgot where they left it.

"Well, speaking of *Fixer Upper*," Pearl says, switching gears, "I'm about to be one myself."

"You booked it?" Suddenly, her mom sounds enthused.

"March thirteenth," Pearl says.

"Oh, sweetheart, I'm so glad you're doing this. It's time. How did you pay for it?"

"Oh, well, actually, I did what you said, took the two watches and that ring Skip gave you."

"Good, so you got enough to cover…"

"Well, I got a little more than fourteen thousand for the Rolexes combined, but that ring of yours—turns out it was fake."

Birdie's heavy sigh fills the living room along with so many old regrets. Pearl fixes her eyes on the family picture of all four Crenshaws—her dad, mom, Ruby, and Pearl—dressed up for some Easter Sunday past, the girls smiling in their white patent leather Mary Janes, both clinging to matching baskets full of brightly colored plastic eggs.

"That seems impossible," Birdie says. "I distinctly recall, at one point, he took it to be appraised for insurance. It was valued at something around twenty thousand dollars."

"Well, not anymore, Mom. The jeweler said it was worthless. Wouldn't give me a dime for it."

Birdie sighs once more. "Well, I'm glad the watches were enough. You tell Ruby yet?"

"I did," Pearl says.

"And?"

"And she says she's coming to help."

"Good," her mom says. Pearl hears the relief in her voice. "Nice to know she'll be with you for that. The two of you were always so close when you were little. Maybe this'll rekindle some of that closeness."

"I have my doubts," Pearl says. "I mean you don't have to try to sugarcoat things, Mom. She's not coming because she wants to. She's coming out of guilt."

"Pearl, try to remember, actions speak louder than words."

"I'm well aware," Pearl says. "But what about you? Have you talked to Ruby lately?"

She already knows the answer, but for some reason, Pearl asks anyway—her way of reminding her mom how fractured their family became once Skip Benzer entered their lives.

"I've pretty much given up on trying to reach your sister," Birdie says. "After twelve years of all my letters being returned unopened and all my calls going to voicemail, I got the message. Hopefully, one of these days, she'll come around. Anyway, we only have four more minutes, and I want to hear more about you and this surgery. What all do you have to do to get ready for it anyway? Don't you have to start losing weight now, in preparation? I think I read something about that."

"Yes. And I'm on my way," Pearl says, stuffing the truth. "I had a salad for lunch."

Chapter 9

Sprawled out supine on her four-poster bed, stuffed into a pair of Ruby's brand-new back-to-school jeans, Pearl stares up at the popcorn ceiling, giving her right hand a rest. For the better part of five minutes, she's tugged at the zipper to no avail. Examining the small cut on her index finger, she gives it a lick, smoothing out the rough skin injury she's incurred trying to force the metal pull over all those resistant teeth.

"We're gonna be late," Ruby yells from the bathroom. "And it's your fault if I get a tardy," she adds.

"One second," Pearl replies. "Mom isn't even back yet."

Even with the door closed, Pearl can hear the water running in the bathroom, which reminds her that she'll have to hold it all day long at school, because once she gets these jeans zipped, there is no way they're coming off until she gets back home.

"She just went to get gas, Pearl," Ruby says, rummaging

through her pink Claire's Caboodles case. "We're supposed to be waiting out front in two minutes."

Pearl doesn't reply. Instead, deep as she can, she inhales, trying to flatten her tummy enough to get the zipper to slide all the way up. But try as she might, it just isn't happening.

In the mirror of the Jack-and-Jill bathroom they share, Ruby effortlessly smears on some cotton-candy-flavored Lip Smacker and quickly slides a bobby pin into the side bangs of her *There's Something About Mary* bob before making one final inspection. By this time, Pearl is no longer able to keep her breathy struggle a secret.

"What are you doing?" Ruby says, appearing at the foot of the bed. "Hey, aren't those mine?"

"It's stuck," Pearl says, sufficiently red-faced. "The zipper is messed up."

Pearl knows what Ruby is thinking—that the jeans aren't even hers, let alone her size, and besides, she didn't even ask to borrow them. But she must look too defeated to debate these matters, because instead of getting mad, Ruby shows mercy. Pearl suspects it's mercy mixed with a big pile of pity—especially after their recent back-to-school shopping trip at the Gap and Pearl's frustration in the dressing room when everything Ruby tried on fit and most of what Pearl tried on did not.

"Look, dummy, even if you're only in fifth grade, everyone knows you have to plan your outfits ahead of time," Ruby says, noticing their Mom's Suburban pulling up in the driveway. "That means you have to try things on the night before, Pearl."

"But *Oprah* says we are skinniest first thing in the morning," Pearl explains, taking another lick of the blood on her worn-out finger.

Quickly, Ruby mounts the bed.

"Here, let me try," she says, straddling her sister. "Now suck in your belly," she adds.

Best she can, Ruby tugs on the zipper, but it barely budges.

"Told you it was messed up," Pearl says.

The horn honking out front signals Birdie's impatience. Ever since their dad died, it's been like this: their mom burning both ends of the catering candle in a constant state of multitasking, even on their morning commute.

"Don't you know? You have to button it first and then zip," Ruby explains, knowing full well that what she's saying may or may not be true. "Just let me do it, and then we gotta go!"

Pearl takes one final deep breath and holds it, doing her best to flatten her tummy. From this position, Ruby is at last able to secure the button, and with one final yank, she slides the zipper into place.

"There!" she says, sliding off Pearl, back to the floor. "Now come on!"

With the jeans properly secured, Pearl rolls off her bed and takes one look in the full-body mirror hanging on the back of her door.

"Do they look too tight?" she asks, turning side to side.

There is no doubt about the answer to this question, but Ruby just doesn't have the heart to tell her the truth. And besides, their mom is honking again.

For the rest of the day, Pearl suffers in silence. In homeroom, when they recite the Pledge of Allegiance, she tries to ignore the way the jeans bite into her waistline, creating an uncomfortable muffin top. And at lunch, although she finishes every last bite of her pepperoni Hot Pocket as well as a sleeve of Oreos she bought in the vending machine, she takes only a few small sips of her Capri-Sun because she knows she'll have to wait until at least 3:45 to pee. The worst is PE. As durable as the denim may be, the super snug fit doesn't offer the stretch she needs to give it her all at kickball. So instead, Pearl finds herself hanging out on the sidelines, doing her best to be invisible. With her face smooshed between the holes on the chain-link backstop, she watches the other kids run the bases, counting the minutes until the bell rings when she can, at last, free herself from the bondage of her stupid borrowed pants.

The steady flow of traffic along the perimeter of the playground is little more than white noise until the sudden screech of tires causes everyone on the field, including Pearl, to turn and look. It's another near miss at the busy intersection, one Pearl is all too familiar with. She watches for a moment, noticing how the cars involved have come a to standstill just inches from collision, as though some kind of invisible force field seems to have blocked one from broadsiding the other. As she watches, she thinks about her dad, wonders why him and not them.

"Not fair!" She hears one of her classmates scream to some kid trying to alter the kicking order.

For completely different reasons, Pearl wants to scream those very same words. She may not be the only one in her class being raised by a single mom, but she is the only one in her class with a dead dad. And that is definitely not fair. He's been gone for nearly two years now, and when Pearl tries to account for all that lost time, she feels her stomach growling. Sometimes there just aren't enough Oreos.

The tallest, skinniest, prettiest girl in her class lobs one off to the outfield, and Pearl watches her skip over toward first base with everyone cheering.

Not fair, she thinks again. There is nothing about not having a dad or not even fitting into these stupid jeans, much less this stupid school, that is one bit fair.

Chapter 10

Pearl spends the last weekend of January ditching a decade's worth of clothes she's had crammed into her closet. The rule is if she hasn't worn in it a year, she tosses it. By Sunday evening, the amount of stretchy fabric she's amassed is enough to fill eleven Hefty Cinch Saks. The nurse at the clinic reminded her she'll need to keep at least some of her presurgery clothes so she'll have things to wear in the months to come, as she begins shrinking.

Unlike Ruby, Pearl doesn't have the income to hop online and restock her soon-to-be-evolving wardrobe. She can't afford to play Perry's "Add to Cart" game and actually proceed to checkout, either. At least not yet. So she's sorted what's left into two piles: ugly and uglier. In the end, only the ugly clothes, the ones that made her feel the least bad about herself, got returned to her closet. She feels a twinge of sadness as she realizes there isn't one single item of clothing she actually likes to wear. The abstract notion of a favorite pair of jeans, power suit, or a sexy dress seems as far away as the feet she can no longer see from a standing position.

Appraising the heavy bags on the floor of her bedroom, she knows it will take at least two trips in her Altima to get all of it loaded up and off to Goodwill. Mentally, she adds this task to her list of things to do and moves on to another one she's been avoiding all weekend. For tomorrow's psych consult, she's supposed to complete an electronic document titled "Intake History for Bariatric Evaluation." She's scheduled to meet Dr. Lisa Field, the clinical psychologist whose name appears at the top of this form next to the letters PhD and MS PsyPharm. Sitting on her bed, Pearl enters some of the easier answers into her laptop: name, phone number, marital status, address, date of birth, occupation, age, gender, and ethnicity. She stalls for a moment at the blanks labeled current weight and height, but knowing she can't really fudge on these ones, she reluctantly enters the numbers 531 and 5'10".

The rest of this intake form consists of questions categorized as patient history. Pearl scrolls through six pages all the way to the bottom, and realizing this could take some time as well as an uncomfortable amount of introspection, she decides to move herself and her laptop to the bar in the kitchen where she'll be more comfortable—and where can finish the last two slices of pepperoni pizza she left in the box on the counter.

Once she's settled on the stool, Pearl pops the top on a can of Diet Dr Pepper and reads the first question:

Briefly state the reasons you are seeking bariatric surgery.

Stealing pepperonis off one slice to add to the other, she takes a big, cheesy bite and chews on this. There probably isn't enough room in the electronic field to type each and every reason. She thinks about using this space to declare an actual goal weight but has no idea what that might be. Besides, her reasons for pursuing the surgery aren't only about numbers. Finally, she starts tapping away at the keyboard.

So I'll no longer be referred to as "the fat girl."
So I can ride a bike again, like I did when I was a kid.
So I can fit into a single seat on a plane and see the colors
of Bali for real.
So I can tuck in a shirt.
So I can have a shot at living long enough to meet a nice
man and maybe even have a family of my own.

She takes another bite of pizza and presses on to the next question:

List any current stressors, recent or long-standing.

Again, she feels certain there isn't enough space to hold her lengthy answer. From the TV in the living room, she hears someone whistling, and the sound takes her back to Skip, the happy-go-lucky way he whistled his way into their lives, making all three of them fall in love with him and the idea of having a good man as part of their family. Everyone believed Skip was something he wasn't, even after he died. Pearl hates herself for at one time being impressed with anything about him, which was almost everything: his social status; his job as the general manager at Barrow Creek Country Club, which gave Ruby and Pearl an all-access pass to the pools and the tennis courts; that big Suburban, just like their mom's, that he pulled up in the first time he took Birdie on a date, and how gullibly she and her sister believed it was a sign that, unlike some of the sports car–driving dates Birdie had been on before, Skip must be different, the kind of guy who wants to take on more passengers. Pearl mutes the TV, quiets the whistle-triggered flood of bad memories and all Skip's addict erraticism. The self-described golf junkie turned out to be a junkie of a different sort. Fucking Percocet, she thinks, shaking her head.

Scrolling back in time, Pearl recalls with total clarity more bad memories: being eight years old the day her dad died in a car accident, how random and yet how totally her fault it all felt. For a long time, she blamed herself. She remembers Ruby pedaling off to school. For whatever reason, on that day, Pearl had decided to dig her heels in. She didn't have the energy or inclination to pedal up the steep grade of Cherry Lane, so instead, she stayed behind. She remembers the look of exasperation on her mother's face when she discovered Pearl standing outside, remembers kissing her dad goodbye and the smell of that Hugo Boss cologne he always wore to work, how a half-used bottle of it remained in her mom's bathroom cabinet until it was replaced by Skip's bottle of Dior Sauvage. How later that afternoon, while her mom was working a catering gig at the governor's mansion, her dad, who was on his way to pick Pearl up from school, was broadsided by a utility truck. Still, all these years later, she cringes at the hopelessly crushing nature of the word *broadsided*. Before that terrible day, Pearl did not know its meaning.

Now, down to the crust of her last slice of pizza, she contemplates which stressors, with so many blurring in her mind, she should actually mention on the intake form. Pearl pauses. Not since that Halloween night and the days and weeks that followed when she was questioned by police and a court-appointed child therapist has Pearl been prompted to write about her so-called stressors. Since then, she hasn't written so as much as a single detail, not even a journal entry, about the shooting, that pivotal moment when everything in their whole world turned upside down. Stress seems like too small a word to describe the hows and whys of who Pearl has become. She thinks maybe it's best to not get too specific on this form.

*When I was eight, my dad died. My mom remarried when
I was thirteen. And that man died, too. Since then,
my mom has been in prison. These are some of my
stressors.*

Typing that last sentence, Pearl finds herself laughing out loud at the understated, pathetic hilarity of a life filled with so much dysfunction and drama. Her past, just like her current weight, is so fucked up, she can't help but wonder if this psychologist will interpret this as more reason to proceed with the surgery or as a red flag not to. Some of the questions are easier than others.

Please list any diagnosed physical/medical conditions.

Miraculously, despite her morbid obesity, Pearl has not been diagnosed with any chronic illnesses, such as diabetes, which is common among the grossly overweight. She types in *N/A* for not applicable.

Medication list/Dosages (Include any medications for
physical conditions, mental health conditions, and
herbal or natural supplements)

Drugs are as foreign to Pearl as slenderness. The only thing she hates more than drugs are what they do to people. Drugs scare her to death, and again, she enters *N/A*.

Mental health history: Please indicate any current or past outpatient counseling/therapy, inpatient psychiatric hospitalizations, and/or outpatient or inpatient substance abuse treatment and dates of each.

Although she had to meet with a court-appointed therapist for several months after Skip's death, she types in *N/A.*

Family history: Please indicate any history of a blood relative with drug and alcohol addiction, eating disorders, depression, anxiety, ADHD, schizophrenia, or bipolar disorder.

Immediately she thinks of Skip, but he wasn't ever really her family, not by blood anyway. Her dad loved to drink Jim Beam and Coke, and her mom loved chardonnay and margaritas, but as best Pearl could recollect, neither could be classified as having any dependency. And there was never any mention of any family members, past or present, having mental health issues. Both sets of grandparents died of normal things like heart disease and cancer. Her mom was an only child, so there were no cousins on that side. And after her dad died, there weren't many reasons to make the trip up to North Carolina to visit their only uncle, who was married and was a stepfather to his wife's two children. After the car accident, it was just Pearl, Ruby, and Birdie doing their best to get by. She opens another can of Diet Dr Pepper, recalling how sad she was to lose her father, how vastly different her way of coping was from Ruby's. While her sister immersed herself in running, Pearl found comfort at the bottom of a box of Little Debbie snack cakes, especially the Swiss Rolls. Recalling the three boxes she bought a couple of weeks ago, she gets up from the bar and opens the pantry where a single package of Little Debbie Peanut Butter Crunch Bars is sitting right there on the shelf, just waiting to be devoured. A small dessert, Pearl thinks.

No known mental health conditions or addictions, she types onto the form and moves on to the next.

Please list any blood relative with obesity.

Pearl thinks about her dad. Teddy Crenshaw was larger than life, physically and otherwise. But obese? No. She glances back toward the living room to that framed picture of the four of them at Easter; his rounded belly and double chin would be considered more dad bod than morbid obesity. Had he lived longer, she wonders if that might have changed. Both grandfathers had been similarly heavyset. But there is a wide gulf between heavyset and 531 pounds, so she leaves that field blank.

Substance Abuse

Has anyone ever expressed concern about your use of alcohol, drugs, or prescription medication?

There hasn't been anyone around to witness her behavior, but the only addiction she might have is to Diet Dr Pepper, so she types *no*.

> On how many occasions during the past three months have
> you had more than five drinks containing alcohol?

Of all the questions on the form, this one makes Pearl feel like an honor student. She has to go all the way back to boat day with Ruby and Blake on Lake Texoma to think of a time when she had that many drinks in one twenty-four-hour period. She types a zero and keeps going.

Support System

> Who do you consider to be the primary individuals or
> groups that will be providing support for you pre-and
> postsurgery?

Her first thought is her mom. However, considering that her relationship with her mother consists of three weekly fifteen-minute phone calls, which are closely monitored, she reconsiders. Perry comes to mind, but though he's her closest friend, she would never dream of asking him to take time off work and help her. Rightly or wrongly, Ruby is her person. Reluctantly, she enters the following:

My sister, Ruby Crenshaw.

What are your leisure pursuits/hobbies/activities you do to
relax?

Eating and HGTV are the only two things that readily come
to mind, but Pearl tries to come up with a more positive spin.

I have an interest in home improvement and interior design.

On a scale of 1 to 10, with 10 being the highest/best and 1
being the lowest/worst, how would you rate your self-
esteem right now?

Trying to size this one up, she takes the last bite of the Little
Debbie and swigs some Diet Dr Pepper before throwing out a
number.

4, she types.

She stares at that number on the screen for a long time,
trying to decide whether it's really an accurate measure. Like, if
1 is "I want to kill myself" and 10 is "I'm fucking amazing," then
4 seems only somewhat generous. But she deletes it anyway and
types the number 3 instead.

Have you already started any lifestyle changes, and if so,
what are they?

Glancing at the now-empty pizza box, the cellophane wrapper from her snack cakes, and the two cans of soda, she wrestles with this one, wondering if the fact that she hasn't started any lifestyle changes might disqualify her from being deemed mentally stable enough to proceed.

I've recently started to incorporate more vegetables into my diet, she types, thinking back to that singular beet salad she shared with Perry last week. It's not a lie, she tells herself.

What are your goals postsurgery?

What a loaded question, she thinks. How to put into words something she can't fully imagine? Pearl looks around the kitchen at the dated colors, the faded curtains, and the so-yesterday nature of her childhood furnishings before entering her answer.

I'm a fixer-upper: my goal is to look good on the outside and feel good on the inside, for once in my life.

Chapter 11

Nervously, Pearl picks the chapped skin off her winter lips as she sits in the lobby at Dr. Lisa Field's West Austin clinic. The spacious room has a certain nondescript quality about it: a white leather love seat, a small, oval cherrywood table, a faux ficus tree in one of the corners, a water cooler in another. Various framed black-and-white landscape photographs featuring sunsets over Lady Bird Lake hang on the walls. Pearl wonders what the point of sunset photography is if the images are such that you don't see all the rich colors but rather just the harsh glare. Joanna Gaines would have a field day in this space, Pearl thinks.

While it's true that on any given Monday, she would rather be searching for snakes at Glenwood Manor, if she can just make it through this three-hour psych consult, she'll be one step closer to the actual surgery. And it's this forward momentum that has her feeling simultaneously excited and terrified.

She scrolls Instagram, trying to calm herself, mindlessly scanning slews of selfies when, suddenly, the door opens. Dr. Lisa Field appears holding a clipboard.

"Pearl," she says, inviting her toward her office down the hall.

"Hi," Pearl says, slowly pushing herself up and off the cushy love seat.

Through the maze of hallways, they exchange polite chit-chat. When they arrive in Dr. Field's actual office, Pearl is pleasantly surprised by the ceiling-to-floor windows facing the sunny outdoor courtyard. This space is so much more intimate and inviting than the lobby.

"Nice view," Pearl says, looking out at the stone fountain surrounded by a thoughtfully designed garden. She eases herself down on the couch. "You have so much natural light."

"Yes. I like to watch the mockingbirds. They use that fountain out there as a birdbath," Dr. Field says. "I noticed from your intake form that you really like design. It seems like appearances, at some level, are very important to you."

Oh boy, here we go, Pearl thinks. One comment about the outdoor patio and already Dr. Field is getting all gestalt.

"Well, I just like to watch home-improvement shows, that's all," Pearl says, remembering the fixer-upper analogy she used on the electronic intake form.

"We'll get to some of the specifics in just a little while, but I was so intrigued by the way you answered that last question on the form, the one about postsurgery goals. Tell me more about feeling like a fixer-upper, Pearl." Dr. Field smiles and waits.

Pearl swallows hard, fully aware she's in store for a very long three hours.

"Well, as you can see, I'm big as a house. So the home remodel thing just seems like an obvious comparison, right?" Pearl says with nervous laughter.

"This is a great place to start. Why don't you tell me more about what you think needs fixing?" Dr. Field holds her pen, poised to take notes.

Chapter 12

The sign on the ladder says *Closed for repair*. Orange duct tape stretched and zigzagged across the stainless-steel handrails of the diving board prevents anyone from trying jackknifes or cannonballs. But Pearl and Ruby know the truth; there's actually nothing wrong with the diving board.

At Barrow Creek Country Club, a lush expanse of four rolling green golf courses and state-of-the-art tennis courts, the Fourth of July family fun day is well underway. Toward the deep end of the club's Olympic-sized swimming pool, a South Congress cover band perched under a blue-and-white-striped cabana offers a Savage Garden soundtrack to all the splashing. Even without access to the diving board and with the Par Buster Golf Tournament in full swing, the pool is packed. On this day especially, it's the place to be—a see-and-be-seen kind of scene filled with those privileged enough to be able to afford a pricey family membership.

Overlooking miles and miles of Texas hill country live oaks, red cedars, and bald cypress, the pool perimeter is dotted with freshly manicured moms sipping margaritas and sun-kissed teenage girls lounging on chairs. In the water, kids of all ages compete for prizes by collecting coins off the bottom. It's a members-only annual event but a first for Pearl, Ruby, and their newly married mom.

Skip Benzer, their stepdad and Barrow Creek's general manager, has let them in on a little secret: whenever he expects to exceed maximum capacity in the pool, as a safety precaution, he closes the diving board.

At thirteen years old, Pearl is too old to dive for coins but also too young to be the all-day tagalong to Ruby and her friend Claire, both of whom seem perfectly content to bake in the sun, ignoring everything and everyone around them in the solitudes of their respective Sony Walkmans.

"Mom, can I order a snack?" Pearl asks, rolling onto her side.

"Sugar, we just ate lunch a little while ago," Birdie explains from under the brim of her big, floppy hat.

"But I'm still hungry," Pearl insists.

For Birdie, this rare day off from catering a holiday event means she gets to recline poolside on the club's monogrammed towels, pretending to be among the idle rich, even if she's neither. Plus, she's engrossed in the latest issue of *Texas Monthly*, and Pearl can tell she would rather not be disturbed. Since she and Skip got together, it's been like this—her mom more preoccupied than ever.

"Pearl, why don't you go swim?" Birdie encourages, flipping through a few pages.

Pearl doesn't answer. Instead, she pouts, letting her eyes drift back across the pool where a boy she vaguely recognizes from school licks the edges of an ice cream sandwich, trying to devour every last quickly melting bite.

Lying there between her mom and Ruby, with no umbrella for shade, Pearl begins to feel like she's melting. In a way, she even wishes she would. Maybe sweating poolside could slim her down some, help erase the new, unsightly marks at the top of her thighs. Looking side to side from her mom to Ruby, Pearl compares herself, wondering why she's the only one with these strange lines.

"Mom, what are these?" Pearl asks, trying to rub one away.

From above her dark cat's-eye sunglasses, Birdie glances over to her daughter's thigh.

"That is a stretch mark," Birdie says matter-of-factly.

"Why do I have them?" Pearl asks. "I mean, don't you only get those if you're pregnant or something?"

"It just means you're growing. That's all."

Pearl considers the veracity of Birdie's reply but can't square it with the deeper truth she knows without even asking—that stretch marks are scars from getting bigger, and in Pearl's case, already bigger than most girls her age.

She sits up a little higher on the lounger, scanning, trying to find someone she might know from school, but only spots a small cluster of girls who would probably never talk to someone like Pearl—someone who was already too big to wear cute red, white, and blue Fourth of July–themed bikinis like theirs.

Reluctantly, she rises from her chair and wraps a towel around her chest.

"You gonna go cool off?" her mom asks, still glued to her magazine.

"I'm bored," she says. "There's nothing to do."

"Oh, Pearl, honestly, how can you say that?" her mom asks, taking a sip of iced tea. "You're surrounded by kids your own age in the middle of summer at a country club. Surely, you can find a way to make the most of such desperate circumstances."

Pearl hears the sarcasm, and with no way to refute her mom's mostly accurate points, she just rolls her eyes and heads off to the edge of the pool. For a little while, she sits there letting her legs dangle off the side, waiting. At least a dozen of the club's inflatable watermelon pool rings bob around on the surface, but most are already taken. Patiently, Pearl bides her time until a young girl, easily half her age, abandons one for a foam noodle instead. Before anyone else spots the lone ring, Pearl takes a deep breath and slips underwater. She swims, eyes open, past the bobbing bodies, all the way to the shallow end, where she pushes off from the bottom of the pool and torpedoes up through the ring.

As she catches her breath and wipes the chlorine from her eyes, she feels momentarily victorious for having the stamina and stealth to employ such impressive underwater tactics to seize the only unoccupied watermelon ring in the entire pool. But the celebration is short-lived as she begins to sense that she is stuck. The circumference of the ring is such that, even standing up in three feet of water, it's a struggle to push it down around her waist. Quickly, before anyone else notices her dilemma, Pearl tries to problem solve. With as much nonchalance as she can muster while being cinched in a ring of PVC, she moves back toward deeper water, hoping to, more gracefully, mermaid her way out from underneath the float. But it's no use. There is no way she's getting out of this ring unless she first gets out of the pool.

With so many kids and grown-ups swimming and splashing all around her, Pearl surveys the irony of her situation; although she's above water, she fears she could very well drown from embarrassment if anyone catches on. Exiting the pool with a watermelon ring stuck above her bulging belly is simply not an option. Instead, Pearl drifts into the deep end, where her bind is a little less obvious.

For what seems like a very long time, she stares at her mom on the lounger, still flipping through her magazine. Only twice over the course of the next half hour does her mom look up from the pages to scan the pool. And when her eyes find Pearl, she smiles and waves. Like everyone else, including the two lifeguards perched high on the stands above her, Birdie is completely oblivious to Pearl's distress.

Compulsively, Pearl keeps checking the large clock mounted above the snack bar, but even more than the digital display, her pruning fingers tell her she's been in the pool for far too long. Already she's tried to discreetly bite her way out of this fix. Resting her chin on the plastic and using her folded arm as a shield, she's made repeat and wholly unsuccessful attempts to pop the PVC with her incisors. And no matter how hard she's tried to feel for the air valve, she can't find it, which can only mean it's in the back, out of reach. Sunburned and now sorry she ever dipped her toe in the water, Pearl feels totally helpless. She wants to cry but figures that would only attract attention. So instead, with no way out, she resigns herself to spinning in circles in the deep end.

Finally, Ruby and Claire emerge from their prone positions on the loungers. Together, they stroll over toward the bathroom. Within a few minutes, they're at the snack bar placing orders, and Pearl's mouth waters as she watches them saunter back to their side-by-side chairs, sucking on matching red, white, and blue Bomb Pops. Before sitting down, Ruby says something to their mom, who then motions toward Pearl, waving. Pearl waves but, under the circumstances, can't bring herself to smile back at them. Instead, she leans back until her ears are submerged. With her long brown hair fanning out in the water, she closes her eyes to reality.

"Hey," Ruby says from the edge of the pool. "What are you doing?"

Pearl squints her eyes at the unexpected sound of her sister's voice coming from directly above. From this vantage point, Ruby towers overhead, her tall, slender form blocking the sun, casting a shadow over them both.

"Oh, nothing. Just hanging out," Pearl says, reaching out toward the coping.

"Liar," Ruby says, splashing feetfirst beside her.

When Ruby's head pops back up, she swims up to Pearl, grabbing the watermelon ring until they are floating together, face-to-face.

"You've been in here forever," Ruby says. "Why aren't you getting out?"

"Maybe I prefer swimming to sweating," Pearl says.

Her sister isn't buying it.

"Did you start your period or something?" Ruby says, fishing for the truth.

"No!"

"Pearl, Bomb Pops are your favorite, and you've been out here forever. C'mon, what gives?"

Pearl's bottom lip trembles, and tears pool in her eyes as she admits the hard truth.

"I'm stuck," she whispers. "I swam up into this ring, and now it won't come off."

Ruby's face softens.

"Good grief, Pearl. Why didn't you say something?"

"You weren't looking."

"Well, don't cry," Ruby adds. "You'll just draw attention."

Pearl nods as Ruby takes a breath and dips underwater long

enough to uncap the valve on the back of the ring. Together, they swim toward the nearest ladder, gently squeezing on the plastic as the watermelon slowly deflates. When it's sufficiently soft, Ruby gives it a tug, offering just enough pull for Pearl to slip back out the same way she got in.

Dripping wet, Pearl and Ruby head back to the loungers. As they pass the diving board with the duct tape and the sign, Pearl asks Ruby for one more bit of mercy.

"Don't tell Claire, okay?"

"I wouldn't do that, Pearl. It's weird that you even feel like you have to say that. You should know by now your secrets are safe with me."

Later, with Birdie off joining Skip for a drink at the bar and grill and Ruby and Claire playing tennis, Pearl waits in line at the snack bar, trying to choose between the unhealthy options on the menu. She orders cheese fries, an ice cream sandwich, and a Diet Dr Pepper. She knows better than to take her items back to her lounger and eat them in broad daylight. If her mom or Ruby came back before she was finished pigging out, both would give her an earful. Instead, Pearl ventures into the air-conditioned comfort of the women's locker room. Walking all the way to the back, she settles on a long, narrow bench where she can eat in peace—alone.

Chapter 13

Eight hours separate Pearl from check-in at the Austin Sleep Center, and as she walks out of her psych consult, she's feeling a bit more confident than she did when she walked in. Dr. Field didn't venture too far off script the way Pearl feared she might. Instead, almost verbatim, she stuck to the questions from the intake form and took lots of notes. In addition to encouraging Pearl to seek out therapy over the course of what Dr. Field refers to as her "transition," she also tried to impress upon her the importance of attending the postoperative group meetings Dr. George had mentioned during her last appointment. The biggest takeaway from her consult is that she passed. Dr. Field had deemed Pearl just troubled enough to explain the 531 pounds but not so troubled that she would be mentally unfit for such a major operation. And Pearl celebrates this win by plodding fifty steps or so into the café next door.

But for as much newfound confidence as she felt walking out of Dr. Field's office, the minute she steps into this shop, she feels out of place. The tatted-up baristas are wearing nothing but sports bras, exposing their bare midriffs and navel piercings. It's a hipster spot where everyone, including the customers, is annoyingly fit and fixated on the chalkboard menu hanging over the counter. Standing in line, Pearl searches for something familiar like French fries or chicken strips, but apparently all they sell here is something called kombucha. That's it. No food. Just some mystery liquid concoction that is apparently so good it warrants the line of customers she finds herself standing in. For a split second, she contemplates turning around and finding the nearest Taco Bell, but the space is so small that getting out of line would mean disrupting everyone around her. So she stays put. When it's her turn, Pearl peruses the chalkboard, trying to decipher the difference between something called the Lychee Dragon, the Purple People Eater, and Hallah at Me. But since the base of these mystery beverages consists of kombucha, Pearl has no clue which one to order, let alone what this so-called kombucha even is.

"What can I get you today?" The barista is beautiful and looks like she just ran a marathon in record time.

"Hmm...I'm just trying to decide what exactly I want," Pearl says, head craned up toward the menu.

"You know we don't serve food, right?"

Pearl levels her gaze to meet the barista's, offers her best fuck-you face. But standing there at the front of the line, surrounded by all these health nuts, she's off her game and can't think of a single snarky remark.

"I came for the kombucha," Pearl says lamely. "You have kombucha, right?"

"Twenty-two flavors on tap," the barista says, pointing up to the bright chalk menu.

"Perfect," Pearl says. "I'll have the Slim Shady. A twelve-ounce."

What had felt like a victory lap walking in had turned into the walk of shame. As Pearl makes her way out of the café, trying not to jostle any of the other customers with her sheer circumference, she already regrets this seven-dollar liquid purchase. It's not until she's standing outside, taking in the fresh late-January air, that she takes her first sip of the Slim Shady. And despite the powerful thirst she worked up in that three-hour therapy session, Pearl can barely bring herself to swallow. It's that bad. The kombucha, even infused with ginger, elderflower, and lemon, actually tastes like ass, she thinks, even though she's never tasted ass before.

"Holy..." she says out loud, pursing her lips. "Fuck you, Slim Shady," Pearl says, tossing the still-full cup into the trash.

Moments later, she is rounding the corner off South Lamar onto Barton Springs, where her go-to drive-thru is calling her name. There's a long line, but she knows the loaded tiny tacos and the seasoned curly fries are worth it, so she pulls in, mouth already watering, telling herself, what with tonight's sleep study and all, she'll probably skip dinner, so logic dictates she should take full advantage of this Jack in the Box picnic and pig out properly.

"Welcome to Jack in the Box. How can I can help you?"

The friendly, twangy voice from the drive-thru speaker is one she recognizes.

"Hey, Willie Mae, it's Pearl," she says, grateful to be talking to the one person she knows in Austin who weighs close to what she does.

"Oh, hey, girl," Willie Mae says. "You want the usual?"

"Yes, but add on one of those Sourdough Jacks for me this time, will you?"

"You bet," she says. "So that'll be a bucket of tiny tacos with the avocado lime dippin' sauce. Two orders of curly fries, a Sourdough Jack burger, and a jumbo Diet Dr Pepper. That gonna do it for you today?"

"Yes, ma'am," Pearl says, pulling ahead.

As she waits, fourth in line from the window at Jack in the Box, she's wondering if she'll ever be a kombucha-swilling skinny girl. And just as she's imagining her face and hair on her sister's barre-class body, her phone rings. It's Ruby.

Although pleasantly surprised by this unexpected call, Pearl doesn't answer it right away. Instead, she gauges how much time she thinks she has before Willie Mae takes her credit card. The last thing Pearl needs is Ruby knowing she's on a fast-food run.

"Hey," she says, taking her chances. "What's up?"

"Oh, you know, same shit, different day," Ruby says, her voice cracking.

"Are you crying?" Pearl asks, mystified.

"No. Of course not!" Ruby says, sniffling.

Pearl listens as her sister gasps for air, clears her throat, and blows her nose.

"That sounds like crying, Ruby. What happened? You're scaring me."

"Oh, I'm just having a moment, that's all."

As her car rolls into second position, Pearl fumbles with the phone, puts Ruby on speaker so she can readily access the mute button when she pulls up to the window.

"Did what's-his-name break up with you?" Pearl asks, racking her brain to remember the last time she'd heard Ruby mention the investment banker from Houston.

"Huh?" Ruby says, confused. "Oh please, Pearl, you think I'd be ruining my lash extensions over a guy? If you're talking about Richard, I broke it off with him right after Christmas. I told you that."

"Oh, my bad," Pearl says, knowing full well her sister rarely elaborates about her love life. Most of what Pearl knows about Ruby's life in general are just snippets, brief mentions of "so-and-so's" and "off to's," a world filled with galas, fundraisers, premieres, and after-parties.

With her sister still sniffling, Pearl taps the mute button and pulls up to the window.

"I'm just so fucking exhausted, that's all," Ruby says. "It's like I'm hitting a wall or something..."

"Hey, Pearl," Willie Mae says. "How you doin', girl?"

"Oh, I'm fine," Pearl says, smiling, pointing to her phone.

Willie Mae nods, hands over two full sacks and one jumbo Styrofoam cup.

"That'll be $26.79, Pearl. Oh, by the way, I threw in some extra ketchup for those curly fries."

"Where are you anyway?" Ruby asks, suddenly sounding an awful lot like the barista back at the kombucha bar.

Pearl looks down at her screen, realizing she hadn't properly pressed the mute button.

"I'm just grabbing a quick bite to eat," she confesses.

"Are curly fries part of your new weight loss strategy?"

Pearl fumbles to position her drink in the holder on the middle console. Her flesh spills over, completely blocking one of the receptacles. Knowing this call will be rising with intensity and knowing, too, that she just wants to sit alone and eat her tiny tacos in peace, Pearl pulls into one of the parking spaces.

"For your information, I wasn't getting the curly fries for me, Ruby," Pearl says, lying. "I'm taking lunch back to the office."

"Right," Ruby says.

"Damn right I'm right," Pearl adds. If she's gonna lie, she might as well be emphatic about it. And like all little lies, the one Pearl is telling somehow keeps growing. "Since you're so concerned about my consumption these days, it might interest you to know that I already drank my lunch. As soon as I got out of my three-hour psych consult, I got a twelve-ounce Slim Shady kombucha."

"Then why did you just tell me you were out getting a bite to eat?" Ruby asks pointedly.

Fuck! Why are lies so hard to keep straight, Pearl wonders.

"I meant I was getting a bite to eat for everyone else, Ruby. But that shouldn't even matter. I shouldn't have to itemize what I eat in a single day, especially to you."

"Oh, what's that supposed to mean?"

"It means if you actually cared about all the curly fry details of my miserable life, you would call once in a while to chat."

"Is it not enough that I'm putting my life here in Dallas on hold so that I can help you?"

Seething, Pearl slides her hand into one of the sacks, tries untangling a curly fry from the rest, but just like most conversations with Ruby, she can't seem to separate her emotions before they spiral out of control. Tossing the big blob of fries back in the bag, Pearl loses it.

"Why is it that every time—every time!—I talk to you I feel like shit?"

Pearl is shouting, which surprises even her.

Ruby is momentarily stunned into silence.

"I was actually calling to tell you that I am going to come early so I can help you prepare," she adds, still sniffling.

"Really?" Pearl asks, somewhat shocked.

"I've told DALLUX I'll be taking a leave of absence so I can be in Austin to help you."

The news takes Pearl off guard. She's not used to Ruby sounding so magnanimous.

"Anyway, I still have some things to wrap up here, but I'm hoping to get down there sometime next week or so."

"Um, you do realize my surgery isn't until March thirteenth, right?"

"Yes."

"And you realize there is a whole month between January and March, right?"

"Yes."

"I mean I'm grateful you're coming soon and all, but I just, well, it's just that I'll probably need you more post-op than pre-op."

"Right," Ruby says. "So I'll be there for both. Is that okay?"

"Okay," Pearl says. "I mean, thank you."

"Look, I gotta run," Ruby says. "I'll ping you later."

"Wait, Ruby! You still never told me why you were crying."

"It's nothing. Just a moody Monday, that's all. I'll talk to you soon."

"Bye," Pearl says, hanging up.

Sitting there alone in the car, still processing the news of Ruby's impending arrival, Pearl rummages through the bags of food beside her. She unwraps the Sourdough Jack burger, removes both pieces of bread, and uses the wrapper to hold the mushy mess, eating only the meat and cheese. Everything else, she will throw away.

It's not exactly kombucha, but it's a start.

Chapter 14

Frantically, Pearl hauls ass down I-35 to get to the Austin Sleep Center for her study. Another last-minute wardrobe malfunction has her running late, and if there's one thing Pearl hates to be, it's late, because being late means she has to struggle to get out of her vehicle and get to wherever she's going without arriving all breathless and sweaty. But she's so nervous about the prospect of trying to sleep in front of total strangers that she got stuck at home on the toilet for much longer than she'd planned. Already, she's called to tell them she's behind schedule, and at this point, as she makes the exit toward the clinic, she prays to God she won't be so late that they'll want to reschedule.

Preparing for this study was nerve-racking enough: she had to pack an overnight bag, and she'd be surrendering her cell phone on arrival, then putting on her pajamas in front of complete strangers, who would then cover her with electrodes.

Then she was somehow supposed to fall asleep. She found herself stressing over the idea that if they could monitor her pulse, her oxygen saturation, and her apnea hypopnea index, it stands to reason they might also be able to read her mind, to not only see her very dreams but be able to interpret them as well. It's an irrational fear, but it's real. These are the all-consuming thoughts driving her to distraction as she pulls up to the sleep study center and parks her car. With her overnight bag in tow, Pearl heads in, 100 percent certain this whole thing will be a colossal waste of time.

There's an Alice in Wonderland feel to the whole thing: the surreal juxtaposition of clinical and cozy occupying the same real estate. Once she is checked in, she is led to a locker room, where she is instructed to change and lock up her belongings. From there, she is led into a dimly lit sleep chamber and asked to make herself comfortable on a queen-size Tempur-Pedic. As she lies there, a couple of technicians begin applying gel and electrodes from her feet to the crown of her head. She distracts herself by taking in the Hampton Inn quality of the space: the cheap bedding, the bedside table and lamp, the television set into a small armoire across from the bed, the generic landscape paintings on the wall. As she takes in the cameras bolted to various crossbars installed below the corrugated ceiling, she remembers that this isn't a hotel but a lab. When the technicians are done prepping her, a voice comes from somewhere outside the room she's in.

"Hi, Pearl. Are you comfortable?"

Pearl isn't sure she's supposed to move, now that her body is crisscrossed with wires.

"I guess so?" she responds nervously.

"We're going to turn off the lights and pipe in some ambient sounds that will help you relax and will make you feel sleepy. So just let yourself drift off, and we'll wake you up when we've got the data we need," says the disembodied voice.

Pearl has no confidence that she'll be able to relax, let alone sleep, but the lights dim, and before she knows it, she is in total darkness, and slowly, she becomes aware of the lovely quiet strains of Celtic music being played so softly it feels almost like a whisper. Pearl falls into a deep sleep and begins to dream.

She's eight years old again, and she's watching Ruby ride her bike to the top of Cherry Lane. Pearl waves at her sister.

"Come on, Pearl!" Ruby hollers. "If you don't come now, we're gonna be late."

But Pearl just stands there watching and waving. Then her mother calls from inside the house, "Pearl Jane, are you still here? I thought you already left with your sister."

Pearl shakes her head.

"I'll drive you to school, but your father's going to have to pick you up."

Pearl walks inside, grabs her lunch box and backpack.

Then she's in school, and the bell rings and she goes outside to wait for her father. It's not like him to be late...

The next thing she's aware of is a gentle tap on her shoulder.

"Where am I?" she asks.

"You're here at the Austin Sleep Center, and your test is finished." The tech smiles at her. "Good morning."

Once she's dressed, she meets with Dr. Ames, the head of the sleep center, in his small but well-appointed office.

"So, Pearl," he says, smiling kindly at her. "You do have severe sleep apnea, which means you aren't getting enough oxygen while you sleep. This may explain any tiredness you might experience during the day." He pauses.

"Does this mean I don't qualify for surgery?" she asks nervously.

"No, it doesn't mean that at all. But we can help." He reaches down and pulls out a box with a photograph of someone wearing some kind of cross between orthodontic headgear and a snorkel. "This," Dr. Ames goes on, "is a CPAP machine, and it will help you get a full night's sleep."

"Oh." Pearl takes the box that he slides across his desk.

"Before you leave, a technician will show you how it works. It's a little clunky, to be sure, but it will be a game changer for you in terms of getting some quality sleep." He stands and shakes her hand.

After working with a tech for about a half hour and grasping how to "mask up" at bedtime, Pearl leaves the sleep center feeling good: she is now one step closer to surgery.

PART TWO

Losing It

Chapter 15

The temperature in the room is set to ninety-two degrees. This far into her sixty-minute yoga class, the steam of twenty or so sweaty students makes everything slick, including Ruby's mat. Even covered in towels, her soaked spot on the hardwood doesn't feel safe enough for some of the poses, especially wheel.

"Push into your heels with palms pressed flat on the floor, toward the back wall. Raise your buttocks high in chakrasana," the instructor says, demonstrating from her mat at the front of the room. "When you're ready, lift your head off your mat to form your wheel."

Ruby huffs and puffs, tries pushing just like Pam, the instructor, but it's so much harder today. Her focus is on yesterday and the video that got her fired.

"This is a great heart opener," Pam adds, her voice perfectly unstrained despite the upside-down nature of her face. "Wheel pose helps us maintain emotional stability, helps us feel more empathy for others. In wheel, we find equanimity, a sense of fulfillment. I want everyone to savor this burst of positivity. Breathe it in. Feel the love in the room."

Fuck, Ruby thinks, her feet slipping out from under her. Did she say that out loud?

"Now, for an advanced variation, interlace your fingers behind the base of your skull, and rest the crown of your head on the floor."

Again, Pam demonstrates. Ruby scans the room, watches as at least a third of the class advance to this next level, leaving Ruby behind, head still stuck on her soggy towel-covered mat.

Pam flattens her own wheel and rolls to the side, surveying her students. Ruby can feel her eyes, feels Pam noticing the very non-wheel-like, partially flat, semi-squished tire of her very soul.

"Remember," Pam says, rising to her feet, threading barefoot through the mats. "What happens on our mats is a reflection of what's happening in our lives. When we struggle off the mat, we struggle on our mat. Wheel is a way of dumping our challenges."

Above all, Ruby does not like to have others witness her struggle, and not to be outdone a moment longer, she braces her palms and pushes off, finally extending.

"There," Pam says. "So as you hold this pose, feel your heart opening, feel the warm love of the universe supporting the very arches of your spines. Now, find your *drishti* on the back wall, and allow yourself to hold this pose for a few more seconds."

Ruby blinks away the sweat running down her face, finds some speck on the back wall, and fixes her gaze. But instead of feeling light and love, all she can see in her mind's eye is a reenactment of her rage on full display in that fucking TikTok video.

"I don't hear your *ujjayi*," Pam says, reminding everyone to breathe. "With every exhale, allow your heart to open and expand."

Ruby replays the whole thing in her head—how she was on mile five when she saw that same chubby dude walking his mutt up ahead. Lazy prick. Who lets their dog shit on a public trail, paid for with my taxpayer dollars, and doesn't bother to bend over and clean it up with the sacks they give away for free from the fucking dispenser right there at the trailhead?

The TikTok video doesn't show that Ruby, on at least three separate occasions in the past month alone, had the misfortune of stepping right into a steamy turd dropped by that exact mutt on the Katy Trail. It doesn't show how, on three separate occasions, she was the victim—having to scrape off all that caked-on poo before she could even get back in her Lexus. Nor does it show the three times she, very politely, asked the dog's owner to be more aware of his own dog's public defecations. Nope. None of that. All the TikTok video shows is Ruby finally losing her shit. True. Maybe she should have at least tied off the plastic bag before she launched the steamy turd at the dog owner. At least if she'd done that, he wouldn't look like such a victim. But with all that poop running down his face and shirt, of course everyone's going to sympathize with him. But what about her running shoes? And how was Ruby to have any idea that, of all people, he happened to be the developer of the Shoppes at Highland Park Village, one of DALLUX's biggest advertisers? Under the strain of wheel pose and her ignominious termination, Ruby's arms begin to twitch. The weight of it all is coming down hard on her.

"Remember, shaking is growth," Pam says. "Trembling is progress."

Ruby presses on, now desperate to hold her footing, to prove something, but she doubts how much more opening up her walled-off heart can even take.

"When we approach our practice with gratitude, we derive a sense of fulfillment," Pam adds, dimming the lights for final savasana. "And our hearts fill with peace."

In the dark, Ruby lets herself collapse onto her mat, trying to quiet her pent-up rage. Vaguely, she recognizes the old Jewel tune. And in her mind's eye, she pictures the beautiful snaggletoothed singer strumming away on a spotlit barstool at the front of the yoga class, posing the primal question of her chorus.

It's a profound question, one she hasn't given much thought to until now. And lying there in corpse pose, tears streaming down her face, Ruby Crenshaw realizes she has no clue who will save her soul.

Chapter 16

After two full days away from the office, Pearl is eager to be back at work. February is the shortest month of the year, and she knows how quickly it will pass. With the countdown to her EGD test and her surgical date approaching, she needs to keep her mind off the details and the very real risks involved in what she's come to think of as her "transition."

"It sounds so Caitlyn Jenner, don't you think?" she asks Perry as they search Suite 9 in the memory care unit for Mary Margaret McDonald's missing dentures. "Like I'm going into surgery as the old me and coming out a new me, right?"

"Well, Caitlyn Jenner got the cover of *Vanity Fair*," Perry says, riffling through a potted ivy on the windowsill. "I mean did you see her hair and that strapless silk bustier? She's, like, living proof, Pearl. A transition that puts you more in alignment with your authentic self can be jaw-dropping. It's that whole mind, body, spirit connection thing. It's confidence, and once people achieve it, it's sexy as hell."

The thought of this makes Pearl pause the tooth hunt for a moment. Silently, as she fluffs Mary Margaret McDonald's pillows, she imagines what she might wear for her own Annie Leibovitz cover shoot—tries to imagine not only looking sexy but feeling it, too.

"The therapist I met with the other day told me to focus on my tuck-in weight."

"Huh," Perry says. "Explain tuck-in weight."

"So my tuck-in weight is that point in my weight loss when I can actually tuck in a shirt. I guess that will be when my metamorphosis is complete."

"I like that. Your tuck-in weight," he says, trying it on for size. "So intuitive. Check the closet," Perry adds.

In the closet, Pearl checks the built-in drawers, a couple of Ms. McDonald's bags, and all the pockets of her robe and sweaters.

"Not there," she says. "Maybe she left them in the craft room."

"Well, she can't eat without them, so no stone unturned," Perry says, motioning Pearl out of the way. "Step aside. I have radar for this kind of thing."

"So I found out yesterday my sister's coming to stay with me starting sometime next week," Pearl says.

"Girl, that will be the biggest transition of all," he says, laughing. "Am I right?"

"I'm not sure what scares me more—the thought of Ruby

and I living under one roof again or me dying of a propofol over-dose while I'm getting my scope EGD procedure."

"Aha," he says, holding the dentures between his index finger and thumb. "Told ya."

"In her slipper?" Pearl asks. "That's a new one."

"New, but not the strangest," Perry says, dropping the dentures into a plastic baggie. "Last fall, I found Mr. Vasquez's dentures in the tank behind his toilet."

"Hmm. Well, at least that kept them moist," Pearl says, giggling.

"True. Now, I'm putting you in charge of sanitizing these before the lovely Ms. Mary Margaret realizes she's missing her teeth."

"Thanks for helping me find them," she says, taking the bag. "And, Perry, thanks so much for everything."

"What everything?" he asks.

"Mostly just being so understanding about the time off I'm taking. You've just been super cool about the whole thing, and I just want you to know how much I appreciate your support as I go through this."

"I'm a sucker for change for the good." Perry returns her smile. "I'm rooting for you, Pearl. I want the world for you." He gives her shoulder a squeeze as he leaves Suite 9.

Down the hall, in the break room, Pearl dilutes vinegar with some water. The smell makes her grimace, taking her straight back to that Slim Shady kombucha from yesterday. She drops Ms. McDonald's dentures into a clean bowl and watches as the vinegar and baking soda solution bubbles around this missing set of teeth, dissolving all the bits of food that shouldn't be there. It's gross yet oddly fun to watch. And she's wondering to herself if that's how kombucha works, too, if it disintegrates, say, an undigested Wendy's honey butter chicken biscuit in the same way. Her reverie is broken when she hears Esmerelda and Loraine, two of the cafeteria ladies, laughing hysterically behind her.

Pearl turns around to see both of them sitting at the break room table, staring into a phone screen.

"What's so funny?" Pearl asks.

"Oh my gosh, Pearl," Loraine says. "Get yourself over here. You got to see this. Some lady throwin' dog shit at somebody on a jogging trail."

Pearl approaches the table and leans in for a look, but the video is almost over.

"Wait. Play it again. I wanna see," Pearl says.

Esmerelda turns her phone horizontal so the image will fill the screen and hits Play.

Pearl recognizes the voice right away. From the very first "fuck you," she knows that this beautiful but completely unhinged woman is none other than Ruby. Even with the baseball cap and sunglasses, there is no mistaking it. Mortified, Pearl tries to pretend it's as funny as Esmerelda and Loraine still think it is, but inside, she's dying. The part where Ruby, still yelling at some guy and his large yellow dog, bends over and actually picks up the pile of poop leaves no question as to what will happen next, and Pearl almost can't bring herself to watch, but she has to. She has to see the windup of the pitch, which on TikTok has been drawn out in slo-mo for added drama. Whoever produced the video even went so far as to set it to music with "Take Me Out to the Ball Game" playing on an organ in the background. But it's when the shit hits the target that things really get ugly. The poop from the inside of the little baggie splats all over the man's chest, sending some of it onto his face and glasses. And as if that's not bad enough, the entire pitch gets shown over and over again, like a replay on ESPN.

Pearl tries to laugh along with Esmerelda and Loraine, who are both slapping their scrub-covered knees, but inside she wants to cry just like Ruby was yesterday on the phone. Now she knows.

"That's one angry bitch, right?" Loraine says, chuckling. "She don't take no shit. That's for sure."

"So funny," Pearl adds, doing her best to look amused. "Where did you find this? You have to send it to me."

"No need," Loraine says. "It's all over Twitter at #shityounot."

Speechless, Pearl remembers the dentures. Without saying another word, she collects Ms. McDonald's teeth, all the while keeping a smile planted on her face until she is out of the break room. The muffled baseball organ music lingers down the hall along with the fading laughter. And for the first time in her entire life, Pearl utters these two words to herself—*poor Ruby*.

Chapter 17

It's only the first day of their summer break, and already it's too hot to walk barefoot. As she and Ruby wait for their ride, Pearl tosses her black Steve Madden platform sandals onto the front porch and slips them on, one at a time, using Ruby's arm for balance.

"Why are you wearing those shoes to go to Barton Springs?" Ruby asks for the third time. "They're too tall, Pearl. You look like a stripper."

Once again, Pearl protests. "No, I don't," she says, examining her feet, feeling secretly proud at the prospect of looking so grown-up.

Although she doesn't share this with Ruby, nine-year-old Pearl also likes the way the higher heel elongates her legs, making them appear less stocky. Plus, they are the first pair of not-flat shoes Pearl has ever owned, ever been allowed to wear. Along with the black funeral dress, they were a gift from Birdie—a purchase her mom would have only made under duress. Pearl had worn them to her dad's service, stumbling down the aisle for the viewing of his body like a little girl playing dress-up. In more ways than one, the Steve Maddens represented a loss of innocence, an end to Pearl's childhood.

"We're going swimming," Ruby reminds her, checking the time on her dad's old Casio G-Shock. Since the accident, Ruby hadn't taken it off. "If you wear those with wet feet, you're gonna fall flat on your face, and don't expect me to pick you up."

"There they are," Pearl says, altogether ignoring her sister's warning, pointing toward the burgundy Toyota Camry turning on to Cherry Lane.

With their mom off prepping for a fundraiser luncheon at the Lady Bird Johnson Wildflower Center, Ruby and Pearl have been assigned to spend the whole day at Barton Springs with Autry Atwood and his older sister, April. Since Teddy died, the girls have been the recipients of way too many awkwardly forced sympathy outings like this. It's as if all the moms in the neighborhood feel sorry for Birdie and the girls, and since food is never in short supply for a caterer, they instead organized a long and seemingly never-ending string of playdates. But at nine and eleven years old, Pearl and Ruby don't have much say in the matter. So despite the fact that Pearl has never liked Autry, Birdie's working-single-mom shuffle means that for the foreseeable future, whether she likes it or not, they're stuck with the Atwood kids for the whole day at Barton Springs.

"Climb on in, girls," Mrs. Atwood says cheerfully over the loud music. "Barbie Girl" spills onto the block as Pearl and Ruby slide into the back seat next to Autry. Pearl can't decide which annoys her more—the lyrics to her sister's new favorite song or having her sweaty thighs rub up against Autry's as she's stuffed into the middle of the back seat.

For Ruby, it's different. Although April isn't an athlete like Ruby, she is pretty and popular. Like Barbie girls in training, the two of them have this much in common—which at twelve years old is practically everything. However, all Autry and Pearl share is a long-standing mutual disdain for one another, which is obvious by the way Autry looks out the window for the entirety of the twenty-minute drive to Zilker Park.

When they arrive, Mrs. Atwood hands April a twenty and reminds them all to stick together.

"Stay away from the topless hippies, okay?" Mrs. Atwood says before they get out.

"Autry's the only pervert in the car, Mom," April says, glaring back at her brother. "He's the one you have to worry about. Not us."

"April, shut up!" Autry says, slamming his door, not even waiting for Pearl to scooch over and exit.

With Autry doing his best to lag behind and avoid being associated with Pearl, they make their way into the fourth-largest natural swimming hole in Texas. The nine-hundred-foot-long strip of spring water is flanked by lush, mostly shaded sloping St. Augustine grass—most of which is already occupied. Pearl does her best to keep up with the girls, but in her chunky Steve Madden slip-ons, this proves to be more of a balancing act than she imagined. As they search the grassy knoll for an available spot near the water, Pearl wobbles along, and Ruby has to keep catching her so she doesn't fall.

"Told you not to wear those," Ruby says, exasperated. "As if!"

With most of the public and private schools already out for summer, the three-acre park is packed, and they have to hunt for a slice of grass large enough to accommodate all four of their towels.

"There's one," Pearl says, spotting some college kids abandoning their spot.

Within half an hour, all four of them have taken their first plunge in the sixty-eight-degree water, and Pearl finds herself alone on their towels, shivering in the light breeze. Somehow, it was just understood that Pearl would be tasked with holding their spot while Ruby and April strut down the concrete catwalk next to the pool, looking for people they know. With his mask and snorkel, Autry said he was going to check out the catfish, but Pearl knows better. From her lookout post on the knoll, she watches him drift down toward the dam where two topless women are floating side by side on rafts.

Pearl wouldn't mind sitting all alone if it weren't for the obnoxious group of three high school boys who just moved in behind her. Lined up in a row, with their board shorts and reflective Ray-Bans, they perch facing the concrete poolside runway, scoping out all the girls walking by—some the same age as Ruby and April. In between their snickering and predatory grunts, Pearl can't help but overhear their observations.

"Check out the rack on the girl in the pink over there."

"Dude, her bush is showing through those bottoms."

"Hella fly. I'd do that."

"Dude, we know you. You would do anything. Rack. No rack. Bush. No bush. You fuck anything that moves—including that fatty down there."

As their conversations descends into more laughter, Pearl cringes. She's almost sure they're talking about her—the fatty. Casually, she covers up with the towel beside her, trying to pretend not to hear them. But after a few more lewd remarks, it becomes clear they're referring to someone else—a heavyset woman her mom's age who is bent over with her broad backside on full display while she straightens her towel.

"Lookee there, Kirk! She's ready to take it from behind. You don't even have to look at her ugly face."

Pearl looks around, wishing a grown-up was here, wishing her dad was here, wishing anyone was here to hear this. But with Autry still swimming and Ruby off with April, she is forced to make a choice—either sit here and listen to the creepy boys or get up and make her way over to the food truck for a hot dog.

As she rises and slips into her black platforms, she can feel the boys watching her, sizing her up. Modestly, she secures the towel under her fleshy arms and fishes a five-dollar bill out of her wadded-up shorts before leaving the spot she's supposed to be guarding.

As she totters away in her platform funeral shoes, Pearl, too, becomes the brunt of their muffled, under-the-breath jokes.

"Nah, maybe this fatty right here is more your speed, Kirk," she hears one of them say.

"At least she's closer to your age."

Their sick, sinister laughter rocks Pearl with a sudden jolt of shame. Ruby was right, she thinks, blushing. Maybe her shoes do make her look like a stripper. With a warm rage spreading like a rash on her skin, she takes off the sandals and carries them, beelining barefoot for the safe company of the small crowd gathered next to the food truck.

After the hot dog, Pearl nurses the sweet, sugary syrup from a rainbow-colored sno-cone as she makes her way back toward the towels. Thankfully, the high school boys are gone. Pearl sits long enough for the ice to melt, but once the white paper cone becomes too soggy to hold, she tosses it in a nearby trash can and heads back to the water. At the widest part, Barton Springs is no more than 150 feet across, and Pearl swims back and forth a couple of times until she spots Ruby and April walking back toward the towels with those creepy high school boys trailing right behind.

From the pool, Pearl can see them checking out her sister and April, watches them ogling their still preteen bodies. She waits by the ladder, spying as the girls take a seat on the towels and the three boys plop down beside them.

Despite the chill from the spring-fed water, once again, Pearl feels that familiar heat spreading across her skin. One singular thought sends Pearl up the ladder and out of the water—Ruby does not need to be with those boys.

Fast as she can walk without actually running and wearing only her red-and-white-checkered one-piece, Pearl winds her way past dozens of empty towels and clusters of poolside people until she reaches Ruby.

Standing there, red-faced and dripping wet, Pearl has just interrupted whatever amusing conversation they were having. For a second, Ruby seems annoyed by her baby sister butting in.

"Where'd you go?" Ruby asks, taking a long sip from her straw. She's sucking from a jumbo Styrofoam cup. Pearl doesn't have to ask to know it's her sister's favorite, cherry limeade. "You were supposed to be watching our spot. Someone could have stolen it," she adds, scolding.

"I did watch the spot," Pearl says, her eyes darting to the three boys. "You were gone forever."

"Who's this?" one of the boys says, like she's nobody.

"That's my little sister," Ruby says, not liking his tone one bit.

"Little?" one of them says, sneering. "Not so much."

One of his friends elbows the mouthiest one.

"Come on, dude. Pick on someone your own size."

"You're the one who called me a fatty," Pearl says bravely. "Earlier when I was guarding all the towels." She's forcing back tears, but she's standing her ground, fists clenched, giving all three of them the evil eye.

Unfolding her crisscrossed legs, Ruby gets up with her cup

and stands beside Pearl. As if she doesn't want to see what's about to happen next, April covers her face while Ruby levels her gaze at the loudmouth.

"Is that true?" Ruby asks sharply. "Did you really call my little sister a fatty?"

Stunned by the accusatory boldness of Ruby's tone, the teenage trio sit there smirking.

Taking two deliberate steps in their direction, Ruby bends over to be perfectly sure this dickweed in the middle can hear whatever she says next.

"My little sister may just be a little bit fat, but you—you're ugly. And there's no fixing that. Pearl can always go a diet, but you—you're stuck this way for life."

With that, Ruby pops the plastic lid on her cup and dumps the entire jumbo cherry limeade on top of his head.

"What the hell?" he says, flicking his head like a wet dog. "You need to try taking a chill pill, you...you little..."

"You wanna try calling me a name?" Ruby dares him.

With a small crowd of people now staring from all directions, he blinks away some more of the limeade and bites his tongue.

"Come on, dude," one of his buddies says, standing. "Let's bounce."

For the rest of the afternoon, right up until Birdie picks them all up, Pearl is no longer assigned towel duty. Instead, she is included in delicious girl talk, which, like her Steve Madden sandals, makes her feel much older than her years. While Autry swims around, supposedly still looking for catfish, the three of them tan in the sun on their small patch of grass as Ruby coaches Pearl on how not to take shit from assholes.

"If you can't outrun the dickheads, sometimes you have to be ready to embarrass them in public," Ruby explains, popping a big bubble with her gum.

In Pearl's estimation, Ruby is the smartest girl she knows. Even at eleven years old, she's always in control, wise beyond her years. Pearl isn't sure why Ruby's that way and she isn't, but she does know one thing—she wishes she were more like her.

"The thing is, Pearl," Ruby says, rolling onto her side, propping up on her elbow, "if someone's messing with you, you either have to run away or draw attention to it. If you just sit there and take it, it will only get worse."

Chapter 18

As Pearl sits on her bed, putting on the clunky headgear for her new CPAP machine, #shityounot is all she can think about. Over the past few days, she's watched the video no fewer than fifty times, trying to square Ruby's explosive rage with the always-in-control way her sister has moved through her entire life, rising to such a point in her career that, at twenty-eight, she could afford to buy her own home. How had Ruby become so utterly unhinged?

It took a couple of days before Pearl could muster the courage to talk to Perry about this, to explain that the shit-throwing star of the infamous viral video was none other than her sister, Ruby, who was about to come to town. Perry tried hard to stay calm, but he was literally jumping up and down.

"No way! No way! That's your damn sister?" Perry was now doubled over.

Pearl surprises even herself when she hears herself defending Ruby. "She's really not like that. She's…she's…" Pearl actually has little to no idea what Ruby is like these days. But she does remember, in a flash, how in the weeks and months after their father died, Ruby was always there for her.

She remembers running into Ruby's room and spooning her big sister in the middle of the night and Ruby letting her, even comforting her. She remembers both of them standing in the bathroom they once shared, looking into the mirror, Pearl asking Ruby, "Do you think I'm fat?" And Ruby, without missing a beat, responding, "It's just baby fat, Pearly. You'll definitely grow out of it."

And Pearl had believed her. She remembers, too, the sweet way Ruby always offered to French braid her hair, calling Pearl's long brown mane worthy of a Clairol Herbal Essences commercial.

But tonight, as Pearl evaluates her reflection in the same bathroom mirror they once shared, what she sees saddens her even more than the #shityounot TikTok video of Ruby. She looks like a fat, unhappy character out of a cheap sci-fi movie with her CPAP gear on.

She shuffles back to her bed to finish reading the instructions, doubting that this hideous device is going to help her get a good night's sleep.

"Give it at least a week." That's what the tech at the sleep center suggested. So she dutifully plugs in the CPAP, arranges the tubing and headgear, and allows herself to settle in for what she is convinced will be the worst night's sleep of her life.

Pearl wakes the next morning after eight glorious hours of uninterrupted sleep. Feeling more rested than she can remember, she rises with a burst of energy. Unstrapping her headgear, she fluffs her hair and stretches. Sunlight beams through the blinds in her room, sending dust particles dancing in the air. It's Saturday, and other than getting up to pee, she has nothing pressing to do. Despite how cumbersome it is, she has to admit that if every night is as restful as the last, the CPAP just might be her new best friend. And despite the fact that she hasn't yet lost a single pound, this one night of great sleep alone has her feeling healthier, somehow lighter, than she's felt in ages. As she's making her bed (something she mostly neglects to do), her cell phone chimes. It's a text from Ruby:

Leaving Dallas now. Will be there by noon.

True to form, Ruby rolls into the driveway on Cherry Lane at exactly 11:55 a.m. Pearl hears the car and checks the blinds in her bedroom. Standing there, peeking through the slats, her voyeurism safely obscured, Pearl watches her sister, sees the disappointment on Ruby's face as she appraises the weed-filled yard and chipped paint on the trim of the house she left so many years ago. Pearl observes Ruby lean against her leather headrest in something that looks like resignation or dread, possibly both. Whatever it is, Ruby appears to be in no rush to exit the vehicle, and Pearl imagines her sister mustering the resolve to come home again, to step foot in the place she swore not to—the calm before the storm.

As much as it pains her, Pearl can't help but notice Ruby's stylish, freshly cut bob, her hair blown into silky, smooth, voluminous perfection, making Pearl feel shaggy by comparison. Closing the blinds, she imagines they're both thinking the same thing: this is gonna suck.

"Hi there," Pearl says, waving on the front porch.

Ruby is wrestling with her laptop bag and a yoga mat in what appears to be the first of many loads. But hearing Pearl's voice, she looks over at her even-more-inflated-than-last-time sister and tries not to say what she's really thinking. Yet because they are sisters, she doesn't even have to not say it for Pearl to already know it. Ruby is thinking: *Holy shit! Did you eat every taco in Texas or what, Pearl?*

But instead, she says, "So think you can give me a hand with some of these bags?"

"Wow," Pearl says, approaching the car, noticing the jam-packed, filled-to-the-roof contents of her sister's SUV. "Is this your entire wardrobe or just the spring/summer collection?"

"Ha ha," Ruby says, reaching for a laundry basket overflowing with shoes. "Let's just say I came prepared."

With their arms loaded, before they walk into the house, they exchange an obligatory neck hug and air kiss. After not seeing one another for so long, the gesture seems simultaneously perfunctory and proper.

"Well, I'm glad you're here," Pearl says, approaching the front door. "But please leave your judgments right here on the doormat, because I didn't really have much time to tidy up the way I hoped to."

"Oh please, Pearl," Ruby says dismissively. "You're one woman living alone with no children and no pets. How bad can it possibly be?"

Chapter 19

A dense morning fog hangs over Travis County, making Ruby's morning run through Tarrytown feel like unfamiliar territory. Not being able to see more than a block in front of her, not being able to clearly anticipate the approaching turn or the approaching anything else has her brain working overtime. With such limited visibility, instinct tells her to cut this six-mile route in half, but her OCD won't let her. To Ruby, halfway is just another way of saying half-assed. Not completing what she set out to do, not finishing, not jogging all the way over to Low Water Bridge and back to Cherry Lane would feel like utter failure, one that has the potential to send her whole day spiraling into a miserable, unproductive waste of daylight. Frankly, with that stupid video, her recent termination, and this relocation to Austin (however temporary it may be), Ruby's run is part exercise, part post-traumatic shock therapy. Every heel-toe is an opportunity for her to face her demons, to scour the very pavement for all kinds of land mines. Quite simply, she does not want to step in any more shit, so the fog and the diminished visibility have her looking down more than she's looking ahead. Metaphorically, this can't be good.

Normally, she wears her wireless earbuds, but today, on this first full day of being back in her hometown, she's skipping the music and practicing something close to meditation. She listens to her own breathing, and with every exhale, she watches the fog coming out of her mouth, each puff more proof that she is alive and well. And not just Pearl's version of alive and well; not slug-it-in-bed-and-spend-half-your-day-watching-other-people-remodel-their-homes alive and well, but something better than that. Unemployed though she may be, at least Ruby has the self-discipline to get up and out of bed and get moving. Just seeing Pearl in person again only reinforces the compulsion she feels to stay active—anything to avoid becoming what her sister has become, what their mother has become.

As she rounds the last half mile to the old house, she practices her own brand of mindfulness: not so much exhale stress and inhale peace but more like no pain, no gain. The irony is not lost on her: this home, this place she swore she would never step foot in again, and yet here she is, at this very moment, running straight back to it. How she had managed to screw up her career to the point where she had no other choice but to list her condo in Dallas and come back to Austin is beyond her. The video, she tells herself, could have happened to anyone. At least Pearl doesn't know. And it's best to keep it this way. With her sister's myopic focus on her rapidly approaching weight loss surgery, Ruby takes some comfort in knowing that the house on Cherry Lane, however unkempt, is at least a safe space, a little shell she can hide under until the viral nature of her #shityounot moment begins to dissipate.

Although she's only been here twenty-four hours, she's already crawling out of her skin with anxiety: all the same old furniture—even the bedding!—nothing in the house has changed. It's as if Ruby got caught in a time warp and everything, right down to her mom's old *Don't Mess with Texas* mouse pad, is still in the same place it was fourteen years ago. Literally the only new things are Ruby being here and Pearl occupying even more space.

Now back and on the front porch, Ruby checks her time and mileage, compares them to both the time and distance recorded in her weekly and monthly log. Sufficiently sweaty, she pulls off her moisture-wicking shirt and heads back inside. Based on what she saw when she left for her run, she doubts her sister is even awake yet. An hour ago, when she passed Pearl's slightly open bedroom door, she caught an unfortunate glimpse of her 531-pound little sister, the hugeness of her body eclipsed only by the long, plastic snorkel stuck to her face. Ruby forgets exactly what the tubular apparatus is called but knows it's some kind of prescription breathing device that, from what she understands, only fat people need in order to sleep without snoring. In the kitchen, she surveys the old pots and pans hanging over the island, one of the only still pleasant reminders of happier times and Birdie's exceptional cooking.

When she arrived yesterday, she'd done her best to get right back out and stay out as long as she could. After unpacking a whole SUV full of items into her old bedroom and a quick visit with Pearl, Ruby left to run some errands. Really, she ended up taking a two-hour walk around Lady Bird Lake, followed by a one-hour walk in the Whole Foods on North Lamar. That left an evening alone with Pearl, the two of them sitting at the same kitchen island where they both lost their first tooth. Over a couple of grilled salmon and quinoa bowls she'd picked up at the Whole Foods deli along with a bottle of cabernet, Ruby had made an earnest effort to reconnect. But the sight of Pearl, the space her sister occupied in the room, was just too distracting. The entire time Pearl was talking about work and her friend Perry and the wait-till-you-see good looks of her bariatric surgeon, Ruby was holding her breath. At any moment, she fully expected the barstool, wholly hidden by her sister's mass, to give way and come crashing to the floor.

And now, as she chugs water at the kitchen counter, Ruby can't help but notice all the wadded-up paper towels and the two empty cans of Diet Dr Pepper cast off in the sink.

Why, when only ten feet away in the pantry, there is a ten-gallon Rubbermaid receptacle just waiting to be filled, why, for the love of God, can Pearl not put trash where it goes? She doesn't even recycle!

Laziness, she thinks. The same laziness that gets a person to weigh a quarter ton is the same laziness that causes them to use the kitchen sink as a trash can.

The almost empty pantry and fridge do little to shed any light on her sister's substantial size. In fact, by comparison to Pearl's poundage, the lack of snacks and stocked shelves are a paradox. Although this mystery gnaws at her, other disappointments are plain to see. By Ruby's estimation, her sister has allowed the formerly lovely house they grew up in to fall into a state of dated disrepair. With Pearl still in bed, she takes a moment to inventory every nook and cranny. It's hard to guesstimate the last time the wood floors met up with a mop. And flicking the light in the half bath, previously the one used by guests, she inspects the grimy toilet, the hard water–stained bowl, the noticeable crack in the toilet seat. There's an acrid fusion of mildew being masked by some strategically placed magnolia-scented candles, and throughout the house, the formerly white baseboards are covered with a sticky gray lint. Looking up, Ruby's eyes land on the ceiling fan in the living room, the blades of which are weighed down with a thick layer of dust.

On the back patio, once a lively place for barbecues and birthday parties, several years' worth of dried leaves clog the concrete corners. The outdoor table, caked with bird droppings, is its own little ecosystem. Draped with cobwebs between the iron legs, Ruby spots a bird's nest in the base just below the tabletop. The yard used to be a source of pride, and Ruby stares out at the sad, vacant flower beds where Birdie's roses used to bloom and at the remnants of the old tire swing their dad hung for them from the massive live oak. All that's left of it are two stringy weather-worn ropes and a single sliver of black rubber tire. She remembers she and her sister being small enough to sit on the tire swing together while their dad pushed them higher and higher. Looking up at the branch, Ruby wonders how much weight it could support and feels certain that with one squat, Pearl would snap the substantial limb right off the tree.

So much work to do here, she thinks. And frankly, she doesn't know which needs more help—the house or Pearl. Moreover, she can't begin to understand why anyone would willfully choose to inhabit the same space where their stepdad was shot dead. Above all, that was the main reason Ruby chose to stay away for all these years. This house, the very kitchen she's standing in, is just bad juju. However, whether she likes it or not, this is where she is: stuck in some limbo between her own self-made shit show and the hot mess of her baby sister's life.

Making her way down the hall toward the shower, she passes Pearl's door and peeks in.

"Hey," Pearl says, averting her eyes from a very loud episode of *Fixer Upper*. Still very much in bed, Pearl is propped up on pillows, the snorkel now sunken to the floor. "Did you go for a run?"

"Yep," Ruby says, barely able to mask the still-simmering

scorn for all the muck and her sister's blatant lack of standards. In one syllable, she's managed to convey so much. Ruby's yep packs a powerful punch. It's a yep that says, *Yep, I already ran six miles while you're lounging in bed, and yep, even if it is the weekend, I am annoyed that you, a grown woman, are still lollygagging around at 10 a.m., and yep, I've only been here one day and already I'm so over all of it: the way you've just let all of it—the house, the yard, yourself—go.*

"What, pray tell, have you been up to?" Ruby asks, and considering her sister's current location, the implication is quite clear. Pearl has been up to not much at all. In fact, there's a strong case to be made that Pearl isn't even technically up.

"Just watching a little Chip and JoJo before I get the day started," Pearl says joyfully, altogether ignoring her sister's snarky tone. "Looks kind of nasty outside."

"It's just a little early-morning fog, but we can't go around letting the weather dictate our day or stop us from getting things done," Ruby explains.

Pearl averts her eyes, trying to ignore Ruby's efforts to start shit so early in her stay.

"Just trying to encourage you to, like, carpe diem, Pearl. No time like the present to—"

"To what?" Pearl says, interrupting. "To take myself on a one-hour sprint around the neighborhood? To be more like you?"

Ruby rolls her eyes and walks away before she says anything she might really regret. In their shared bathroom, she shuts the door to Pearl's room a little too aggressively but makes no apologies. Saying sorry is simply not Ruby's style.

The only update Pearl appears to have made to the entire house is yet another sad reminder of her sister's runaway obesity. A plastic shower curtain has replaced what, once upon a time, was a sliding glass door, presumably a retrofit so her sister could more easily squeeze into the stall. Standing there, letting the steamy hot water soak her hair, Ruby tries to get ahold of herself.

I am not my sister.

This is not my life.

She is in no way a reflection of me.

I am not the boss of her.

I cannot control her choices or her behavior.

It's a free fucking country, and people can live like pigs if they please.

And the talking to herself does seem to calm her some, right up until she reaches for the shampoo. Four different bottles of shampoo, but three are totally empty. What kind of person lets empty shampoo bottles collect for God knows how long in the confines of their shower? Like, when she puts a new one in, why doesn't she throw the old, empty one out? "Fuck me," Ruby says under her breath.

Dripping wet, Ruby tiptoes across the tile floor, dumping a menagerie of plastic containers into the trash before making her way to the still-open suitcase in her room to fish out her own toiletries. With the shower sufficiently restocked, Ruby lathers up, rinses, and repeats, doing her level best to avoid looking at all the long brown hair collecting near the drain and the soap scum and mildew between the tiles. Pearl knocks on the bathroom door.

"What?" Ruby says, somewhat startled, still irritated.

"Brought you a cup of hot tea," Pearl says, making her way to the vanity. "Thought you might like some Earl Grey with honey after that run in the fog."

Ruby turns off the faucet, wrings the water out of her hair, and steps out onto the green fuzzy mat. As immodestly as a two-year-old in the tub, she reaches for a towel and begins to pat herself dry. For a second, the tea, this gesture of kindness and thoughtfulness, throws her off, makes her forget about what a slob her sister really is.

"Thanks," she says. "Tea does sound good. Hey, by the way, are empty shampoo bottles something you've started collecting? Is that, like, a new hobby or something?"

"Oh, my bad," Pearl says. "I just keep forgetting to toss out the old ones, but there should be some of the Pantene left."

Standing there in her nearly worn-through stretchy black leggings and tattered T-shirt, her lush long hair a tangle around her pillow-wrinkled face, Pearl looks, to Ruby, especially sloppy. She's not sure if her sister's shambolic appearance is an extension of the house or if it's the other way around, but tea or no tea, Ruby can't stand to see everything so dirty and disheveled. It's as if her sister gives no fucks whatsoever about her appearance or anything else.

"Pearl, it's not just the empty shampoo bottles," Ruby says, bending over, twisting her wet hair into a tall towel turban on top of her head.

"Oh, here we go," Pearl says, crossing her arms in front of her chest. "Nothing is ever good enough for Ruby. I forgot. You know, if I had a little more notice you were coming yesterday, I might have had more time to tidy things up around here."

Ruby walks to the vanity, reaches for a sip of tea.

"Oh, knock it off with the nothing's ever good enough, Pearl. The level of filth you're willing to tolerate should have no bearing on whether or not you're expecting company."

"Wow," Pearl says, taken aback. "Someone woke up on the wrong side of the bed today."

"Oh, don't wrong side of the bed me, Pearl. For two weeks, you've known I was coming. You could have, at the very least, I don't know, swept off the front porch or something. It's just about being considerate."

"Well, excuse me, Miss Perfect. Forgive me for being so inconsiderate. I guess it's just flat-out rude of me to bring you some fresh hot tea with honey!"

"Pearl, the tea is very nice," Ruby admits, trying to temper her temper. "It's just…"

"It's just what?"

"It's just, like, why the hell can't you throw your used paper towels and leftover Diet Dr Pepper cans away? Why do you use the kitchen sink as a personal dump? And what is up with the ripped wallpaper right behind your head? Was that a project you started and just forgot to finish or something? And while we're talking about all of this"—Ruby sweeps an arm wide—"what's up with the toilets in the house, Pearl? All the seats are cracked, and they're all stained and nasty. Do you even own a toilet brush? A vacuum cleaner? All this filth, it's just so fucking weird! Honestly, I'm surprised *Hoarders* isn't your favorite show instead of *Fixer Upper*."

"Oh, so this is how it's gonna go today," Pearl says, rolling her eyes. "It's pick-on-Pearl day. Point out all the many ways I don't measure up to you, count all the many miles I've never run. Is that what day it is, Ruby? Gee, all along, I thought it was Sunday, but turns out it's Pearl-sucks day?"

"Oh, come on," Ruby says, rolling deodorant onto her pits. "For once, Pearl, you've got to stop acting like such a victim. I came down here to help you get your life back on track. How many other people do you know who are willing to take time out of their busy lives to come move in with you while you try to lose a few hundred pounds? News flash, Pearl: zero. That's the number! I'm the one who showed up. Actions speak louder than words, remember? Those are words of wisdom from Birdie herself. So you may not like my approach or the way I basically point out the obvious, but this is one of those times in life when somebody's got to talk about the elephant in the room!"

Pearl's eyes squint, and she shakes her head in disbelief at her sister's hurtful words. The look on her face says it all. For as much as she loves Ruby, for as much as she longs for the kind of sisterly simpatico they shared when they were younger, at this very moment, Ruby can feel it—Pearl hates her guts.

"Fuck you, you self-righteous bitch," Pearl screams.

"What did you just call me?"

"You heard me," Pearl says, her voice echoing off the bathroom walls. "Only a total bitch acts this ungrateful for a cup of tea!"

And with that, Ruby loses it completely. Still totally naked except for the turban on top of her head, she takes the porcelain cup, aims it straight for Pearl, and launches it clear across the bathroom. Hot tea trails through the air as Pearl ducks. Due to Pearl's quick reflexes, the cup misses its target, instead shattering directly behind her, hitting the mirror on the wall, sending shards of cracked glass all over the tile floor around them.

For a moment, it's all quiet, both women standing perfectly still, slack-jawed in the what-do-we-do-now wake of their fiery feud. Carefully, so as not to inadvertently step on something sharp, Ruby unfurls the damp towel from her head and throws it on the floor, covering the broken glass, creating a safe place for both of them to stand.

"Nice pitch, Ruby. You've got that windup down pat. Hashtag shit you not," Pearl says bluntly. "Too bad nobody caught this one on video."

Chapter 20

By Sunday evening, Ruby is the one bringing hot tea to Pearl. All day, they avoided one another by busying themselves trying to spiff up opposite ends of the house; this was their silent but very productive way of conceding some mutual accountability for the current state of their respective unfortunate circumstances. Sweaty and spent, Pearl is doing one final Swiffer over the hardwood floors in the living room when Ruby emerges from the kitchen to extend an olive branch.

"Here, made you some tea," she says, swapping the cup for the Swiffer.

"Thanks," Pearl says, somewhat surprised.

"Look," Ruby says, walking toward the hall closet to put away the mop. "I owe you a huge apology for lobbing that teacup at you and breaking the mirror. I promise I'll replace it first thing tomorrow. Why don't we take a break and sit down for a little while," she adds, motioning toward the sofas.

"Okay, I'll take a break from all this cleaning and scrubbing and join you on the sofa, but only if you don't accuse me of being a couch potato."

"Deal." Ruby kicks off her sneakers and plops down on the faded love seat. "It does feel good to take a load off." She motions for Pearl to do the same, and her younger sister lowers herself onto the sofa opposite the love seat.

Together, they scan the results of their labor, both feeling an unexpected sense of satisfaction.

"I admit, the house looks way better than it did this morning," Pearl says, propping her swollen bare feet up on the coffee table.

"Yep," Ruby says.

"So is now a good time for me to ask what really happened with the flying dog poop video?"

Ruby closes her eyes and sighs.

"I don't know," she says finally.

"You don't know what happened or you don't know if this is a good time for me to ask?"

"I mean I don't know why I lost my mind the way I did and threw dog poop at that guy."

"Well, it wasn't like some kind of random assault, right? You didn't just suddenly start flinging shit at that guy for no reason, right? So, like, what was the run-up to all that?"

"Well." Ruby sits up straighter, becoming thoughtful. "I run the Katy Trail all the time, if not daily at least every other day," she says. "The signs are posted everywhere, and they all say the same thing: Pick up after your dog. But for a few weeks, that same guy decided he was going to be the exception to that rule, and he kept letting his big mutt take these gigantic dumps right in the middle of the path. In the mornings, when it's still dark outside, poop is hard to see, and I had already stepped in it a few times before. Anyway, I mentioned it to him the other times, tried pointing at the sign, lifted up the bottom of my shoe, the whole bit. He didn't care. But when it happened again, I just lost it. And as you know, we can't exactly go around losing it in public. Cell phones make everyone part of the paparazzi. So there I was, caught on camera, acting erratic."

"At least you know you were acting erratic," Pearl says sheepishly. "Does the video have anything to do with you taking this sabbatical?"

With both index fingers, Ruby sweeps under her eyes, ostensibly rubbing away any smudged mascara but also putting pressure on her tear ducts. For a few seconds, she's silent, but finally she nods.

"So were you fired?" Pearl asks cautiously.

Too proud to say it out loud, once again, Ruby nods, now battling back tears.

"I'm so sorry that happened," Pearl says sincerely. "Seriously, that just sucks."

Still speechless, Ruby turns her head, and her gaze lands on the old framed family photo on the credenza. Even from where she's sitting, the details captured in that shot are easy to see— right down to the scuffs on their white patent leather Mary Janes.

"Remember how excited we used to get when it was time to shop for new Easter dresses?" Ruby asks, waxing nostalgic.

"And remember how we would hide and then re-hide and then keep re-hiding those plastic eggs?" Pearl adds, laughing. "Mom and Daddy probably couldn't wait for Easter Sunday to end, right?"

"How is she anyway?" Ruby asks.

"Who, Mom?"

"Birdie. You still keep up with her, right?"

"We talk twice, sometimes three times a week, and about once a month, I go for family visitation."

"And?"

"And she seems good. Complains about the food, but other than that, she mostly just wants to talk about us," Pearl says, draining the teacup.

"And what does Birdie have to say about us these days?" Ruby asks somewhat bitterly.

"By and large, she just talks about how much she wishes she could be here, how sad she is to be missing so much of our lives, how sad she is that you don't seem to want to have anything to do with her. You know, stuff like that."

"We are two very different people, Pearl," Ruby says, tucking a loose strand of hair behind her ear. "I'm not you and you're not me, and I don't get you and you don't get me, and for the love of God, I have no ability to comprehend how or why you could just keep living in this place after what happened right over there." Ruby swivels and points at the back door.

Pearl doesn't speak. It's so rare to hear her sister being so simultaneously introspective and calm, and despite the intensity of the content, she doesn't want to cut her off.

"Birdie could have made so many other choices, Pearl. I know we all fell for Skip in the beginning, but after they were married and he had that back surgery… Once he got hooked on the Percocet, he was never the same, and neither, frankly, was Birdie."

"But what choice did she have, Ruby? I mean, they were already married, and she loved him, and the truth is, she was probably more afraid of Skip and his addiction than you and I were." Pearl is scrambling to defend her mother but has the sinking feeling she's failing at it.

"If I was a single mom with two girls to raise and I married some guy who ended up becoming addicted to opioids, there would be only one good option, and that would be to leave. I mean, c'mon, Pearl. Wouldn't you choose your two daughters over some junkie? The problem with Birdie is she wasn't decisive enough. She gave Skip one too many chances, and look what happened. Look what it cost her. And you. And me," Ruby whispers.

Pearl can't help but look over toward the back door, where her mind flashes on the memory of Skip lying there, lifeless, in a pool of blood.

"I don't disagree that she gave him too many second chances, but I don't believe her staying married to him meant she didn't love us. I know for a fact she loved us—loves us—I mean," Pearl replies.

"Right, Pearl. Keep telling yourself that. You sound just as delusional as Birdie, almost as delusional as Skip, and that's pretty effing delusional—the opioid junkie who very nearly mistook his wife for a piñata. I mean props to Birdie for getting a shot off before he smacked her upside the head, but it didn't have to come to that. Think about it. Hell, I just wonder how different your life would be, how different all our lives would be if only Birdie had had the good judgment to kick him out once his back was healed and it became clear that he was abusing those painkillers. Instead, she waited too long, and look what happened."

"You weren't even around, Ruby." Pearl feels anger building within her but manages to sound calm.

"Am I supposed to apologize for accepting a track scholarship to SMU?" Ruby replies.

"No, that's not what I mean," Pearl says. "Look, I don't want to fight about this, Ruby. I'm simply saying you had another place to go, but I was still in high school, and Mom and I had no choice but to stay. It's just the way it was."

"But that was twelve years ago! You could have made choices that would have gotten you out of here, Pearl, and you just didn't make them! It just seems like you froze when Birdie went away, and you've been stuck in place ever since." Ruby shakes her head.

"Well, I'm hoping to not be stuck much longer," Pearl says. "You think I don't see what I've become, but I do. I live it every day. I'm almost thirty years old now, Ruby. As many years as it took me to end up this way, it's gonna take a minute to get myself out of this mess," she says, shaking her head in disgust.

For the first time in years, Ruby seems sanguine. With a sympathetic smile, she studies her sister.

"What?" Pearl says.

"I'm just sizing you up, That's all."

"And that's exactly what I don't need you to do."

"I meant I'm sizing up the level of courage it takes to do what you're about to do, Pearl. I'm proud of you. There. I said it. And look, I may not have been here then, but I'm here now," Ruby adds. "So besides cleaning the house, what can I do to help?"

For a little while, Pearl considers this question, and for the first time all day, she smiles.

"Just try not to break any more mirrors, okay?"

Chapter 21

With just a week to go before the dreaded EGD scope procedure, Pearl has checked off every other item on the pre-op prep list. The psych consult, the sleep study, the cardiac evaluation, and her lab work—all of it is behind her. And truth be told, she's formed quite the attachment to her CPAP machine, which, after giving her the seven best nights of sleep in her life, she affectionately refers to as Mr. Winky.

"I'm not kidding," Pearl says to Perry. "Mr. Winky makes me feel like a new woman!"

They're walking toward Ms. Sullivan's suite on what has become a daily mission to deliver a fresh package of candy cigarettes before Ms. Sullivan starts begging for the real thing.

"Are you sure Mr. Winky isn't really a sex toy?" Perry asks, elbowing her. "You just seem a little overly enthusiastic to be wearing a snorkel to bed."

"Perry, I had no idea how tired I was all these years," she says. "It's like night and day. Literally. In fact, I think everyone should sleep with a Mr. Winky."

"Only if he's tall, dark, and handsome," he says, grinning.

At the entrance to Suite 7, Perry knocks.

"Yoo-hoo, Ms. Sullivan," he singsongs cheerfully. "May we come in?"

"Where are my smokes?" she rasps. Seated in her wheelchair with the ever-present nasal cannula from her oxygen tank strapped to her face, smokes are the last thing Ms. Sullivan should be asking for, but Pearl has found a clever way to assuage her cravings and her persistent demands, and it's a trick she's employed with great success with all the smokers in this smoke-free facility.

"I need my nicotine, dammit!"

"Here you go, Ms. Sullivan," Pearl says, passing over a single white, cigarette-shaped stick of sugar.

Together, Pearl and Perry watch Ms. Sullivan position the candy cigarette between her trembling fingers and eagerly bring it to her mouth for one long, seemingly gratifying smoke-free drag.

"Have I told you yet today that you are a genius?" Perry says this to Pearl each and every time they make this delivery, and each time, Pearl soaks up the flattery.

"I still can't get over how many employees that mean old biddy scared off with her nicotine withdrawals before you showed up with the fake cancer sticks and tamed the beast," Perry adds.

"I seem to be doing a lot of beast taming these days," Pearl says, grinning.

"Do tell," Perry asks as they walk side by side toward the activities room. "Has Ruby stopped throwing things?"

"Cold turkey," Pearl says. "Actually, it's kind of nice having her around. The house hasn't been this clean and organized since my mom went to prison. And she's already started trying to stock the fridge with health food."

"My, how quickly we adapt to change," Perry says.

"What do you mean?" Pearl asks.

"I mean, it's just a fact. We adapt. Ms. Sullivan and her candy ciggies are a perfect example, Pearl."

"Do you think me adapting to Ruby being around is a bad thing?" she asks.

"As long as there are no projectiles involved and she's treating you with respect, it could be the best thing in the world," Perry says. "Look at the progress you've made in such a short amount of time, Pearl. Like, your new friend Mr. Winky is just one part of a much bigger picture, and though you may be so close to it that you can't see it, I can. Less than a week ago, you were complaining because Ruby threw that cup of hot tea at you and shattered an enormous mirror right behind your head, but now you're saying she's dazzling you with her domestic goddess skills, right?"

"Um, pretty much," Pearl says meekly.

"That's adapting," he says, stopping just shy of the activity center doors. "You and Ruby are learning to coexist. And buckle up, butterfly, because the changes are coming, and the more layers you shed, believe me, the more things are going to start coming to the surface."

"Like what things?" Pearl asks. "That sounds kind of scary."

"All kinds of things," he says. "Nothing to fear, Pearl. It's like when I came out. I made the choice to change the way I presented myself to the world. Instead of hiding, I started owning who I really was. And as soon as I did that, the people around me, my family especially, they had a choice to either adapt and embrace me or get out of my way. For every big change we go through, there's a yin and a yang. It's the duality of life. You and Ruby. Yin and yang. It's when opposite or contrary forces actually become complementary, interconnected, even interdependent. Yin and yang are seen in all forms of change. I'm not making this shit up. It's ancient Chinese philosophy. After all these years apart, Ruby arrives on your doorstep weeks before you undergo life-changing surgery. Coincidence? I don't think so. Teacup hissy fit aside, I think Ruby arriving is the universe conspiring on your behalf."

Chapter 22

It is still dark and a bit chilly as they walk through the automatic glass double doors at the outpatient surgery center adjacent to Austin Weight Loss Specialists. Pearl is Dr. George's first case of the day, and she's scared speechless. Although it's considered a minor, outpatient, pre-op test, the esophagogastroduodenoscopy feels as huge as it sounds. It may be her last clinical hurdle before her actual sleeve surgery on March 13, but for Pearl, who has never been sedated in her entire life, the idea of propofol being pumped into her veins is as frightening as the notion of never eating another chimichanga. Ruby can't relate, but she's doing her best to coach her sister through the fear.

"Are you okay?"

Ruby has asked this at least a dozen times since they left the house, but all Pearl can manage is a nervous nod. Before they approach the reception desk, Ruby pivots and faces Pearl.

"Remember what we discussed. Three quick breaths in through the nose, then slow exhales through the mouth. Do it now," Ruby says assertively.

Pearl does as she's told, trying anything to avoid a full-scale panic attack. She's fighting a strong impulse to turn around and walk right back out those double glass doors.

"You are not Michael Jackson," Ruby says calmly. "This is a perfectly safe procedure. They do this all day, every day, Pearl."

"Right, but not on people who weigh what I weigh," Pearl whispers.

"That's another lie you tell yourself," Ruby says. "If they didn't think this was safe, they wouldn't have scheduled you. They would have told you to lose more weight first, but they didn't. We've been through this six ways from Sunday, Pearl. This is just your fear talking. Do the breathing one more time."

Ruby waits patiently for Pearl to finish the breathing exercise. And once she has, once Pearl seems to have steadied herself enough to walk to the counter and hold a pen in her hand without dropping it, they approach the desk together.

"Good morning." The cheerful receptionist is dressed for the holiday. A cluster of red heart-beaded necklaces adds a pop of color to her gray scrubs, reminding both Pearl and Ruby what day it is.

"Hi, this is Pearl Crenshaw," Ruby says for her sister. "She's a patient of Dr. George."

With her enormously long scarlet fingernails, the receptionist clicks Pearl's name into her keyboard.

"Yes, we have her down for an esophagogastroduodenoscopy, right?"

Pearl nods.

"Have you had anything to eat or drink since midnight?"

She shakes her head.

"No. She hasn't," Ruby says, compensating for her sister's muteness. "She's a little nervous," Ruby explains, smiling at the woman behind the counter. "Never had any kind of surgery before so…"

"Well, Pearl, you're in for a nice little beauty rest," the receptionist explains. "Now, if I can just get you to sign right here, I'll have someone out front with a wheelchair in just a moment. We'll get your temperature and blood pressure, and you'll be on our way."

Pearl reaches for the pen, and that's when Ruby and the receptionist can plainly see exactly how terrified Pearl really is. Her hand is shaking so hard, she can barely steady the pen to meet the paper.

"I'll get to go back there with her, won't I?" Ruby asks, gesturing toward Pearl's wholly illegible signature.

"Yes. You can sit with her while they get her prepped. Once they wheel her back, you can wait right out here, and we'll call you just as soon as she's awake and ready to go home."

In the patient holding area, a friendly older nurse, who bears an uncanny resemblance to their mom, Birdie, walks Pearl through the pre-op instructions and hands her a gown and a plastic bag for her possessions while Ruby sits unobtrusively in the chair next to the bed.

"Pearl, I'll give you a moment to change and get comfortable, and I'll be back shortly to start your IV. Dr. George is usually right on time, so he'll be by along with Dr. Galvez, your anesthesiologist, to go over everything before they roll you back."

Once the nurse pulls the curtain, Pearl stands there holding the bag, motionless.

"Don't chicken out," Ruby says. "You've come this far, Pearl. Remember, you've got the Mr. Winky thing going, you did all that lab work, the therapy session, and let's not forget, you've already paid in full for next month's surgery. This is the last little hurdle."

"I know, I just…I'm afraid to have my clothes off in front of total strangers," Pearl mutters, holding up the flimsy hospital gown. "And what if this doesn't fit?"

Seeing Pearl so afraid musters all Ruby's long-lost big sister instincts. Suddenly, she's ten years old again, encouraging Pearl to pedal harder on Cherry Lane.

"It's one size fits all, Pearl. It's going to fit," Ruby says, standing. "Here. Do you want me to help you?"

Slowly, Pearl tugs her sweatshirt up and over her head. It's the first time she's undressed in front of Ruby since they were in high school. Ruby does her best to avert her eyes, but there's no missing the expanse of her sister's stretch mark–covered flesh. She holds up the gown as Pearl unfastens her bra, lets it fall to the floor, and slips her arms through the holes.

"Don't forget this," Ruby says with an evil grin, handing Pearl the stretchy blue hair cap.

"I don't want to put that on until after Dr. George comes by,"

Pearl says. "And I'm serious. You should put on more lipstick. He is that effing cute."

Ruby is relieved her sister is thinking about something other than being naked or the sedative that's to come.

"Pearl, your teeth are chattering. Good Lord. Get under the covers, and calm the fuck down," Ruby insists, fishing lip gloss from her purse.

Once Pearl is situated on the gurney, the nurse reappears holding an IV bag.

"All settled?" she asks, hanging the bag on a stainless-steel pole next to the bed. It doesn't take a medical professional to see that Pearl is in no way "settled." Sensing this, she tries to distract and help tamp the look of terror on Pearl's face by chatting away the whole time she's finding a good vein and inserting the needle.

"So around here, we let the patients pick their favorite song to listen to in the OR," she explains. "When we get you back there, there will be several people in the room getting everything ready, and it's just kind of nice for you to lie there and listen to your favorite tune until you fall asleep. So, Pearl, what song should I tell them to load up for you?"

"Um," Pearl says, grimacing at the needle poking her skin. "Natassssha Bedingffffield's 'Unwritttttten.'"

"I don't know that one, but we've never had a song request we couldn't find, so I'll go tell them to make sure they've got that cranked up loud and clear when they roll you through the door, okay? Is there anything else I can get for you?"

Pearl shakes her head.

"Okay, well, I hear Dr. George's voice down the hall, so he should be by shortly."

"Thank you," Ruby says.

And just as soon as the curtains are yanked closed again, Pearl begins to cry.

"Oh no, Pearl," Ruby says, reaching for her sister's chubby hand. "No waterworks. You don't want your mascara to run in front of Dr. George, do you?" Ruby is standing over her sister, patting away her tears with a tissue when Dr. George makes his appearance.

"Good morning, ladies," he says, reaching toward the wall-mounted antiseptic dispenser.

He is undeniably gorgeous, and his looks alone are enough to render both Ruby and Pearl momentarily awestruck. Dr. George is like the last few seconds of a blazing sunset—he's hard not to watch.

"Pearl," he says, approaching the bed opposite Ruby. "You ready?"

And something about that simple question floods Pearl with another wave of fear, and she begins to sob.

"It's absolutely normal to be a little nervous," Dr. George says as he takes Pearl's hand. "And if I'm not mistaken," he adds, checking her chart, "this will be your first sedation, right?"

Pearl nods affirmatively while continuing to stare into Ruby's eyes.

"She's afraid of propofol," Ruby says. "You know, Michael Jackson and all..."

"Oh, well, that was a bizarre situation that did not take place in a well-run outpatient clinic like ours," Dr. George says, now beginning to appraise the dynamic between these two women. "You must be Ruby, Pearl's sister?" he says, once again checking the chart.

"Yes, that's me." Ruby nods, smiling.

"Well," Dr. George says, leaning in closer to Pearl, "I promise we're going to take very good care of you. And remember, Pearl, this little scope helps me map the inside of your stomach, so we'll be ready for that sleeve next month." Dr. George holds up a tiny lighted filament. "I simply send this light down your throat, take some pictures, and we're done for the day. All in, it will take about fifteen minutes. So what do you think? Are you still up for it?"

"Yeeessss." Pearl is visibly shaking now, but she manages a thumbs-up.

"You are sisters, right?" he asks, looking at Ruby, then back to Pearl.

"Yeeessss," Pearl manages again.

"Pearl and Ruby," he says, trying the names on for size. "Two rare gems. I like that. Your parents chose well."

His comment makes both of them blush, but it's what he says next that makes Ruby swoon.

"There's no sense in feeling so stressed, Pearl," he says. "Your comfort is important, so let me talk to Dr. Galvez, your anesthesiologist, and we'll see if she can't give you a little something now to take the edge off. How does that sound?"

"If you thiinnnkkkk sooooo," Pearl says, managing a partial smile.

"Good," he says, giving Pearl a gentle pat on her arm. "So, Ruby, you'll be here waiting for her when she wakes up?"

"Yes," she says, standing.

"Great. Any questions?"

They both shake their heads.

"Okay, so when we're done, I'll come find you, Ruby, and give you an update," he says, smiling at her. "Pearl, I'll see you in a few minutes."

As soon as the curtain is pulled and the two of them can hear Dr. George walking away, Ruby looks directly into Pearl's face and mouths the words, "OH MY GOD!"

Again, Pearl nods.

"Tolddd yooouuu sooooo." She shivers, tugging the sheet up around her neck.

Patiently, they wait until Dr. Galvez makes her appearance with her own introductions and a bump of diazepam to save the day. Almost immediately, Pearl's nerves mellow, and to Ruby, the instant contrast is hysterical.

"Better now?" Ruby asks, giggling.

"He winked at you," Pearl says. Her placid expression is one Ruby has never seen on her sister's face.

"No, he didn't," Ruby says.

"Uh, huh," Pearl says, giving her a slow-motion thumbs-up. "I distinctly saw him winking at you. He likes you."

"Don't forget your beautiful bonnet," Ruby says, changing the subject. Gently, she scoops Pearl's thick hair into a twist and slides the cap over her head.

"Maybe he can be your valentine," Pearl says.

She's drunk on the diazepam, and her shivering speech is already beginning to slur.

"When Mom calls, will you be sure to tell her I'm okay?"

Ruby's eyes widen. She wasn't expecting this.

"Will you?" Pearl asks again softly.

"Are you expecting her to call this morning?"

"No," Pearl says drowsily. "But you would talk to her if you had to, right? Like if I couldn't?"

Before Ruby can answer, the curtain rips open again, and the Birdie look-alike nurse reappears.

"They're ready for you, Pearl," she says, tugging at the foot of the bed. "Time for your nap."

Not even forty minutes later, as Ruby is scrolling mindlessly through her phone in the lobby, Dr. George appears before her, still wearing his surgical cap.

"She did great," he said, clapping his hands together.

"Wow," Ruby says, standing. "That really was fast."

"No signs of bacteria or any infection, so as far as her surgery goes next month, as long as she commits to the two-week pre-op fast, she's good to go."

"That's good news," Ruby says, trying not to hold his gaze for anything longer than normal.

"So let me give you my card." Dr. George reaches into his scrubs shirt pocket and pulls out a business card. "Oh, and let me just write my cell on there. I don't expect she'll have any trouble, but don't hesitate to call me if you or Pearl have any questions or need anything at all." With a smile, he hands the card to Ruby.

"Thank you, Doctor," Ruby says, inspecting the card. "I appreciate that. And thanks for taking such good care of her. I've never seen her so focused on something, so she'll be glad to know there's nothing holding her back."

"The sleeve is a big surgery," he says. "She'll need your support. Hopefully you live nearby? I mean, I noticed on her chart she lists you as her designated caregiver, so…"

"I live in Dallas. I mean, I'm taking some time away from work to help Pearl. So I'm actually staying with her."

"That's great," he says. "What I see with my patients is the more family support they have, the better the outcomes."

"Well, I know she's hoping for big results," Ruby says. "And I've got my fingers crossed, too."

"Okay, well, until next month," he says, extending his hand. "It's nice to meet you, Ruby."

"Nice to meet you, too, Dr. George," Ruby says, trying not to notice the ever-so-subtle extra squeeze she feels in his grip.

"Please," he says, "just call me Henry."

"Okay, Henry. Thanks again. I'm excited to see where all this goes."

"So am I," he says, smiling.

Chapter 23

Just like the morning after her first night with Mr. Winky, Pearl can't believe how good she feels the morning after the EGD. She expected to wake up groggy and spend the rest of the day crashed out on the sofa. Instead, she's riding shotgun in Ruby's Lexus, strapped in with the seat belt so tight it's literally jamming her jugular, on her way to the Domain, one of Austin's more upscale, high-density office, retail, and residential concepts. With its expansive, parklike setting, the Domain is like a prefab city within an actual city.

"You've got this awesome opportunity in front of you, Pearl," Ruby says, pulling into a parking garage. "Your sleeve surgery and the weight loss that will follow offer you a way of rebranding yourself to the world. So you don't have to wait until March to start shopping for ideas."

"I get that you're trying to help me, but at this point, it's really hard to even imagine what type of clothes might look good on me because I can't visualize how I'll look. Besides, this is a process. It's not like I will come out of the OR three hundred pounds slimmer."

"That's valid," Ruby says, scanning the aisles for an empty space. "But this is yet another reason why you should feel lucky I'm here, Pearl. Trust me, we are at the Domain, and style is my game! Oh, here's one," she says, eyeballing a parking spot.

"Um, would it be okay if you try to find a parking space that's on the end?" Pearl says, noticing the tight fit between the cars. "It's just that it's a little hard for me to get out if I can't open the door all the way."

"Oh, right," Ruby says, driving on.

On the next level, it's not as crowded. Mercifully, Ruby slips into a space at the end of a row, with no parking on the passenger side. Pearl wants so badly to move at her sister's pace, to hop in and out of a car with Ruby-like ease, to wear cute little Lululemon leggings and lace-up tennis shoes and be able to sprint from one makeup counter to the next, sourcing the best gifts with purchase. But this is not where she is—not yet anyway. From the more strategic parking spaces she's forced to find to the way she tries to hide all the slack she's created on the now stretched and worn-out seat belt, Pearl hates the way even simple daily tasks like getting into and out of a car and buckling up take so much effort. Normally, no one is with her, so she's free to absorb the awkwardness of functioning in the world as a fat person all by herself. Being with Ruby only serves to amplify her ampleness in a way that Pearl finds absolutely annoying.

Although, shopping at the Domain wasn't the first thing she had in mind after yesterday's EGD, she does feel good enough to keep Ruby company, and besides that, she 100 percent does not want to quash this rare "girl-time vibe" they're enjoying by being a stick-in-the-mud.

"This will be fun," Ruby says, sliding her sunglasses into headband position. They're approaching the entrance to Nordstrom, and their side-by-side reflection in the glass doors is too brutal for words. Neither one of them comments. Instead, they both avert their eyes.

Inside, it's clear that Ruby really is in her domain. As she bounces from rounder to rounder, feeling fabrics and checking price tags, Pearl thinks about what a perfect name the Domain is for an upscale shopping center. For the Rubys of the world, stacks of skinny jeans and racks of spaghetti-strap silk camisoles are like a tree-lined natural habitat. But Pearl feels totally out of her element.

And Ruby's no dummy. She knows Pearl is plus size, and she very eagerly takes her over to the section of the store filled with a big selection of big-people clothing. The only problem is, Ruby doesn't fully comprehend what Pearl already knows; that she outgrew the plus-size clothing at Nordstrom about two years ago. It's a not-so-fun fact that Pearl doesn't really feel like sharing, especially because she knows it will burst Ruby's enthusiasm bubble.

"Rachel Zoe says style is a way to say who you are without having to speak," Ruby says, sifting through a rounder full of flowy tops. "How do you feel about this?" she says, holding one up to herself. "What does this say to you?"

"That says my sister has been swallowed by a lightweight nylon jacket," Pearl says sarcastically.

"Come on," Ruby says. "I'm trying to help you. This isn't just an army-green, lightweight, hooded nylon jacket, Pearl. This is a sporty wardrobe staple. It's a go-with-anything, semi-structured topper that will hide bulges even after you've lost them."

"It's cute," Pearl says. "But what size is it?"

"So this is a twenty-six," Ruby says, inspecting the tag. "What do you wear?"

"They don't have my size here," Pearl admits. "Look, I wear a thirty-two, and that's, like, on my skinny day. Most department stores don't carry anything above a twenty-eight."

"What about Lane Bryant?" Ruby says. "Maybe they have one there?"

"Lane Bryant only goes to size twenty-eight, too, Ruby."

"Are you sure? I thought plus-size clothing was, like, their whole business model?"

"Trust me. I weigh five hundred and thirty-one pounds, Ruby. Plus-size clothing is my domain. There's a store I shop at called the Avenue, but it's nowhere near here. And they don't sell 'styles.' They basically just sell jersey-knit tents."

Standing there empty-handed yet surrounded by so many

outfits, it's hard to tell which one of them feels more defeated. Like a deflating balloon, a perfectly good shopping spree cut short feels a little sad. But Ruby remains steadfast in her mission to help Pearl reimagine herself.

"Okay, fine," Ruby says. "You know what? The clothes can wait. Why don't we hit the makeup counter instead? All we need to salvage this spree is some new lipstick and mascara."

And that's exactly how they spend their day after Valentine's Day afternoon: with Pearl happily perched in front of a hand-held mirror at Nordstrom as one of the makeup ladies makes her over. The finishing touch is a generous swipe of Chanel's most iconic lipstick—Rouge Allure Pirate—a classic red. And as she checks out her new look and the powerful perfection of her own luscious red lips, Pearl feels a faint flutter, the soft stirrings of her very soul, a feeling she hasn't felt in ages. With just weeks to go until her surgery, for the first time in years, she feels almost pretty, and it's that feeling, not the lipstick, that makes her smile.

Chapter 24

On her way home from work, Pearl fights a strong urge to whiz through the Jack in the Box drive-thru and say hi to Willie Mae. Although Ruby texted her to say she's making some kind of grilled chicken and riced cauliflower for dinner, Pearl can practically smell her favorite bacon cheese potato wedges. So as nice as it is to have their mom's pots and pans being put to use once again and despite how truly tasty Ruby's menu sounds, the fact is, old habits die hard.

"Welcome to Jack in the Box. How can I help you."

"Hey, Willie Mae, how's your day, girl?" Pearl asks.

"Hey, Pearl. It's just gettin' started. What can I get you, sweetheart?"

"I just want an order of the bacon cheese potato wedges," Pearl says, already hating herself.

"That gonna do it for ya?"

"Um, yes. I think so. Wait. You know what? Go ahead and throw a couple egg rolls in there, too."

"And a jumbo Diet Dr Pepper?"

"You know it, girl."

From start to finish, it takes Pearl exactly six and a half minutes to consume all that food and wash it down with her soda. And once all of it has landed in her stomach, sitting there in her stinky Altima, Pearl catches a glimpse of herself in the rearview. Her grease-stained lips don't look as pretty as they did a few days ago at the Chanel counter.

Ruby would lose her mind if she witnessed this little binge. And paranoia makes Pearl look around her car very carefully to be sure her sister hasn't hidden a camera in here somewhere. It would be like her to do that, she thinks.

The rest of the way home, Pearl tells herself all kinds of dangerous lies:

It's okay to pig out while you still can.

You're about to have a tummy the size of a banana, so you owe it yourself to indulge a little.

Who are you trying to fool? The surgery probably won't even work. Just stick to what you know—which is being fat.

And the lies lead her to thoughts about her mom, who is sitting in a prison not more than two hours north of this very spot. Tonight is the night Birdie's supposed to call, and Pearl wonders if there's any chance at all that Ruby might surprise her and join in the conversation. But as she pulls into the garage, noticing how much tidier it looks since her sister got here, she tells herself another one of her go-to lies:

There's no sense getting my hopes up.

Inside, she can already smell the sautéed garlic and onion on the stove. Ruby is flitting about in the kitchen wearing one of their mom's old aprons. Normally, the TV is on. But since Ruby arrived, the TV, at least the one in the living room, is always off. Instead, Ruby's background sound of choice is a Spotify station called French Jazz Café, which can be heard all over the house from her tiny Bluetooth speaker on the island.

"Hi," Ruby says.

"Hi, yourself," Pearl says, shuffling toward the kitchen. She plops a stack of mail on the counter and sifts through it. It's nothing but bills and direct mail pieces, two of which are still addressed to Elizabeth Crenshaw.

"Smells great in here," Pearl says.

"Hope you're hungry. I'm obsessed with riced cauliflower. It's all the sticky, starchy goodness of actual steamed rice without the carbs. Have you ever had it?"

"No, but I'm excited to try. It's on the list of the new foods I'm supposed to be able to eat post-op."

"Well, it's all ready, so I say we go ahead and dig in," Ruby says. "By the way, don't look at the mess down the hall or this near-empty bottle of chardonnay. I started cleaning out closets today, and it literally drove me to drink."

Pearl cranes her neck to see the piles of stuff on either side of the old steamer trunk.

"Wow, you were busy," she says. "And thirsty," she adds, noticing the short splash of chard still left in the bottle.

"Honestly, Pearl, after spending the better part of the afternoon sifting through four years' worth of Birdie's Catering bank statements and a truckload of Barrow Creek Country Club Koozies and golf tees, I've come to the conclusion that the shit you hold on to says more about you than the stuff you let go of. Like, why haven't you purged all that stuff before?"

"I guess I just thought all that stuff belongs to Mom, and it's not really mine to toss," Pearl explains.

"Pearl, news flash: she got a twenty-year sentence for manslaughter. You'll be almost forty before she gets out. And even though I don't talk to Birdie, I'm pretty sure she wouldn't miss the Koozies."

They sit at the old breakfast table. Ruby has gone to the trouble to use actual place mats and linen napkins. She's even lit a candle.

"This is nice," Pearl says, taking her time with her bites. She's trying to stay on pace with Ruby.

"I know, right? I'm glad you like it. I just thought it would be nice to dine instead of eat, you know?"

Pearl doesn't know, but she understands the distinction.

"So did you come across any keepers while you were weeding things out today?" Pearl asks.

"I didn't get rid of any photos, but I probably should have. Came across that picture of the four of us standing in front of Skip's blue Suburban when we were at that beach house in Galveston, remember? So creepy."

"We were so convinced he was, like, dad of the year with a big family car like Mom's."

"Can't judge a book..."

"Right. Boy, did that ever backfire," Pearl says, moving some of the cauliflower around on her plate with a fork.

"You wonder why I don't have anything to do with Birdie, but to me, all things considered, it seems like an obvious choice. Who lets their daughters go on ride-alongs with their stepdad when he's heading over to East Austin to score Percocets from his dealer? We told her about this, Pearl, and she still didn't leave him. I just can't get passed how fucked up it all became."

"I think she was just trying to hold our family together," Pearl says, getting up from the table.

"Well, that really worked out for her," Ruby says, collecting their plates.

Pearl's phone rings. She recognizes the numbers and flashes the screen toward Ruby for her to see, too.

"Speak of the devil," Ruby says, tossing their plates in the sink. "I'll let you two have a moment while I keep working on the mess back here."

Pearl answers and puts the call on speaker. Over the French jazz, the kitchen fills with the familiar recording.

"This is a call from inmate Elizabeth Crenshaw Benzer at the Mountain View Prison Unit. Press one to accept."

Ruby says she doesn't want to have anything to do with Birdie, but Pearl wonders if maybe the sound of their mom's voice might change her mind.

"Mom, you there?"

"Hi, sweetie," Birdie says. "How's everything? How'd the procedure go?"

"All good," Pearl says. "I passed with flying colors, so I guess that means my stomach looks good enough to cut out."

"Well, that's what you still want, right?"

"Want and need are two different things," Pearl says.

"True," Birdie says. "What's that sound? You listening to some music?"

"I'm not," Pearl says. "But Ruby is."

"Is she there?"

"Uh-huh," Pearl says.

"But you're surgery's not until March thirteenth, right?"

"Uh-huh," Pearl says.

"Well, that's great that she came down early. I hope she's going to be able to stay a while. I love the idea of my girls back together."

"I think she will be here for a while, Mom," Pearl says, raising her voice to be certain Ruby can hear. "She's on a pretty big sabbatical from her job."

"A sabbatical? You mean like a leave of absence?"

Pearl pauses to consider her words. "It's more like a leave from her life..." She lets her voice trail off as she joins her mother in silence.

Finally, Birdie speaks. "Well, Ruby always knows what she's doing, so I for one can't wait to see what she decides to do next."

From down the hall, where she's pretending to be busily paring down the piles from their past, Ruby is listening intently to every word Birdie says. It's the first time she's heard her voice in twelve years, and she's shocked by the lump that's growing in her throat, especially when she hears her estranged mother's vote of confidence, even after all this time.

"So, sweetheart, what's next before your surgery? You've done all the tests, right?" Birdie seamlessly shifts the conversation, having mastered the art of maximizing these fifteen-minute chunks of time she gets with her child.

"Next is the hardest part of all, my two-week presurgical fast," Pearl continues. "Basically, I think the next two weeks are going to suck, but it is what it is. I either fast or forget all about the sleeve."

Ruby listens to her little sister and her mother until a loud beeping signals that their time is up.

"I'm here for you, Pearl. Maybe not physically, but just know I've got little else to do all day every day than pray for you and Ruby. I don't know why I have such a strong feeling about this, but I do. To me, it feels like you're both on the cusp of a happy new chapter in life. Think positive, and hang in there, you hear?" Despite the bars and emotional barriers that separate these women, the love in Birdie's voice is like a song they both know by heart. Even all the way down the hall, Ruby hears the harmony, and although she still refuses to sing along, she can't help but listen.

"I'll do my best," Pearl says. "Bye, Mom. I love you."

"I love you, too, sweetheart. Give Ruby a hug for me."

Chapter 25

February 26 is Pearl's D-Day. It's the last day before her March 13 surgery when she can eat like a no-holds-barred fat person. Once the clock strikes midnight, she'll begin the two-week pre-op fast, which will then be followed by another two-week post-op fast, which will then be followed by a lifetime of seriously restricted and forever changed eating.

For Pearl, it's been a philosophical day filled with curiosity about what the future will hold for her, agonizing spells of self-doubt, and an anxious run-through of the foods she knows she'll miss most, like the fresh jelly doughnuts brought to work this very morning by a colleague. She knows she'll miss those for sure, so she had not one but two when the break room was empty, earlier in the day.

As she finishes her room inspections at Glenwood Manor, Pearl finds herself paying way too much attention to the leftovers in some of her residents' rooms: the half-eaten dinner rolls, the perfectly good cold but untouched fish sticks and tartar sauce. All of it looks too good to waste. Like a bear about to go into winter hibernation, food, and the soon-to-be scarcity of it, consumes her every thought.

"So," Perry says, popping his head into Suite 12 before he takes off. "Is six thirty still good? I can't wait to meet Ruby."

Like an inmate on death row, Perry encouraged Pearl to pick her final "fuck it" meal, her what-she's-gonna-miss-most favorite dish. It could be anything in the world, and Perry told her he would not only make it from scratch but also deliver it right to her house, where he, Pearl, and Ruby could savor her "last supper" together.

"Can't wait," she says, joining him in the hall. "I can taste your amazing three-cheese lasagna already."

"And don't forget about the garlic bread, girl. It's going to be a one-two punch carbohydrate knockout."

And just then, the tears come. Pearl's been going through her day, just like it's any other day, but she's on the verge of leaving her furtive, food-obsessed lifestyle behind—forever. The magnitude of this new reality hits her hard.

"Oh, Pearl," Perry says, reaching for her hand. "Look, I know this is unbelievably daunting."

Pearl looks at her dear friend, unafraid at least for him to really see the terror in her eyes. They stand there for a few moments, locked in an unspoken moment of acknowledgment of the great unknown that Pearl is about to step into.

"You are, Pearl Crenshaw, one of the bravest people I know. And one day soon, you're gonna love beets. I swear," Perry says while wiping away his own tears. "So don't you get me started, because I've got work to do, including putting together a meal that would make even Gordon Ramsay smile."

As promised, at exactly 6:30 p.m., Perry, dressed to the nines and cradling Pearl's last supper, rings the doorbell.

"I come bearing gifts," he says as Pearl shows him inside.

To set the mood, Ruby's selected a Roman Holiday station from Spotify. With lights dimmed and candles lit all over the house, the place almost looks elegant. And as they make their way to the kitchen, Pearl makes the introductions.

"Perry, this is my sister, Ruby."

"Oh my gosh," he says, extending his arms for a hug. "It's so fun to finally meet my favorite person's sister."

Pearl bites her lower lip, waiting for Perry to betray in some way that he knows this is the infamous woman from the #shityounot video. But of course, being Perry, he never lets on. Instead, he immediately begins to pepper Ruby with the kind of affectionate banter he uses with everyone as a way to break the ice.

"Is that top from French Connection?" He looks at Ruby with satisfaction. "Because it's certainly connecting!"

Ruby can't help but smile, impressed that Perry knows his labels.

And it's only at this very moment, as she watches the two of them embrace, that Pearl realizes Ruby doesn't have a Perry in her life. She doesn't have that one person who's willing to chef it up in the kitchen preparing her a last supper, a special someone who loves her through thick and thin.

Pearl watches as Ruby and Perry move around the kitchen as though they've known each other for years.

"I set the oven at three hundred to keep the lasagna warm while I whip up a salad. Does that work, Perry?" Ruby nods toward the built-in.

"I'd say that's perfect, Ruby. What else can I do to help?" Perry replies.

Pearl sets the table in the dining room, which, until Ruby's arrival, was the repository for years of unfiled paperwork and junk mail. She can't recall the last time they used this room for a family meal, but somewhere, way back in the recesses of her mind, are the vague recollections of happy gatherings around Birdie's excellent food. She finds herself smiling as she places freshly laundered napkins on the polished table. Ruby, who'd moved on from the closets to the tangled, overgrown yard, had managed to pull together a handful of roses from an overgrown bush and had placed them in a vase that now sits at the center of the table. Pearl realizes that this is only one of a handful of meals that she has eaten at the table in more than decade, and all those have been in the weeks since Ruby's arrival. "Perhaps things really can change," she muses as she lays out the silverware for their celebratory meal.

By the time they are seated, these two long-estranged sisters and one extraordinarily discreet man, they are breaking bread as friends.

"So, Pearl," Perry says, raising his glass, "I want to make a toast to your metamorphosis. We are all only one decision away from a totally different life, and I'm so proud of you for making this one. Cheers to your future tuck-in weight."

Half-embarrassed, Pearl smiles and thanks Perry. Soaking up this much attention is like sopping up the sauce on her plate; she loves every last drop but hates feeling like all eyes are on her.

"What's a tuck-in weight?" Ruby asks, truly curious.

"It's that number on the scale that signifies when you can actually tuck a shirt into your waistband for the first time," Perry chimes in. "It's not about hitting a goal number: it's more of a feeling number, a number that signifies you're now on the other side. You're now in the realm of the healthy." Perry goes on, "For me, this is the moment when my confidence really kicked in. When I knew I was in charge of me—that I could take actions that were self-loving, not self-harming."

Ruby is now super curious. "So, Perry, have you had this sleeve surgery too?"

"No, but only by the grace of God. I somehow managed to get my weight under control before I got to that point, but losing eighty-seven pounds was still no joke."

"Amen to that." Pearl raises her own glass to her friend.

Ruby nods, understanding, and raises her glass, too.

At that moment, the three friends clink their glasses, and before they resume eating, Ruby blurts out, "One more toast, please! To my baby sister, Pearl, whose bravery has always inspired me—even if I haven't always shown it."

Pearl can't recall the last time her sister said something so tender, and although she suspects Ruby would have never said it without an audience, it still feels good.

Long after they've finished their feast, the three of them linger at the table, chatting and laughing. To Pearl, it's almost magical the way this sad, old, lonely house feels so full and happy tonight. At 9:00 p.m., after all the dishes are put away, Pearl walks Perry out to his car, with all the leftovers carefully packed up so he can take them away, and she believes, for a wonderful, fleeting moment, that she's actually got this.

"I'll see you in the morning." Perry kisses her cheek.

"Yep, see you in the morning." Pearl allows herself to bask in the glow of her friend's love.

But much later that night, long after midnight and when Ruby is sound asleep, Pearl sneaks back into the kitchen and opens the refrigerator. She reaches her arm deep into the back of the bottom shelf and pulls out a big slab of lasagna, one she'd separated from the leftovers she so readily handed back to Perry. Without even warming it up, she sits alone in the dark, devouring every last bite of it.

Chapter 26

Although it's not mandatory, it is strongly encouraged that bariatric surgical candidates attend group therapy. Reluctantly, Pearl decides to attend this evening's session, one facilitated by Dr. Lisa Field, the same woman who conducted Pearl's psych consult. Pearl arrives early, and as other bariatric patients file into the room, she can't help but appraise each and every one, trying to estimate which phase of the process they're in. Just seeing the various shapes and sizes of the other attendees intrigues her. The demographics of the attendees are all over the map, too, but all these people have one thing in common: they had all reached a weight that prompted them to make a decision of life over death, to choose a surgery that was not without risk.

And somewhat shamefully, Pearl is silently thrilled as she counts a total of three attendees who easily outweigh her. There is just something delicious about not being the fattest person in the room, and savoring this feeling, she's glad she came.

For the past four days, she's lived on nothing but water, Premier Protein shakes, sugar-free Jell-O, and vegetable broth. Although the first two days without solid food gave her wicked headaches, since then, she's been pleasantly surprised by how quickly the human body adapts to change—even radical change, like fasting.

In the conference room, the layout is more like a classroom designed for really large students, with sturdy, cushioned chairs positioned in several slightly curved rows all facing the front of the room. Behind the podium, there's a dry-erase board, which is where Dr. Lisa Field is writing her name in black marker.

"Okay, folks, I'd like to go ahead and get started," Dr. Field says. She does her best to make eye contact with each and every one of the nineteen people in attendance.

"For those of you who are new and as a reminder to those who aren't, I'm Dr. Lisa Field. I work very closely with the bariatric surgeons at Austin Weight Loss Specialists to provide pre- and postsurgical counseling to patients who are either considering weight loss surgery or who are recovering from it. I want to welcome each and every one of you tonight, and I always start these group meetings by emphasizing the importance of privacy and anonymity. I like to say what happens in group stays in group. So without further ado, let's start by welcoming those of you who are new tonight. Just with a show of hands, anyone about to have their surgery?"

Pearl feels a flush. She hates being put on the spot and didn't expect to have to do any public speaking. She waits until five others have raised their hands before raising her own.

"Okay, welcome to each of you," Dr. Field says. "We hope that by hearing some of the struggles and victories of those who have gone before you, it will make this journey more bearable and, ultimately, more successful for you all. And with that, I will take a seat. I'm available to field any questions as they relate to the mental health components of weight loss, but beyond that, this is your time, so who would like to start us off?"

In the front row, an older woman rises and slowly walks to the podium. With her white hair and solid build, she looks like former First Lady Barbara Bush, right down to the pearls she's wearing around her neck.

"Hello, most of y'all know me by now, but for those who don't, my name is Beverly Hollings," she stammers. "I live right here in Austin and have my whole life. My husband is Roy, and we've been married goin' on thirty-five years now. My sleeve gastrectomy was December twenty-second. So far, I'm down fifty-seven pounds—"

She's interrupted by a hearty, heartfelt round of applause. Several people popcorn their attagirls and way-to-gos. Pearl studies Beverly's face, sees the blush emerging and the smile forming. And even though she's a perfect stranger, Pearl can tell her expression is more than joy; it's peace, and as Pearl smiles and claps along, without knowing why, she begins to cry.

This is it, she thinks. She's jumped all the required preoperative hurdles, passed every one of the tests that deemed her a perfect candidate for bariatric surgery, and despite all this trouble, there is just something in Beverly that Pearl fears she may never see in herself. For as much as she craves the sound of all this thunderous ovation, since she's never heard it directed at her own jaw-dropping weight loss, it seems too pie in the sky, too lofty for any further serious consideration.

Up until now, the actual surgery was still a ways off, still down the road enough for Pearl to largely ignore the voice inside that kept telling her that the notion of being able to lose weight was nothing but a big, fat, stupid fantasy, as unreachable a goal as, say, tying her own shoes. Yet sitting there with tears streaming down her cheeks, the whole room abuzz with bravos for Beverly, Pearl wills herself to deny all that bullshit doubt keeps telling her. Someday soon, instead of being the clapper, she will be the clappee, and she closes her eyes, imagining her own curtain call.

Chapter 27

It's only a twenty-minute drive to the specialty hospital on West Thirty-Eighth, and Pearl is spending every one of those minutes practicing her deep-breathing exercises. Repeatedly, she inhales three quick breaths through the nose followed by one long exhale through her mouth.

"Holy shit, Pearl, you would think you're about to go into labor or something," Ruby says, teasing her.

Pearl ignores the comment and stays absolutely focused, sniffing and blowing in the passenger seat as Ruby winds her way through early-morning traffic in West Austin.

"Here, I've teed up your favorite song," Ruby says, tapping the display. "It's like your new personal anthem. Just try to relax and enjoy the rest of the ride."

Although it's sprinkling outside, Ruby rolls down the windows, letting some of the March mugginess fill the car, cranking the volume.

Right away, Pearl recognizes the tune and taps her thighs to the beat of Natasha Bedingfield's "Unwritten." From the first lyric, all of them—Ruby, Pearl, and Natasha—are singing in unison, belting it out. As she sings, Pearl thinks back to the day she sold the watches, considers all the many steps she's taken since then to arrive at this point, and she can't help but be emotional. It's been this way for two weeks, as the pre-op fasting seems to have unleashed an emotional roller coaster. The clinical goal of the fast was to lighten her fatty liver just enough so Dr. George could efficiently lift it up and off her stomach in order to make his dissection, but to Pearl, although there's no way to measure it, the fast also seems to have lightened her heart. As nervous as she still is, after two weeks of militant liquid dieting, she's tapped into some transcendental self-awareness that she didn't see coming, and for the first time, she actually feels bigger than her body, not fatter but stronger. It's weird but cool.

"Well, here we are," Ruby says, rolling up under the overhang. A valet with a very wide wheelchair approaches the car, and Ruby turns down the music.

"I'll go park and join you inside," Ruby says. "Before you get out, I have something for you." She reaches into the back seat and produces an envelope with Pearl's name on it, in her mom's unmistakable handwriting.

"What's this?"

"It came in the mail. It was inside a larger envelope addressed to me. Anyway, she asked me to give it to you before your surgery this morning."

Pearl wants to ask more questions, wonders what exactly her mother sent to Ruby, but the valet has already opened the passenger side door.

"Are you ready?" Ruby asks as she rubs Pearl's arm.

Unclicking her seat belt, Pearl takes a couple extra beats, a final gut check to see if there's any inner voice telling her to close the car door and get the hell out of here. But if there is, she can't hear it. She turns to her sister.

"I'm ready," she says, though it feels like someone else's voice forming the words.

"Good. You wait in the lobby, and I'll go park and be back in a sec." Ruby smiles tenderly at her younger sister.

With that, Pearl lifts herself out of the car and walks toward her future.

Inside the enormous, glass, ten-story hospital, it's all *Honey, I Shrunk the Kids* surrealism. Every detail, from the cavernous atrium to the oversize furnishings, is designed to make patients feel small, to make obese patients feel welcome. As Ruby trails behind, carrying Pearl's overnight bag, a uniformed valet pushes Pearl in a wheelchair toward a cluster of cargo-sized elevators. It's a spare-no-expense piece of real estate, and Ruby marvels, slack-jawed, at the notion that all they do, every day, is bariatric surgery: an entire facility dedicated exclusively to curing obesity. The patient rooms are equally ample, with doorframes easily twice the size required to meet code and a hospital bed that looks closer to queen-size than twin.

While Pearl changes out of her clothes and into her hospital gown, Ruby's doing some mental math, multiplying the number of overweight people she thinks it would take to keep the lights on in such a pricey piece of real estate. By her staggering guesstimate, she wonders if it's really possible that there are, in fact, enough overweight people in Texas to make her figures compute.

Once Pearl is dressed in the hospital gown, a surgical nurse appears.

"Okay, Pearl, before we get any further along, I need to get a final weigh-in," she says. "If you'll follow me, we've got a scale right here outside the door."

A look of fear washes over Pearl's face, but she does what she's told. As she approaches the scale, despite the two weeks of fasting, she doubts there will be any numerical proof of her sacrifice and self-discipline, worries there will be not a single pound to show for her efforts. But as she steps on the scale and looks up to the digital display, her worry gives way to a moment of pre-op triumph: 494 pounds.

"Let's see, Pearl," the nurse says, comparing that weight to the last recorded on her chart. "That's great! Since your initial consultation in January, you've already lost thirty-seven pounds, and fourteen in just the past two weeks. Congratulations!"

Although Pearl completely understands that 494 is nothing to brag about, she can't help but be slightly thrilled that she is no longer a member of the 500+ Club, and this, on the day of her bariatric surgery, feels like major progress.

Back in the room, Pearl dances a jig for Ruby and the nurse.

"I have lost thirty-seven pounds! I have lost thirty-seven pounds!" Pearl sings the words as she sashays in her cap and gown over to the bed. And she's still celebrating when Dr. George walks in.

"Wow," he says, smiling. "Do I have the right room? You are Pearl Crenshaw, right?"

If she wasn't so truly pleased with herself, she might be a little embarrassed to be caught acting goofy, especially by someone as hot as Dr. George. But with the weigh-in, Pearl seems to be taking everything in stride.

"Hi," she says, taking a seat on the edge of the bed. "I'm just glad to see all my fasting paid off."

"I can tell," he says, checking her chart. "You're off to a fabulous start."

With a backpack slung over one shoulder, there's a casual, approachable ease about him that has Pearl feeling not one bit self-conscious, which is a particularly yummy feeling considering the sudden flush on Ruby's face. Pearl knows what she's thinking. Dr. George's website picture does not do him justice. He is way hotter in person.

"How are you, Ruby?" he says.

It is not lost on either of them that he called her by name.

"Me? I'm okay," she says, blushing.

"Okay, well, ladies, the fact that nobody is hyperventilating is a really good sign," he says, grinning. "I do have some things to go over with you, Pearl. I know we've already walked through the whole procedure, and you're probably sick of those videos we made you watch, but I like to make it a habit of going over everything again step-by-step with you and your family the day of, too."

From the backpack, he produces the familiar plastic model, a three-dimensional puzzle of abdominal innards, and begins to explain.

"So here's another quick review. And, Ruby, feel free to ask any questions." He clears his throat and begins his thorough demonstration. "As you know, our stomachs expand after we eat. But what lots of people don't know about is this right here—the portion of the stomach that expands to store the food. It also produces a hormone called ghrelin that stimulates hunger. This area of the stomach," he says, pointing. "We call it the fundus, remember?"

Pearl nods and Ruby leans in closer. From the presurgical videos she had to watch, Pearl could write a how-to manual about every step. But, for Pearl, hearing the clinical play-by-play repeated, yet again, by such a sexy surgeon, is almost as electrifying as watching Lenny Kravitz shred a solo on stage. And judging by her sister's rapt attentiveness, she's 100 percent sure Ruby feels the same.

"Once you're sedated, I'll make several incisions, probably five or so, and this will allow me to pass several instruments and a camera into your abdomen. I'll lift the liver," he says, demonstrating by removing the brown plastic piece in his hands. "Then I seal off and remove some blood vessels and insert this little guy, the bougie."

He fishes yet another prop out of his bag, a plastic tube that looks like a tiny, clear garden hose.

"And this bougie helps make sure the appropriate amount of your stomach remains in place. After that, I'll divide and seal your stomach and permanently remove the part you don't need from the abdomen."

He puts the model back in the bag before going on, as if the whole process really is as simple as his demonstration seems to suggest.

"And postoperatively, that reduced ghrelin level is what will keep any sensation of hunger in check. With a much smaller stomach, you'll experience a quicker sense of fullness upon eating and drinking. Now all that will take some adjustment and getting used to, but if you follow our post-op guidelines, jump right into one of the post-op therapy groups, and get your support system in place, I believe you're not only going to meet but exceed your goals. Any questions?"

Pearl can't think of any, and Ruby is too tongue-tied to speak. Dr. George's hero factor looms large for both of them. For Pearl, he's the man who is helping her to save her own life. For Ruby, he's the man who is helping save the life of her sister. So unless something goes wrong during surgery, he can't lose with either of them.

"Before I go, I need to make a few marks on your belly with my trusty Sharpie so I'll have my bearings once we're in the OR."

There's an awkward pause. Pearl did not .anticipate this moment of pre-op humiliation, hates the notion of this gorgeous man having to get a sneak peek at her wide girth. It's a necessary but totally evil presurgical step. Ruby excuses herself to lessen the intensity.

"I'm gonna grab a cup of coffee down the hall," she says. "Be right back."

When Ruby returns, Dr. George is gone, Pearl's IV is already hooked up, and she's ready to be wheeled back. Ruby giggles at the sight of her lying there with her paper bonnet.

"I know," Pearl says. "You don't have to say it. I know I look ridiculous."

"Okay, I won't say it," Ruby teases, taking a seat beside the bed.

"I read Mom's card," Pearl says.

Ruby nods but says nothing.

"I'm sad she's not here," Pearl confesses.

"Well, I have something for that," Ruby says, pulling something from her pocket. "Red lipstick—your signature color," she says, uncapping the sleek black tube. "Remember what Lady Bird Johnson always said: flowers in the city are like lipstick on a woman—it just makes you look better to have a little color." Ruby gently applies a small amount to Pearl's lips. "I'll be here when you wake up," she says.

"You gonna tell me what Mom sent to you?" Pearl says.

"We've got time to talk about that later," Ruby says. "You don't think he recognizes me from the viral video, do you?"

"Who? Dr. George?"

Ruby nods.

"You were wearing sunglasses and a ball cap," Pearl says. "You were totally incognito."

Ruby considers this, chewing on her lip.

"I mean, the only way he could possibly know it was you in that video is if I showed it to him and told him so," Pearl says with a sly grin.

"You wouldn't," Ruby says, her eyes widening.

But before she can say anything else, the nurse reappears.

"Okay, Miss Crenshaw, they're ready for you," she says.

"Don't worry. Your secrets are safe with me," Pearl says to Ruby, winking. "Thanks for being here. I know we don't ever tell each other this, and you don't have to say it back or anything, but I figure now is as good a time as ever—I really love you."

Ruby squeezes her sister's hand. As the nurse pulls the bed toward the door, Pearl looks back at Ruby's face just in time to see the tears pooling in her eyes.

A few hours later, Ruby hears her name called over the intercom in the family waiting room. She shoves the letter Birdie sent to Pearl back into her sister's purse and collects her own, making her way toward the recovery room, still trying to process what Birdie meant, especially that one line: *I'm learning that secrets aren't good for anyone's health.*

It's so cryptic. What secrets exactly is she referring to? Ruby thinks about the equally cryptic line in the note Birdie wrote to her: *Your sister has carried this burden for far too long.*

She has no idea what Birdie means by that. What burden? And what secrets? Again, she hears her name over the intercom and picks up her pace. Why are they calling her name twice? *Is Pearl okay?* she wonders. *Oh my God, is my sister okay?*

Although it's a popular surgery, it's also a major one. General anesthesia isn't 100 percent safe even with the healthiest of patients, but for someone Pearl's size… The gravity of what may have happened, the possibility that something might have gone wrong, that her sister might not ever wake up, quickens Ruby's step and has her subconsciously holding her breath. Frazzled and almost bracing for bad news, she pushes through the door marked *Postsurgical Consultation Lounge.*

Dr. George is waiting for her, smiling.

"She did great," he says.

"Oh my gosh. I'm so relieved," Ruby says, giving herself permission to breathe.

"She's going to be really sore for several days, and I've got some good medicine on board to help her with the pain."

"Opioids?" Ruby asks.

"Yes. Morphine for now," he says. "Hopefully, I can send her home with just Tylenol. That's the goal anyway."

"How long will she have to stay?"

"If she does well, if we can get her up and ambulating, hopefully just a couple of nights."

"That's great," Ruby says, sighing. "Well, I can't thank you enough. This is such a game changer for her."

"It's game-changing surgery for everyone who has it," he says. "That's what I love about it. I get to see these people months and then years postoperatively, living lives they could only dream about before."

"If you don't mind my asking, what made you choose bariatric surgery as a specialty? I mean, I get that it's big business, but..."

"My mom," he says. "For as long as I can remember, she was morbidly obese. Right before my senior year, she was diagnosed with diabetes. And before I left for UT, she'd already had one leg amputated. Didn't live long enough to see my sister or me graduate from college."

"Wow, I'm so sorry," Ruby says. "Do your patients know about that?"

"Some do," he says.

"I just meant it's such an impactful real-life loss, and I would imagine it would really resonate with your patients." Ruby realizes she's overstepped.

"We all have loss," he says, rubbing his smooth chin. "As a rule, I just try not to get too personal with any of my patients or their family members," he adds, clearing his throat. "What I mean is I try to just keep the focus firmly on my patients. And my patient, Pearl Crenshaw, sailed through surgery and should be coming to anytime now." Dr. George's warm smile is irresistible.

Ruby extends her hand. "Thanks so much, Dr. George, really."

"Call me Henry." Dr. George holds on to Ruby's hand a moment longer than necessary. "Your sister is just beyond these doors, second bed on the right. Let me know if you need anything. I gave you my card, right?"

"Yes, you gave me your card and your cell number," Ruby says, smiling.

"Good," he says. "Hang on to that."

"I will," Ruby says.

"Okay, so I'll be sure to check in on you, I mean your sister, later."

"I look forward to that," Ruby says.

At her bedside, Ruby sits quietly waiting for Pearl to wake up. Perry's already sent half a dozen texts, so Ruby sends him an update, promising to have Pearl FaceTime him as soon as she's able. As she waits for her sister to wake up, Ruby watches through the privacy slits in the curtains, sees an older mom sitting at her daughter's bedside, and she's struck by the sad realization that if ever there were a time when Birdie should be here, it's now. Ruby thinks back to their shared past, remembering an encounter with Skip she wishes she could forget: the good-night hug she'd given him long ago, him stoned on some mixture of hydrocodone and Johnnie Walker scotch; how he'd held her a bit too long, and when she pulled away, he'd let his mouth graze her own; how totally creeped out she'd been by the whole thing but how she dismissed it as some drunken mix-up, him mistaking her for Birdie or something.

And Ruby wonders what other drunken mix-ups there might have been after she left for SMU. She wonders what secrets her sister has kept buried under all that weight.

"Are you there?" Pearl says, eyes still closed, half dreaming. "Can anybody hear me?"

"I'm right here, Pearl," Ruby says. "I can hear you," she adds, patting her hand carefully in order to avoid disturbing the IV port.

"It's my fault," Pearl mumbles, still talking in her sleep, in that twilight between a drug-induced doze and coming to. "It's all my fault."

"Pearl? You just had surgery," Ruby says. "Dr. George says you did great. He said everything went exactly according to plan."

A sleepy smile forms on Pearl's face. "Dr. George..." Her voice trails off, and she drifts back to sleep.

Ruby smiles, too. However morphine-garbled Pearl may be, like a vital sign, this smile is the first post-op indication that her little sister is going to be okay.

Chapter 28

For nearly two days, all Pearl's done is sleep. And as Dr. George stops by her room for the fourth time today alone, Ruby can't begin to comprehend how her sister will possibly be able to go back to work by Monday.

"She looks like death warmed over," Ruby says, brushing Pearl's hair off her face. "Is this normal for her to be so out of it still?"

Discreetly, Dr. George lifts Pearl's sheet and gown to check his work.

"Absolutely," he says, inspecting. "It's big surgery. But her incisions look good. We just have to give her a little time. Everyone heals differently."

"She told her manager she would be back at work next week. Doesn't that seem soon to you?"

"Not at all," he says. "Almost all my patients are back in their routine within seven to ten days post-op. Just give her time."

Dressed in jeans and a lightweight pullover hoodie, his thick, dark wavy hair perfectly messy, Dr. George—Henry—stopped by one last time before heading home. Ruby found herself scrambling to find a question simply so she could spend a bit more time with him. But he beat her to the punch by asking a question first:

"So, Ruby, are you a runner?" he asks.

The question makes her heart race. This is it. He's seen the viral video. He knows.

"Umm. Yes. I am. Why do you ask?" she says, sounding more defensive than she meant to.

"Oh, I just noticed your Hokas, and that's the same brand I wear," he says, pointing down toward his feet.

"Oh, right," Ruby says with relief. "Yes, I'm a devoted runner. And these shoes are the best, right?"

"I love mine," he says. "I finally gave up my beloved ASICS for these."

"I don't run quite as much as I did in college, but I still try to get in about twenty to twenty-five miles a week," Ruby says, avoiding any mention of her SMU track scholarship. Too self-promoting, she thinks. Too boastful.

"Same here. I really like running at Lady Bird Lake. I like feeding off all the energy of everyone else on the trail."

"Yeah, me, too," Ruby says. "That trail was the thing I missed most about Austin after I moved to Dallas."

"Well, maybe one of these days, we—"

Before he can finish his thought, Pearl's cell phone rings, interrupting the moment.

Ruby looks over at the screen, and even from where she is standing, she can see the words Gatesville, Texas, under the number and knows exactly who it is. More than anything, she wants to ignore it and hates herself for not thinking to silence Pearl's phone earlier. The last thing she wants to do with Henry standing here is to have a long-overdue chat with her mother. But she promised Pearl she would let Birdie know how the surgery went:

"Looks like Pearl's fan club wants the latest," Ruby says, reaching for the phone.

"Right. No worries," Dr. George says, waving. "I'll check back later," he adds, walking out the door.

Ruby lets the phone ring one more time, then she takes a deep breath and exhales before tapping the screen.

"This is a call from inmate Elizabeth Crenshaw Benzer at the Mountain View Prison Unit. Press one to accept."

Dreading it, Ruby follows the instructions, taps one, and greets Birdie for the first time in twelve years.

"Hello," Ruby says, composing herself, taking a seat in the chair next to the bed.

"Ruby? Is that you?" Birdie asks, surprised.

"Hi, Birdie. It's me."

"Is Pearl…is she all right?" Birdie asks nervously.

"Oh yes. Yes, she's fine. She's just sleeping, and she asked me to answer if you called, so…"

"Oh my goodness," Birdie says with relief. "When I heard your voice, well, I just… I had a moment of panic there. How is she? How did it go?"

"Actually, her surgeon was just here. He literally walked out right as you called, and he says she's doing great. It looks like she might be able to go home tomorrow."

"Well, I am so glad to hear that," Birdie says. "Has she been up walking around much yet? When I spoke to her yesterday, she said they were about to come in and get her out of bed."

"Uh-huh, she's been up twice already today. She walked all the way to the end of the hall and back. She says she's really sore, but that's to be expected."

"Right. Well, I think it's wonderful that you were willing and able to be there with her for this. So I just want to say thank you for—"

"I didn't do this for you, Birdie."

"I didn't say you did, Ruby. I'm simply acknowledging that I know how much Pearl appreciates your help, that's all. Anyway, how long you planning to stay?"

For Ruby, it's hard enough to talk with Birdie about matters related to Pearl, but it's nearly impossible to talk about herself with this person whom she hasn't seen and has barely spoken to since she was twenty years old. Mercifully, she doesn't have to answer Birdie's question because her sister is waking up.

"Well, Birdie, you're in luck. Pearl just opened her eyes. I know you don't get much time on the phone when you're serving time," she says sharply, "so I'll hand the phone over to Pearl and let the two of you catch up."

"Wait, Ruby. It's good to hear—"

Without letting her finish, Ruby hands the phone over to her still-sleepy sister.

"Hello," Pearl says, still dazed.

Wanting to leave but knowing she shouldn't, Ruby walks over to the window and stares outside. Something draws her attention downward, and from the third-floor window, she sees Henry walking into the parking lot adjacent to the entrance of the hospital. While Pearl chats with Birdie, Ruby can't help herself. She watches Henry until the hospital shuttle bus blocks her view. Then, after it passes, she cranes her neck, trying to find him, but he's no longer in sight.

PART THREE

Gravity

Chapter 29

She's only one week post-op, but already, Pearl feels different. Aside from the soreness, which has necessitated a new rolling approach to getting herself out of bed, the most striking change between the Pearl today and the Pearl of a week ago is that she's not one bit hungry. Dr. George meant it when he said that ghrelin, the hunger hormone, would be no longer be in the driver's seat, no longer steering Pearl toward food and away from health. Today is her first day back on the job, and with 84 percent of her stomach missing, Pearl thinks about how much less of her is showing up for duty already.

As if nature itself is aware of Pearl's nascent metamorphosis, the Mexican plum and redbud trees lining the Glenwood Manor parking lot are in full bloom, their fragrant blossoms waving in the breeze. With her windows rolled all the way down, Pearl finds herself noticing things like this more than ever, as if her senses have come alive, and smell is now compensating for the things she will no longer taste. With a fresh swipe of the Rouge Allure lipstick Ruby gave her, Pearl checks her reflection in the rearview mirror: she might not look as glamorous as the day of her makeover, but there is something new there—a blush of self-respect that was previously missing. For the first time, Pearl realizes that lipstick can't give you this sense of empowerment—it can only enhance it. She caps the lipstick and smiles at her reflection. *It's going to be a good day, even if my energy isn't 100 percent yet*, she thinks to herself as she locks her car and heads to the employee entrance.

What happens next utterly surprises and overwhelms here.

As she steps into Glenwood Manor, she's met by her colleagues, who are gathered to greet her with high fives and hugs.

"Welcome back, Pearl!"

She didn't expect this cluster of coworkers to be there, greeting her in unison. It's a pleasant surprise, and Pearl soaks up the unfamiliar attention, trying not to cry. Whether it's the fasting, the physical toll of the surgery, or a combination of both, Pearl's been wildly emotional since her operation, so she does her best to keep her red lips from quivering. Even though she's just beginning this journey and has hundreds of pounds to lose, this warm reception gives her a moment to pause and celebrate the miracle of what she's already achieved. Perry, of course, is front and center, holding a case of strawberry-flavored Premier Protein shakes, festooned with a big red bow on top.

"These are for you," he says. "Ruby told me this is your favorite flavor."

"Oh my gosh, it's all I live on these days," Pearl says, thanking everyone.

"Well, we all chipped in on a little something special for you," Perry explains, handing a card to Pearl. "It's for later, when you're ready to do some 'tuck-in' shopping."

Inside the congratulations card, signed by most of the staff in the memory care unit, is a two-hundred-dollar gift card to Nordstrom.

"This is too much, really," Pearl says, now unable to tamp down her tears. "This is just so nice, and I can't tell you how grateful I am for your support. Thank you all so, so much."

After a few more hugs and warm words, the welcome-back party breaks up, with everyone scattering to their respective posts. With Perry, Pearl walks down the hall toward the activity center.

"I just have one request," Perry says.

"Anything," Pearl responds.

"When you're ready to hit up Nordstrom, promise you're taking me with you."

Pearl stops, turns to Perry, and pulls him in for a soul hug.

"How did I get so lucky to have you as my best friend?" she whispers.

"Back at ya, girl," Perry whispers in reply.

When they continue on down the hall, Pearl hears a familiar Willie Nelson tune and remembers what day it is.

"Hey, are you sure you're up for this already?" Perry asks before they enter the rec room. "I mean, considering everything you've been through…"

"I'm super sore," Pearl says. "But my energy is great. I feel like I'm using muscles I never knew I had. Literally, every part of me aches, but Dr. George—I mean Henry—says that's normal."

"Oh, so it's Henry now? Is that why you're rocking the red lip?" Perry winks at her.

"Let's just say Ruby's on a first-name basis with my surgeon now, and I'm getting really quality care because of it," she says, laughing. "And the lipstick, it's Chanel's Rouge Allure Pirate, my new signature color. You like?" she asks, puckering up.

"I like all of this," he says, swirling his index finger at Pearl. "I'm not kidding. I already see such a major difference in you, and it has nothing to do with your weight."

"Well, I was down thirty-seven pounds the day of my surgery. Can't wait to see what I've lost when I go for my two-week follow-up."

At the activity center entrance, Pearl and Perry pause, smiling. It's as festive as they've ever seen this room with about a dozen residents, all seated in a semicircle, clapping and lifting their voices in a country music sing-along. At the front of the room, the man in a straw cowboy hat is strumming a guitar and leading them all in a rendition of "If You've Got the Money, I've Got the Time." To the beat of the music, Mr. Reynolds taps a tambourine and Ms. McDonald is shaking her castanets. What strikes Pearl are all the smiles. *These people may be old,* she thinks, *but in this moment, damn, they're happy.*

"It's music therapy Monday! Gotta love it, right?" Perry smiles at Pearl.

Pearl can't disagree. And for a moment, from the side of the room, she reflects on what a gift her job is, how lucky she is to work with such good people, people who care so lovingly for those who can no longer care for themselves. It strikes her then that she's still so young and that it's not too late for her to put some of the energy she's put into helping the residents of Glenwood into caring for herself. This thought, devoid of the shame and self-doubt that has literally crippled her, stirs something new in her, and she steps into the room and immediately joins in the fun.

In a rare moment of recognition, Mr. Reynolds waves his tambourine at Pearl.

"Toots, you're back!"

She rushes over to him and impulsively bends to hug him.

"I am, Mr. Reynolds. I am. I'm back!"

Chapter 30

The fresh air blowing in from the back patio is the first thing Ruby notices when she walks in the front door. Leaning her rolled-up yoga mat against the island in the kitchen, she follows the faint scent of honeysuckle all the way to the porch, where Pearl is potting an actual plant.

"Wait! Who kidnapped my sister?" Ruby says, her hands on her hips in mock outrage.

"Ha ha," Pearl says, reaching into the potting soil bag for another scoop.

"Seriously, since when did you develop an interest in gardening?"

"Since today," Pearl says. "Don't ask me why, but I drove by the Barton Springs Nursery on my way home from work, and something made me do a U-turn. Just felt like giving the back porch a pop of color. Thought it might be nice for spring. It's a bromeliad, a Scarlet Star," she says, spinning the pot around for Ruby to inspect. "What do you think?"

"I think you must be feeling better," Ruby smiles.

"I am. So if you were getting your hopes up for Dr. George to have to make a house call or something, you better come up with another plan, because other than being a bit sore, I feel great."

Pearl shoots her sister an evil grin and walks over to the wall-mounted hose to fill her watering can.

"Well, I'm glad you're feeling so well," Ruby says. "I guess I'll just tell Henry he doesn't need to pick me up for our run tomorrow. I can just meet him at the park," she adds, winking.

"Seriously?" Pearl says, so very not surprised. "When did this happen? Did he just call you and ask you out?"

"Nope," Ruby says, perfectly impressed with herself. "I texted him."

"Bold move," Pearl says. "You are fearless, Ruby. And I hope to become more that way myself."

"You are bold!" Ruby says, reminding her sister about how huge this step has been. "Having your stomach reduced by eighty-four percent is as bold as it gets. Now you just need to apply that boldness to other areas of your life, Pearl. Speaking of which, I bought you a ten-pack of classes at the yoga studio."

She produces a small gift card from a hidden pocket on the back of her yoga pants and hands it to Pearl.

"Ruby, I can't possibly… I mean, I'm still too big. I can't even fit on a yoga mat, let alone into a pair of yoga pants."

"There's no rush or time limit," Ruby says, interrupting. "I just thought it might be something to look forward to. It's pretty great if you want that whole mind-body thing."

"And you know I do. Thanks, Ruby." Pearl hugs her sister: "Today really does feel like Christmas. Everyone at work chipped in on a gift card to Nordstrom to use when I reach my tuck-in weight. And Perry got me a four-pack of my fave shakes."

"Nice," Ruby says. "So I take it the first day back went well?"

"It was fabulous. I got a little tired, but it felt great to be back to the routine. But enough about me—I need to know more about this running date of yours. So more deets, please."

"Okay. So I told you how at the hospital he was asking me about my running shoes and dropping all these hints about where he likes to run? So I don't know, it's kind of like the U-turn you made at the nursery today. I just followed my impulse. Anyway, I'm meeting him at Lady Bird Lake tomorrow when he gets out of surgery."

"A day date," Pearl says, nodding. "I like it. You both take separate cars. No commitment. You get to show off your ridiculous legs, and there's the added bonus of seeing how hot Dr. George is when he's off duty."

Ruby laughs but doesn't disagree.

"It's not a hot date, Pearl. It's just a run," Ruby says, walking back inside.

"Just try not to step in any shit this time." Pearl can't resist.

"I'll do my best," Ruby says. "Hashtag shit you not!"

Later, as Pearl is fishing Mr. Winky out of her bedside drawer, Ruby knocks.

"Come on in," Pearl says, busy with straightening out her CPAP gear.

"Hey," Ruby says.

"Hey yourself," Pearl says, lowering onto her bed. As always, Pearl's watching her favorite channel, HGTV.

"Whatcha doing?" Ruby asks, looking over at the TV.

"Just gonna tuck it in with a little Chip and JoJo," Pearl says. "My show's about to start."

Ruby stands at the doorway, listening to the announcer:

"*Chip and Joanna Gaines are helping their client, Dr. Marla Hendricks, find a home in Waco for her and her new husband. They're boomers, but they're young at heart and seeking a home to fit their active lifestyle. Marla is a veterinarian and an ultra runner who wants to be near Cameron Park, an outdoor enthusiast's paradise and a great playground for her pets. She's returning to Waco after a hiatus in California where she met her husband, David, an avid mountain biker and businessman. David will join his bride in a month and is entrusting Marla and the Gaineses to find them the perfect fixer-upper. How will David react when the Hendrickses' fixer-upper is revealed to him the very first time?*"

By the time the show goes to commercial, Ruby is perched at the foot of Pearl's bed, watching along.

"You can't just watch the beginning," Pearl says. "You've gotta watch it all the way to the end to see the big reveal. That's the good part."

"Did you drink your sixty-four ounces today?" Ruby blurts out, instantly regretting that her older-sister tendency to be so damn controlling hasn't just gone away.

"Sixty-four ounces plus the twelve I'm still working on," Pearl says, raising up the cup on her bedside table. "I'm a good patient."

"Hey, now that you're feeling so much better, I've been meaning to ask you about that letter Birdie sent—the one I gave you before the surgery."

"What about it?"

"Well, the one she sent me mentioned something about how you've carried this burden for far too long. What did she mean by that?"

Pearl gulps but tries to act nonchalant. "I don't know. What all did she say exactly?"

"She was just thanking me for taking care of you, for taking time out of my own life to be here with you, but she made a comment about how you've had to carry this burden for far too long. I want to know what she meant by that, Pearl." Ruby is so sincere that Pearl sits up straighter.

"I'm sure she was referring to my weight. Duh?"

"You sure about that?" Ruby asks, studying her sister's face.

"Look at me, Ruby," Pearl says, pointing to her body spread out under the covers. "You try weighing what I weigh and tell me it's not a burden."

Ruby is still staring her down, and Pearl averts her gaze by looking back at the TV. It's clear she would prefer to avoid any further interrogation.

"Why won't you level with me, Pearl?"

"Shh," Pearl says ignoring her probe. "My show is back on. Do you mind grabbing that remote and turning it up some? You've got to watch the big reveal."

Chapter 31

Bundles of bluebonnets flank both sides of the hike and bike trail at Lady Bird Lake. Ruby and Henry have agreed to run just five miles of the ten-mile loop. Side by side, they clip along, passing the full spectrum of humanity that continues to make the city live up to its unofficial motto: Keep Austin Weird. Just like the sauntering barefoot hippies, the guitar-strumming amblers, and the stroller-pushing moms, Ruby and Henry are simply two more glistening beautiful people taking in the lovely spring day.

"I'm not kidding," Ruby says as they approach the mile 4 marker. "I've never seen her potting plants. Not once. Forget the weight loss. My sister taking pride in her surroundings is a first. The bromeliad is like…"

"…a sign of new growth?" Henry offers, finishing her thought.

"Maybe," Ruby says, considering this. "I mean, I think so. Honestly? I was pretty skeptical about Pearl taking such a drastic step and having some kind of irreversible procedure, but now that I've been here and spent enough time with her, let's just say my worldview about obesity and bariatric surgery is changing."

"Well, since that's how I make my living..." Henry begins.

"Oh, no, I didn't mean that in a bad way or anything. I just..."

"No, I totally hear you. Lots of people make the wrong assumptions about morbidly obese people. I felt enough of that growing up. My mom came from this really abusive childhood, and she never really dealt with it. Food became her coping strategy. You would be amazed at the percentage of patients I have who reference some kind of childhood abuse on their intake forms. Of course, I'm speaking in generalities, so I'm not breaching any patient confidentiality or anything, but I would say in my patient population alone, the incidence of abuse is somewhere north of eighty percent."

Ruby ruminates on this information, silently wondering about her own sister's intake form.

"That's terrible," she says finally.

Realizing they've broached a topic neither one of them feels very comfortable pursuing, they cross over the charming wooden pedestrian bridge that traverses this tranquil portion of the lower Colorado River, and Henry quickly changes the subject.

"So anyway, I have to tell you, I think it's great how you took so much time away from work and everything to come help your sister. It says a lot about you and your character, especially with your mom more or less out of the picture."

Ruby cringes. She doesn't know what she hates more: that he doesn't know the truth about why she's here or that he does know the truth about why their mom is not. Either way, her hopes for a lighthearted fun run in the sun with a smart, good-looking surgeon are quickly being dashed by the stress she's suddenly feeling. It's not only Pearl whose life has been so compromised by secrecy. Ruby feels dangerously out of her comfort zone now, aware that this new person in her life has no idea why she's really here and why Birdie is not.

All her life, she's been running from drama, but something about this moment, something she really senses is good and decent about Henry, finally makes her stop.

"Look," Ruby says, slowing to a walk, veering off the trail and out of the way. "I need to just put something out here. I didn't take time away from work to be with Pearl because I wanted to. I did it because I had to."

Henry is all ears, and he squints his eyes, using the bottom of his T-shirt to wipe off his sweaty face, inadvertently teasing her with an unexpected flash of the six-pack he keeps so well hidden under his baggy scrubs.

"What do you mean?" he says.

Ruby bends over, hands on knees, catching her breath.

"I mean, look, I don't know you very well, but you seem like a really nice person, and I just can't go one more step having you think I'm something I'm not."

"Okay?" Henry asks, prodding.

"I was let go from my job at DALLUX. I didn't exactly take a leave of absence like Pearl said. I mean, I fully intended to come and be with Pearl for her surgery, but initially, I was only planning to be here for the surgery itself and then maybe a few days after."

"Okay?" he says, waiting on some more remarkable revelation. "So?"

"Right, so the reason I was fired had to do with a sort of scandalous video I was in that basically went viral."

By his expression, Ruby can tell he has the wrong idea.

"Whoa!" he says, smiling. "Don't be too hard on yourself, Ruby. Maybe I should take a look. Let me be the judge and see just how scandalous your video really is," he adds, winking.

"No. I mean, yes, but it's not like that. I'm not taking my clothes off or anything, I'm just, well, it shows me, more or less…"

"More or less what?"

"More or less throwing dog shit at a total stranger on the Katy Trail." she says sheepishly.

"That was you?!" he says, looking surprised.

"You've seen it?" Ruby asks.

"No," he says, laughing. "But I had you, didn't I?"

Ruby's not smiling. She can't. It's all still just so embarrassing.

"Okay, okay," he says. "Did this guy on the Katy Trail have it coming?"

"No," Ruby admits. "He was a jerk, but he didn't deserve to have me hurl a baggie of his own dog's shit at him. Here," she says, pulling up the video on her phone. "You might as well see for yourself. Plus, I prefer to get this over with so you can decide if I'm too wild to be in your company."

She hands it over to Henry, hardly able to bear watching him watch it.

"Nice pitch," he says, laughing and actually turning up the volume. "Whose idea was it to add the ballpark sound effects?"

"I don't even know who made the video," Ruby confesses. "There were so many people on the trail that morning. It could have been anyone."

"What in the world did this guy do to cause you to lose it like that?" he asks, handing back her phone.

"He kept letting his dog crap on the trail, and I'd asked him several times before to pick it up, and he would just ignore me or flip me the bird and keep walking and talking on his phone, and anyway, I guess I stepped in it one too many times, and I just basically..."

"You basically lost your shit," he says, still grinning.

"Hashtag shit you not," she replies.

"That's seriously the hashtag?" Henry asks, stifling a laugh. "No shit?"

"No shit."

For as nervous as she had been to reveal the public hissy fit she would have preferred to keep private, Henry seems to be taking it all in stride. Cooling off, they walk and talk for the last half mile back to their cars.

"You think I'm horrible?" Ruby asks. "I mean, I feel horrible for doing that, so if you think I'm horrible, I totally get it."

"I don't think you're horrible," he says sincerely. "Bizarre maybe," he adds, teasing. "But not horrible. A word of caution though: we both grew up in Texas, so you know as well as I do that flinging shit at someone can get you shot. So the next time you run across somebody violating a city ordinance, you might want to try calling the police or city hall or something first," he says, smiling.

"Right," Ruby says, biting her lip. The reference to shooting makes her think of her mom, another humiliating private-turned-public matter from her past.

"Sorry," he says, sensing her discomfort. "I didn't mean to… I mean I know about your mom."

"You do?"

He nods.

"How?"

"I've basically googled everything there is in the public domain about Ruby Crenshaw. And hey, good job scrubbing that video from anything with your name on it."

Speechless, Ruby stares at him, not sure whether she should be creeped out or turned on.

"So you were stalking me?" she says finally.

"I prefer to think of it as exploring with rapt curiosity."

"Hmm, you make stalking sound so flattering."

"From the minute I laid eyes on you, I've been curious about you, Ruby Crenshaw."

And just hearing him say her name out loud makes her swallow hard. The more he talks, the more she can't think of any cogent words to string together.

"Don't get freaked out or anything. I just wondered about you. That's all. I mean, you're this really smart, beautiful, super fit woman who once ran track for SMU, and even more impressively, you managed to move beyond your hardships, rise above your circumstances."

"I didn't rise above," Ruby says, looking off toward the trail. "I just ran away."

There's a long pause as Henry takes in the full weight of her comment.

"Well, now that you're back," he says finally, "if you do plan on sticking around for any extended amount of time, I'd like to be the first guy in Austin to ask you out."

Still rosy-cheeked from their run, Ruby blushes to an even deeper shade of red and smiles.

"That looks like a yes to me," he says, grinning. "I'm taking those Ruby red cheeks as a yes."

"When?" Ruby asks.

"How about tonight? You free at seven p.m.?"

"As a matter of fact, I am," Ruby manages.

"Great. I'm glad we got the running out of the way then."

Henry's words, so fraught with meaning, linger as Ruby, suddenly feeling both vulnerable and hopeful, heads back to her car.

Chapter 32

In the two weeks since her surgery, Pearl has subsisted on little more than water and liquid protein. Combined with the two weeks leading up to surgery, today marks one whole month without solid foods. More astonishingly, she doesn't even miss it. To be specific, although Pearl misses the idea of dunking a giant waffle fry in ketchup and the satisfaction of devouring every last one in the bag (including the cold crispy crumbs at the bottom of the sack), she doesn't actually miss the taste. And this is one of the greatest gifts of the sleeve surgery. Her physical hunger has been quelled.

However, her emotional hunger is an altogether different story, which is why, following this quick weigh-in at Austin Weight Loss Specialists, her first since the surgery, Pearl will walk directly beyond the conference room doors and into her third bariatric support group meeting.

"Pearl, today's a big day!" Dr. George says, personally escorting her down the hall toward the examination rooms.

One fun perk of Ruby now dating her surgeon is that Pearl did not have to sit and wait in the lobby for her name to be called, and she rather likes this new, more royal level of treatment, right up until Dr. George asks her to remove her shoes and step on the scale.

"You ready for your moment of truth?" he says, smiling, practically brimming with satisfaction. "I noticed on your chart your blood pressure is already trending down, so that's encouraging."

Despite the glaring fact that she hasn't had solid food for an entire month, Pearl still cannot imagine that she might be smaller. With so much of herself to lose, it's difficult to discern any incremental differences, but the numbers don't lie. And with Dr. George looking right over her shoulder to witness her first post-op feat, courageously, Pearl steps up.

"Lookee there!" he says, patting her on the back. "You're down another eighteen pounds! You should be proud of yourself, Pearl."

Standing there with both feet firmly planted on the scale, she stares at the red digits in disbelief: 476.

Although tears well in her eyes, Pearl is bursting with joy.

"The numbers don't lie, Pearl," he adds. "I think it's safe to say you're on your way."

Overcome with emotion, Pearl steps off the scale and reaches for Dr. George, taking him in an awkward yet warm embrace.

"Thank you. Thank you. Thank you," she says. "Really, I can't thank you enough."

"Hey, I'm not the one losing the weight," he says. "You are."

"I just can't believe it, that's all."

"Well, seeing is believing, right?" he says, turning toward the computer to make a note on her chart.

"I guess so."

"Well, I know your sutures look good from that check-in last week, so other than that, you're good to go, Pearl. Going forward, you just need to stick to those scheduled interval weigh-ins and do your best to really embrace the group therapy."

"That's actually where I'm headed next," she says, pointing toward the conference room.

"Good. That's a great resource. My patients who do the best are the ones who go to group. I think you'll find it very helpful to warm up to some folks who may be a little further along with their recovery."

"I do have a question," Pearl stammers.

"What's that?"

"Is it normal that certain foods I used to love just sound gross to me now?"

"Absolutely," Dr. George says. "I've had patients who lived off hamburgers, but after surgery, they couldn't stand the taste or texture of ground beef. And then I had one lady who loved eggs, scrambled, fried, omelets, you name it. But after surgery, she hated them. Your body is going to have a whole new relationship with food, and in these early days, it's going to be trial and error, so take it slow and be good to yourself. Any more questions?"

Pearl shakes her head.

"Okay, well then, I'm officially releasing you into the wild. Remember, from now on, the goal of eating is to nourish and fuel your body, but you'll only learn how to do that if you proceed with caution, so easy does it."

"Got it," she says, saluting.

"Good luck. I have a feeling you're gonna do really well," he adds with a warm smile.

Pearl shakes his hand and turns toward the conference room but then pivots. "Hey, before I go, I just want to say I'm really glad you and my sister are friends, Dr. George."

"I'm glad we are, too," he says, smiling. "And, Pearl, it's Henry now. Call me Henry."

Chapter 33

Part of Pearl's post-op weight loss success is contingent on exercise, but even now that she's lost more than fifty pounds, it's not like she can start running with Ruby. At Pearl's size, just walking any distance greater than a few blocks still puts such strain on her bladder that she leaks, which makes her just want to piss away the whole notion of treadmills or strolls around the neighborhood.

Swimming was Ruby's idea, one that has led the two of them to the women's locker room at the YWCA where Pearl is, understandably, a bit put out by the dress code.

"You didn't mention anything about a swim cap, Ruby!"

"Oh, stop," Ruby says, adjusting the straps on her sleek black one-piece. "I don't make the rules, Pearl. You have to wear one. Everybody does."

For Pearl, it's bad enough that her swimsuit isn't even actually a swimsuit but rather a pair of light gray knit drawstring shorts with a matching T-shirt, and having to tuck away her single greatest feature inside a flesh-toned rubber cap is demoralizing in a way that Ruby will never understand.

"I look like Dr. Evil," Pearl says, pointing her pinkie to the corner of her mouth.

Ruby can't help but giggle at the striking resemblance between her swim-cap-headed sister and the Austin Powers character, but she's on a special training mission and remains totally undeterred.

"Well, once you're underwater, it won't matter who you look like, so let's go."

For Pearl, wearing this getup makes the one hundred feet or so they have to walk from the locker room through the chlorine-scented hallway to the pool a walk of shame, and she realizes the walk back will be even worse. Silently, she cringes at the prospect of her wet shorts and T-shirt sticking to her when she gets out of the water, and that leads her to an all-new cause for concern—how in the hell will she get out of the water in the first place?

Ruby leads the way. With her racing suit and cap, she looks practically professional, like she's training for a triathlon or something. By comparison, Pearl looks like a swimmer of a different sort—more like a manatee, she thinks. But as they step into the pool and wade neck-deep into the water, any misgivings she had about her swim cap are drowned out by a refreshing, exhilarating feeling of weightlessness.

"It's nice, right?" Ruby says, bobbing around.

Feeling light as a feather, Pearl bobs along on tiptoes, getting used to the water, already loving it.

"It's been so long since I've been in a pool," she says.

"Remember how cool we used to think it was to take all our friends to the country club when Skip was manager?"

"Gross," Pearl says. "Don't remind me. Let's not ruin a perfectly good moment with any Skip talk, please."

Ruby wants to ask more, wonders if Skip ever brushed up against Pearl or lingered a little too long with one of his sloppy, drug-induced bedtime hugs. Skip's downward spiral into opioid addiction, which was well lubricated by booze, was just one of the reasons Ruby never wanted to look back when she left for college, and Birdie's nonstop enabling, her timidity with Skip's behind-closed-doors temper, was enough to keep Ruby away. Their mom never should have stayed with that SOB long enough to let things escalate the way they did. In Ruby's opinion, Birdie should have flown the coop and taken the girls with her long before Skip became deranged enough to go at her with a fireplace poker. But her sister's right; the echoey lap lane at the Y is not the place for this kind of deep discussion.

"Here," Ruby says, handing Pearl a blue Styrofoam kickboard.

"What do you want me to do with this?" Pearl asks, confused.

"Swim, Pearl. That's why we're here. I'll do it with you," Ruby adds, grabbing one for herself.

"Okay," Pearl says. "But it's not a race."

From separate lanes at one end of the pool, they push off the wall. Not since childhood have they splashed in the water together, and something about it takes them back to their younger selves, to a time when doing sisterly things together was the norm and not the exception. As they kick up and down the lane, Pearl's heart rate surges. It's the most exertion she's felt in years, but with her buoyancy and the kickboard, it's doable. In fact, despite the huffing and puffing, Pearl can't stop smiling.

For nearly an hour, it's like this, until both of them, slick as seals, finally float over toward the steps at the corner of the pool.

"Good job," Ruby says, high-fiving Pearl. "Nice little work-out, right?"

Pearl nods, wipes the water from her eyes, and appraises the steps, dreading the way she'll look and feel when she hoists her wet self up and out of the water. Self-consciously, she looks around to see how many people will bear witness to this sight. Mercifully, other than a geriatric water aerobics class at the other end of the pool, the only person paying any attention is the lifeguard. Sensing her sister's anxiety, Ruby goes first.

"Here," Ruby says, offering a hand. "Let me help you."

"Lots easier getting in than out," Pearl says.

"Right," Ruby says, tugging on her sister's arm. "That's true for lots of things, isn't it?"

Chapter 34

The drive from Austin to Gatesville is less than two hours, but it's the longest amount of time Pearl and Ruby have spent together in a car since the day the three of them (Birdie, Ruby, and Pearl) moved Ruby into her SMU dorm fourteen years ago. As they make their way north on Route 183 with the windows rolled down, singing along to a folksy Brandi Carlile playlist, nothing about the mood in Ruby's Lexus suggests they are headed to a state prison. It's only because Pearl accepted Ruby's you-go-to-one-yoga-class-and-I'll-go-anywhere-with-you challenge that Ruby is, however reluctantly, making this first-ever visit to see Birdie behind bars.

Last night, Pearl had caught her sister at a moment of weakness. Half drunk and still half buzzing with excitement after another hot date with Henry, Ruby had come home and plopped down on the sofa, only to find Pearl on the floor sifting through a plastic storage container filled with their mom's old Easter decorations. Sitting there with her legs fully extended, Ruby felt amazed by her sister's remarkable flexibility and was equally blown away when Pearl woke up at the crack of dawn to join her for a seventy-five-minute Bikram session the day before, during which Pearl learned that, even at 470 pounds, she can do a wicked tree pose.

So over dinner last night, when they were joyfully recounting Pearl's successes, Ruby made the comment about how much she loved them being active together again. This was Pearl's opportunity, and she wasn't about to lose it. "So I've done a few things you've suggested now, including walking, swimming, and even hot yoga. So can I ask you to join me in an activity of my choosing?"

Pearl had looked so hopeful and the wine had tasted so good that Ruby was happy to comply. "Of course! Whatever you want to do, I'm all in." Little did she know...

That was what led to the Crenshaw sisters rolling down the highway just outside Williamson County with the blooms of the Texas hill country ablaze around them. On this Easter weekend, the soft pastels of the bluebonnets and the fiery reds of the Indian paintbrushes are the perfect seasonal eye candy, and as they drive along, they notice families and couples parked on the side of the road in order to take advantage of this uniquely Texan springtime photo opp.

"I don't know when I've seen the bluebonnets this thick," Ruby says.

"It reminds me of that picture of us when we were little, with our Easter baskets and white Mary Janes," Pearl says. "I always loved how Mom made such a big deal out of our new Easter dresses."

"And what about her bonnets?" Ruby says. "I swear that woman wore more hats."

"I feel bad for her," Pearl says, staring out the window. "Must be so hard to be stuck inside that prison and not able to enjoy the things she used to love, like fancy Easter bonnets, fresh flowers, and good home-cooked food. By the way, she's lost a lot of weight since you've seen her last, so I'm just warning you."

Ruby makes no comment, just stares straight ahead pensively, eyes on the road.

"Wish we could pick some of these flowers for her and smuggle them inside," Pearl says.

"She sure would like that."

They drive on a little longer until Ruby, in a moment of inspiration, slows the car and veers off toward the shoulder. Loose gravel crunches under the tires until they come to a complete stop.

"What are we doing?" Pearl asks.

"Let's take some pictures," Ruby says.

"Of the flowers?" Pearl asks.

"Of us in the flowers," Ruby says.

"I don't want any pictures of me at this size, Ruby. I'll take pictures of you if you want, but none of me until I lose more weight."

"Pearl, you've already lost nearly seventy pounds. You should be documenting the progression of your transformation."

"Why on earth would I want to remember this?" Pearl says, pointing toward her stomach.

"Are you kidding? The after pictures are only impressive if you have the before to compare them to, silly. Think about it, Pearl: if you keep vanishing at this rate, your transformation could make you a social media icon."

Pearl gives Ruby a look that says she doubts this.

"Seriously," Ruby says. "Pearl, you could be an influencer. Trust me. I do brand management for a living."

"You mean you did brand management," Pearl says, smiling.

"Look, news flash: a picture says a thousand words. Just think about how many words your pictures will say about you one day. You're going to want to look back and see how far you've come."

"I don't like the way I look now, Ruby."

"And that's okay. But let's take the pictures anyway. C'mon, just put on some lipstick and get out of the car," Ruby presses.

They wade through a meadow so purplish blue that from a distance, if they squint, it almost looks like a small lake. Once they're sufficiently surrounded, nearly knee-deep in indigo, Ruby suggests they strike a pose.

"Here, this is good," she says, scooching closer to Pearl. "Okay, look up, and I'll angle the camera down so we get the flowers in the picture."

Repeatedly, Ruby taps the button on her cell phone, and they begin striking poses until they collapse in a fit of laughter.

"Okay, now let's get a few full-body shots of you by yourself," Ruby says.

"No. Nope. Never." Pearl rolls her eyes.

"C'mon, Pearl. I swear I won't post them anywhere. They're for your personal archive. Promise."

"Well, I did tell myself I would start embracing new experiences," she says, relenting.

"That's the spirit. Now, give me some attitude. Channel your inner Beyoncé!"

Just as Pearl strikes a pose, a sudden gust of wind sends bluebonnet petals flying through the air like confetti, and Pearl's long brown hair blows out, billowing away from her like a super model in a shampoo commercial. With the sun shining on her pretty face, already noticeably less plump, even with so much more weight loss still to go, she looks beautiful.

"Wait," Ruby says, extending her phone. "Don't move. You look so pretty, Pearl. I'm not kidding. The light is hitting your face at the exact perfect angle."

Pearl doesn't believe this but reluctantly humors her sister anyway.

"Look," Ruby says, showing her sister the pics. "See for yourself."

Pearl glances toward her image on the screen and does a double take. Never has she seen a picture of herself that made her want to keep looking—in a good way—and this one renders her totally speechless.

"Told you," Ruby says, still staring at it. "Major Texas goddess vibes, don't you think?"

Less than an hour later, they are rolling onto Ransom Road and the grounds of the Mountain View Prison Unit. Despite its name, there is nothing mountainous nor view-worthy about the all-female facility. Instead, everything about it looks and feels as institutional and unapproachable as the aerial photos online. The coiled razor wire on top of the brick fencing surrounding the entire campus serves as an all-too-blatant reminder that this is indeed a maximum-security prison, and as they pull up to the main guard entrance in Ruby's Lexus, she's second-guessing her decision to come. As she rolls down the driver's side window, two prison guards approach her car.

"Good afternoon, ladies," the male guard says. "Do you have an appointment?"

"Hi, yes," Ruby says somewhat nervously. "We're here for visitation with Elizabeth Crenshaw Benzer. We're Ruby and Pearl Crenshaw—her daughters."

"I'll need to see some identification and need to ask you both to step out of the car for a brief inspection."

They do as they're told. Although Pearl has been through the motions of this dozens of times, Ruby has not, and her discomfort, just like every other negative emotion she feels, tends to come out as irritation.

"Wow," Ruby says to Pearl under her breath. "Do they treat everyone like smugglers? I mean, it's bad enough our mother is a felon, but they shouldn't be allowed to treat law-abiding citizens like total trash."

"Look, you've come this far," Pearl says. "Don't bail on Mom now."

Within moments, they are approved for entry and given a parking pass to place on the dashboard, and the gates to the Gatesville prison are opened.

There are two more rounds of security, a pass through a metal detector, and a head-to-toe frisk before the clank of the prison door slams behind them, leaving Ruby and Pearl silently waiting in a hollow family holding room with just five minutes to spare before their 1:00 p.m. two-hour visitation. Ruby twirls her hair, surveying the stark modesty of the space, a mostly white cinder-block square lined with vending machines. Pearl guesses she had expected something closer to what she had seen on TV, like a glass partition to serve as a barrier between them and their mom, and she's sort of seething with Pearl for not telling her that the three of them would actually be sitting in the same room— together. Ruby wants no part of the brief introductory hug the guard reminded them they could each have. The five minutes feels like five hours as Pearl bounces her knees, trying not to let Ruby's obvious discomfort and irascibility bring her down. More than anything, she hopes the visit with their mom will bring more healing than heartache.

The two of them are buzzed to their feet as the metal door opens and Birdie, looking so much older than her fifty-eight years and practically swallowed by her baggy white uniform, enters the room, a guard on each side.

Pearl and Birdie can feel Ruby steeling herself from too much emotion. Ruby's default, her coping strategy, is to rest in her own pent-up resentment to avoid any tearful, long-overdue hug.

"Look at you two," Birdie says, already misty-eyed. "I'm so happy to see you both!"

Pearl approaches her mom's open arms, accepting her brief but joyful embrace.

"Oh, Pearl, you look amazing! I can really tell a difference, sweetheart. I'm not kidding, especially in your face. You look great."

Ruby is still processing the more haggard appearance of their once-beautiful mother: her graying hair, her more weathered complexion. Birdie's weight loss is so dramatic, and to Ruby, she looks somehow shorter than she recalls. In every which way, Birdie appears to be a much lesser version of the woman she used to be.

"Ruby," Birdie says, extending her arms. "I'm so glad you came."

Ruby avoids the invitation and instead nods politely, manages a slight smile, then takes a seat.

"Well, how was the drive?" Birdie asks, trying to put them all at ease.

"It was good," Pearl says. "The bluebonnets are at peak bloom, so the drive was real pretty."

Ruby pulls her cell phone out of her pocket, eyeballs the

ceiling-mounted camera in the corner of the room, and opens the pictures on her screen to show Birdie. The cell phones and a roll of quarters for the vending machines were the only things permitted inside. Everything else—car keys and purses—had to go into a locker. Ruby's grateful that they could at least take their phones. Having something other than one another to stare at makes the visit more tolerable.

"I told Pearl she needs to get plenty of pictures to document her weight loss," Ruby explains, swiping from one image to the next. "This one is my favorite," she adds, landing on the one of Pearl with her hair blowing in the breeze.

"Oh my word, Pearl! You look beautiful," Birdie says. "And my compliments to the photographer, too. Ruby, you always did have an artistic eye."

The comment causes Ruby to swallow hard. For so many years, she has practically pretended to be an orphan, willed herself not to crave so much as a single kind word from her mom, but hearing the same praise Birdie so generously heaped on the girls when they were young reminds Ruby of happier, albeit fleeting times: their lives before Skip—how Ruby and Pearl used to rearrange the furniture in the living room when Birdie was at one of her catering gigs and how impressed their mom acted when she came back home to find the sofa and love seat reconfigured or the bookshelves reimagined.

For the better part of an hour, Ruby and Pearl take turns scrolling through various pictures on their phones, bringing

Birdie up to speed on the current events of their respective lives. It's a bittersweet prison show-and-tell, filled with play-by-plays about the surgery, Pearl's steady recovery, and the cleanup job they've been doing at the house, and before too long, the three of them are all talking like they used to, like old times.

"So, Ruby, when are you heading back to Dallas?" Birdie asks.

"Not sure if or when I am. I'm kind of testing fate to see if my condo sells. If it does, I may just move back to Austin."

This is the first time Pearl's heard Ruby say this out loud. She fights a childhood impulse to tattletale, to spill the tea about Ruby and Dr. George and about hashtag shit you not. Definitely, these are topics they would discuss if Ruby weren't here.

"I mean, what's not to love about Austin, right?" Ruby says. "Plus, I figure Pearl might need me to stick around and help her rebuild her wardrobe once she gets to her tuck-in weight."

"Tuck-in weight?" Birdie asks.

"That's whatever weight I get to where I can finally tuck my shirt into my pants or skirt or whatever."

"I like that," Birdie says. "Makes so much more sense than looking at numbers on a scale. It sort of lets you decide what weight really suits you."

As the three of them chitchat, drain their bottled waters, and watch what little time they have left tick away on the wall-mounted clock, Birdie leans in, offering some parting sentiments for them to think about on the drive home.

"You know what I wish?" she asks rhetorically. "I wish the

three of us could spend the rest of the afternoon out shopping for Easter dresses and some floppy bonnet for me to cover up all this gray hair, and we would get up early tomorrow for the sunrise service and go have our annual splurge brunch on the river at the Four Seasons. They always had the most charming Easter Sunday decorations, the wicker hares on all the tables, and all the children running about in the grass by the water searching for more eggs to put in their baskets. Then afterward, we would go stroll through the botanical gardens, maybe visit the conservatory and while away the whole day surrounded by one another. Anyway, I know I can't be there with you girls tomorrow, but I hope you decide to do something equally lovely. It makes me happy thinking of the two of you, out in the world, living your best lives..."

That last part chokes her up, and Birdie pauses to pat her eyes. Pearl is openly crying. Ruby is fighting hard not to.

"And, Ruby, it means the world to me that you came today. See how easy it was to pick up where we left off? We—"

"I don't want to pick up from there, Mom," says Ruby, cutting Birdie off. It's the first time she's referred to her mother as Mom in more than twelve years. "If it's okay with you, I prefer we just start fresh, okay?"

"That sounds great," Birdie says, reaching for Ruby.

Reluctantly, Ruby slides her hand across the table. But when she touches Birdie's warm skin, feels her own mother's familiar grip, it surprises even Ruby how good it feels, and although she says nothing, she can't help but squeeze tight and hold on.

Chapter 35

They aren't wearing new dresses, but in honor of the occasion, Pearl has talked Ruby into wearing one of Birdie's bonnets as they stroll through the Zilker Botanical Garden on Easter Sunday. Together, with their extravagant pink floppy hats, they take in the wildflowers: Texas lantana, green eyes, and Tahoka daisies. Pearl thinks about their backyard at home and the vacant flower beds where Birdie's roses used to bloom.

"We should resurrect the garden at the house," Pearl says. "Seeing all these pretty flowers makes our yard seem so sad by comparison."

"You sure you're prepared to take that on?" Ruby asks.

"What? Flowers?"

"Yes," Ruby says. "Tilling the soil, planting, watering, pruning? It's hard work."

"I think so," Pearl says. "I don't know why I've never done it before."

"Well, I think it's a sign of your transformation, Pearl. Like a butterfly that's just emerged from its chrysalis, it makes sense that you need some pretty blossoms to enjoy."

Late in the afternoon, after they've spent $400 at the Barton Springs Nursery, Ruby waters a freshly planted bed, filled with fragrant gardenias and day lilies. It was Pearl's idea to stick their mother's old personalized aluminum garden sign back into the ground, and both women view this gesture as a sign that, at least in spirit, their mother is with them.

"It's so much better already, right?" Pearl says, admiring their work. "We need to take some pictures. Mom will be so happy to see her garden coming back to life and her *Birdie's Beds* sign back in action, don't you think?"

"I do," Ruby says, nodding.

It had been a spectacularly beautiful day, and after tackling their first home-improvement project together, which consisted of digging up decades-old decaying rosebush roots and their still spikey branches, Ruby and Pearl are grimy and sweaty and happy.

"Well," Pearl says. "Why don't we get cleaned up, and I'll mash us some avocados with lemon for dinner."

"My, how things have changed," Ruby says, smiling, walking back toward the patio.

From the kitchen, Ruby hears Pearl's phone.

"That's yours. Want me to get it?"

"Please," Pearl says, rolling up the garden hose. "Hey, if it's Perry, just tell him I'll call him back."

At the island, Ruby sees the display on Pearl's screen: that familiar number with the words Gatesville, Texas.

For a moment, she hesitates. The old Ruby would never willfully accept a call from Birdie. The old Ruby would keep her defenses up and simply ignore any of their mother's overtures as too little too late. But weird stuff is happening. After seeing their mom yesterday and holding her hand, and now, looking out back where Ruby watches Pearl practically shrinking by the minute, Ruby tells herself if her morbidly obese sister can have 80 percent of her stomach removed and actively take up a new hobby like gardening, the least she can do is answer the stupid phone.

"Hello," she says, waiting for the familiar recording.

"Hello, my name is Monica Alvarez, and I'm the family liaison coordinator at the Mountain View Women's Correctional Facility in Gatesville."

"Yes," Ruby says, momentarily confused.

"Am I speaking with Pearl Crenshaw?"

"No, this is her sister, Ruby Crenshaw. I'm Elizabeth Crenshaw's other daughter. What's this about?" Ruby says anxiously.

From where she's sweeping off the back patio, Pearl hears Ruby's voice and pauses, broom in hand, studying her sister's face.

"Ms. Crenshaw, I see that you and your sister were just here visiting your mother yesterday."

"Yes, that's right, at 1:00 p.m. Why?" Ruby says, pressing harder.

"I'm afraid I have some terrible news to pass along..."

Chapter 36

There are no flowers or funeral arrangements. Instead, in the days following the news of Birdie's sudden Easter Sunday death, Ruby and Pearl retreat into themselves and into their respective Jack-and-Jill bedrooms, both shell-shocked, awaiting the results of the mandatory autopsy. Like children who've been left behind, they cry into their pillows, trying to fully absorb the new reality that their mother is never coming home.

Thick as early-morning fog, their shared grief hangs in the house, making it impossible for either one of them to see beyond their loss. In between zombielike walks to the kitchen for hot tea, Ruby tries tapping into the resentment she felt for so long, tries mustering her once-familiar, more cynical state of mind where she found it easier to cope with her rage and embarrassment by altogether ignoring her mother, including ignoring her mother's suffering. What kind of a woman values the charade of her marriage more than the near-catastrophic toll it was having on her own daughters? Who stays married to an opioid-addicted lunatic long enough for it to escalate to the point of manslaughter?

Before Sunday, those questions still seemed so righteous. But seeing Birdie so confined, actually hearing the unmistakable disturbing clank of those metal doors closing on any hopes for a normal life now, Ruby doubts her own sanctimony. Privately, she reckons with so much regret: all the calls her mom made that went unanswered, all the years she spent trying to pretend she was already orphaned. Now that she really is, all she can think of is the desperate pleading clutch of her mom's hand, the final gentle squeeze that spoke the unspoken words Ruby could never bring herself to say: *I love you. I love you anyway. No matter what, I will always love you.*

Pearl's regrets are different but equally paralyzing. As she hibernates in front of her muted TV, mindlessly watching Chip and JoJo build dream homes and dream lives for other people, for Pearl, every thought starts with these two words: *if only.*

If only she could have done something to make her mom proud. If only she hadn't worried her mother half to death by ballooning into a 531-pound ticking time bomb. If only she had played possum that Halloween night when Skip staggered into her room. If only she'd been quiet while he groped her in the dark. If only, her mother never would have gone to prison. And the if-onlys go even further back, all the way to 1995, when she stood on the sidewalk watching Ruby ride off to school on her bike alone. If only she had gone with her sister instead of making her mother drive her.

There's no playbook for how to handle the aftermath of a mom who has died in prison. Both Ruby and Pearl, sheltering together but separately while the April showers drench the world around them, are nearly paralyzed with a potent combination of grief and regret.

But by Wednesday morning, there's a break in the clouds and Ruby seems antsy. Although Henry's texted her nonstop asking what, if anything, he can do, Ruby says she just wants her space. For as long as Pearl can remember, her sister has taken comfort in the predictable rhythm of her own heel-toe, heel-toe hitting solid ground.

"I'm going for a jog while I can," Ruby says at Pearl's bedroom door.

Eyes still swollen and red from so much crying, Pearl nods, then averts her gaze back to the silent TV.

"It might make you feel better to get up and move around a little," Ruby says, noticing the pile of wadded-up tissues on the nightstand. "Or maybe you should try and eat something," she adds, noticing her sister's half-empty sixty-four-ounce water jug.

Pearl shrugs but keeps staring at the TV.

"Okay, well, I'll be back in about an hour. Call me if you hear any news," Ruby adds, referring to the yet-to-be-determined results of Birdie's autopsy.

Not since their dad died in the car accident have Ruby and Pearl grieved together. And after all these years, they are simply out of practice. That was the last time they clung to each other in bed, side by side in the sheets, tangled in one another's legs. Although there's a vague sense of some kind of muscle memory for sharing sorrow, at this stage in their lives, they've simply grown used to suffering alone.

By the time Birdie married Skip, Ruby was already an active, popular track star, running circles around Pearl's more muted social life. And when Ruby graduated from high school and raced off to SMU, Pearl was left without cover while Skip slipped deeper and deeper into his addiction to Percocet and hydrocodone. Pearl was the one to witness their stepdad's dark descent into becoming a full-blown junkie.

Outside in the morning mugginess, Ruby considers this, considers, too, some of the things Henry has shared with her about his bariatric patients and how the vast majority of them indicate some form of childhood sexual abuse on their patient intake forms. The farther she runs, the more she can't get away from the gnawing suspicion that there are darker things she doesn't know, that in the dysfunctional jigsaw puzzle of their shared lives, there's a missing piece or two, and that's why Ruby has been unable to put it all together. Up until now, what she didn't know couldn't hurt her: it remained under lock and key, just as her mother did. But now she has questions, and with her mother gone, suddenly it hits her that Pearl is the only one left in the whole world who can possibly answer them. As she stops just shy of Low Water Bridge, watching the rapids surge into Lake Austin below, Ruby is flooded with so many questions and a new sense of urgency to answer them.

As fast as she can, she runs home. Winded and sweaty, Ruby opens the front door, fully ready to confront Pearl, but when she gets to Pearl's bedroom, she's not there. Ruby paces the house and finally spots her through the door, out back, digging up the roots of the dead rosebushes in Birdie's other bed. With her sister sufficiently preoccupied, Ruby goes to Pearl's bedroom to look for that card, the one Birdie sent for Pearl to open before her surgery. Frantically, she rummages through Pearl's nightstand drawers and dressers. Sifting through her sister's things, Ruby can't help but inventory how most of Pearl's prized possessions—the framed family photos, the jewelry box covered in seashells their dad once bought them at a souvenir shop in Galveston, the multicolored friendship bracelets they used to make with their mother, the vacation Bible school yarn-woven God's eyes—all date back to life before Skip. Aside from her hideously huge clothes, the Mr. Winky asleep on the floor, and the impressive bowl-like indentation in the center of Pearl's bed, virtually everything in Pearl's room suggests she simply stopped living, stopped evolving after age thirteen.

As she rifles through the contents of her sister's purse, she finds what she's looking for. Perched on the edge of Pearl's bed, Ruby opens the envelope addressed to her sister and, once again, unfolds the letter:

Dear Pearl,

Although I can't be there today, I am with you in spirit. Please know that I am so proud of you for taking this courageous step. For too long, you've been hiding your light, hiding your inner beauty. I can't help but feel responsible for the heavy burden you've carried all these years. I'm learning that secrets aren't good for your health. They don't go away, Pearl. They fester. I look forward to watching you lighten your load and transform into the beautiful person you are. Praying for all good things as you go into surgery today.

Much love,
Mom

"What are you doing?" Pearl says, taking Ruby by surprise.

Noticing the opened drawers and the contents of her purse spilled out onto her bed, Pearl approaches her sister, yanks the letter out of Ruby's hands, and simmering with indignation, confronts Ruby.

"This has my name on it," Pearl says, raising her voice. "How dare you sneak back inside and start going through my things! What the hell are you hoping to find anyway, Ruby?"

Ruby reaches for the letter, pointing to their mother's cryptic words like they're some sort of evidence.

"This!" Ruby yells back. "I've asked you about this. What secrets is she referring to? What did Birdie mean by burden?"

"Oh, come on, Ruby. Look at me! We talked about this the other night. How do you think I got to be this heavy? Lots of little secrets, that's how. Little Happy Meals. Little Debbie Cakes. Little Caesars pizza. The little bit of the lasagna Perry brought over for my last supper that I snuck off to the kitchen and polished off the night before my fast! All the little secrets, which, if you keep eating them, turn into big, fat lies that weigh five hundred and thirty-one pounds!"

"No, Pearl," Ruby says firmly. "Nice try, but you're still lying. You're lying to yourself and me. Sure, you've been a compulsive eater. I get that. But that's not what Birdie meant in this note. What did she mean, Pearl? What secrets are you keeping from me?"

Pearl backs away, but Ruby keeps walking toward her, until her sister is up against the wall.

"What did Skip do? He did something to you, didn't he? Tell me what happened, Pearl!"

Finally, like an overboiled egg in hot water, Pearl's tough outer shell begins to crack.

"It's my fault," she says, crying.

"What's your fault?" Ruby says, completely mystified.

"Everything!" Pearl screams. "Everything. All this. It's my fault!"

"What? Mom dying?"

Before her eyes, Ruby watches her baby sister regress, sobbing, then sliding down the wall until she's on the floor. Like a wounded animal, Ruby tries to comfort her, but Pearl cannot be consoled.

"Look at me. Look at me. Look at me, Pearl. Just tell me what happened. I'm your sister. And I love you!"

After catching her breath and blowing her nose a few times, finally, Pearl begins to purge.

"That night, the night Mom shot Skip. It wasn't because he went at her with a fireplace poker. It wasn't like what she told the cops. He didn't get mad at her for flushing his pills down the guest room toilet. It wasn't like that."

"What? I don't understand. You have to fill in some more blanks, Pearl. Start at the beginning."

Summoning as much composure as she can, Pearl wipes her nose on her shirtsleeve and, step-by-step, replays the fragmented pieces of that whole ugly night.

"I got home from that costume party before Mom got back from her catering gig, and I could tell Skip was high, because he was saying things to me in the kitchen..."

"What things? Saying what?" Ruby says, pressing her.

"He made fun of my hollaback girl costume, called me Porky Pearl, stuff like that. Whenever Mom wasn't around, if he was high, which, after you left home, was almost always, he would sometimes say mean things or inappropriate things to me. It felt like he was testing me, trying to see if I would call his bluff, rat him out to Mom. He used to say, 'nobody listens to fat girls, Pearl.'"

"Oh my gosh, why didn't you tell me? Or tell Birdie?"

"You weren't ever here, Ruby. And besides, it seemed like your life was great and you were off in Dallas, and I didn't want to pull you back into the shit show you'd left behind. You think I don't understand why you left and never came back, but I do. And besides, don't you get it? Skip's mind fuck worked on me. I stayed quiet."

Ruby hangs her head.

"And as for Mom," Pearl continues, "I honestly thought it was too dangerous to tell her anything. If I told her the truth of how he was treating me, I figured she would call him out on it, and, well, with all his guns and all those illegal prescription drugs around... I guess I was afraid he might hurt her, or she could get into trouble somehow or... I don't know. It's like I had a sense all along that things could get out of control, and it felt safer to just try not to rock the boat."

"Okay, so what happened after Birdie got home that night?" Ruby asks, now gently rubbing Pearl's back.

"So I went to bed, but I wasn't asleep. Mom and Skip were in bed, and sometime after midnight, I hear Skip staggering down the hall toward the kitchen. He used to do that a lot, especially after you left. He would get up and act like he was getting something to drink and then sort of pretend to inadvertently walk back into my room instead of their room. Like he would act stoned or drunk or sleepy and call me Birdie and stuff as if it was all some weird sleepwalking mistake. Fucking creep."

Ruby nods, trying not to punch a hole through the bedroom wall, trying not to cry.

"So he was in my room, in my bed, doing what he always did, just groping me and stuff. And normally I would just pretend to be asleep, act like I couldn't feel what was happening to me. I would just sort of try to roll over with my eyes closed and play possum. I don't know why that night was different, but I pretended to be talking in my sleep, just sort of moaning words like 'no, no, I don't like it,' stuff like that, thinking he might get nervous he was about to get caught by Mom and leave. But he didn't leave, just kept at it until..."

"Until what?" Ruby pushes.

"...until Mom opens the door holding one of his pistols and says, 'Skip, get out of that bed and get your sorry ass out of this house before I pull this trigger.'"

"What?" Ruby is rapt. These are all-new details on a story she thought she knew inside and out.

"So Skip acts like he's just waking up from a dream at first, like he's disoriented or something. But Mom is having none of it. She turns on the lights and backs out of the doorway holding his pistol. So he gets up and starts sort of negotiating with her. He's all, 'Birdie, why don't we talk about this without the gun? This was an honest but very stupid mistake, and I can see how it must look to you, but I swear, nothing was happening. I just went in the wrong door coming back from the kitchen, that's all.'

"And Mom is not buying it for a minute. She's on fire. Like, I've never seen her that angry. She had this crazed look on her face, and even though she was crying, she just kept screaming at him to shut up, told him to stop talking and start walking to the kitchen. And she hollers at me to stay in the bedroom and lock my door. So Skip does what he's told, and I do, too, but by the time they're in the living room, he's back at it, trying to talk his way out of it all. Kept saying 'Birdie, you got the wrong idea,' telling her she should think long and hard about how things could get really out of hand. From right here, crouched down by the door just like we are now, I could hear Mom telling him to shut up and get out of the house, which is what he should have done, but he kept stalling, like a fucking idiot. I think all those drugs just made him feel so bulletproof. Fool was wearing nothing but his boxers, and at one point, I heard him ask if he can at least put some pants on, but Mom's like 'hell no.' Then he starts in about how deranged she's acting and how it's going to look when he calls the cops on his wife.

"And Mom says something like 'You think I'm stupid, Skip? You think I'm just gonna roll over and play dead while you abuse my daughter?' And he's like, 'Seriously? You think I would have any interest in messin' around with a girl like Pearl? Nobody in their right mind would believe that's true.' And I think him saying that to her face, especially while she was pointing a gun at him, made her lose it. And she's like, 'What's that supposed to mean?' And he goes, 'Think logically, Birdie. Fat chicks aren't exactly my type.'"

Pearl, who is almost in a trancelike state at this point, turns and looks Ruby in the eyes. "He actually said, 'I don't think you're stupid enough to pull that trigger, Birdie.' And Mom goes, 'Oh yeah? Seems to me I'd be stupid not to.' And that was it. Next sound I heard was the first shot."

"First shot?" Ruby probes, not understanding.

"She fired another shot right after the first one. I didn't see, but I thought maybe he tried to get up or something. And Mom yells to me, 'Pearl Jane, I'm okay. You stay in that bedroom until the police get here. Don't you come out of that room.' And I hear her flushing the toilet in the guest bath. I figured she threw up or something. I didn't leave my room until the police came in, until I heard her explain the whole thing to them."

"What about the fireplace poker?" Ruby says, still trying to process what's she's hearing.

"She staged that afterward, along with the second shot: right after he went down, she fired another shot and intentionally missed him so she could tell the police he'd tried to attack her and she fired a warning shot before she fired the fatal shot. By the time the cops got here, she'd placed the poker in his hand and emptied one of his pill bottles into the guest bathroom. Told them she flushed his Percocet down the toilet, and he freaked out and that's what started it. But the cops knew that he wasn't holding the poker when he was shot."

"How?" Ruby asks. "I mean, how did they know?"

"The blood spatter all over the handle of the poker. If he'd been holding the poker like Mom said, the handle would've been clean."

Pearl wipes her tears, still trying to shake off the horror of that night like a bad chill.

"Initially, she was hoping to make it all look like self-defense, but the prosecutors insisted her tampering with evidence meant something else was going on. They pretty much had her over a barrel, so she pled guilty to second-degree manslaughter. Didn't want me to have to testify or whatever. Don't you see, Ruby? She didn't want us to be put through any more drama or trauma. I don't think she had plans to kill him. I mean, it wasn't premeditated or anything, but she ended it, you know? I think she just caught him red-handed and lost her mind."

That last part resonates with Ruby in a way that renders her speechless. A wave of shame washes over her as she slides this missing piece into the empty hole of her very soul, and with tears pouring from her eyes, Ruby feels a flicker of recognition, allows herself to accept something she's denied for way too long—that Birdie did love them, that ultimately, their mother was willing to sacrifice her own future to save theirs.

"I've always felt like this was all my fault, Ruby. Like I'm to blame for all this."

"Oh, Pearly, this wasn't your fault," Ruby says, tucking a strand of Pearl's hair behind her ear. "None of that was your fault. How can you even think that?"

"No, you don't understand," Pearl says, choking on tears. "If I had just gone with you when you rode your bike to school that day, Daddy might still be here, and none of this would have ever happened. Skip would have never even walked into our lives, and Mom and Daddy would be living in this house instead of you and me. That's how it would've gone if only I'd ridden my bike to school that day instead of watching you pedal away. You even begged me to come. From the top of the hill. You turned around and told me to hurry up. Don't you remember?"

"Oh, Pearl," Ruby says, cradling her sister's wet face in her hands. "My God, Pearl, that wasn't your fault, either. We were kids. It was a horrible accident. Daddy dying is just what happened. You can't blame yourself for any of this."

Sitting there on the floor of Pearl's bedroom together, the same room where, so many years ago, that whole bloody night began, as their shared sobbing subsides, something in the atmosphere shifts. It's as if Pearl clearing the air about the past somehow altered the barometric pressure in the whole house, recalibrated their senses. Impulsively, Ruby reaches for her sister's hand just as Birdie had reached for her own only days earlier. Clutching Pearl's tear-soaked palm, Ruby tries to convey with the might of her grip alone, with the firmness of her touch, just how very sorry she is.

Chapter 37

It takes two more days before they get the results of the autopsy. Ruby and Pearl are at a car wash running Pearl's Altima through one of the bays when the last call they'll ever get from Gatesville, Texas, appears on Pearl's screen. With pink and blue foaming soap blurring their view, the family liaison coordinator explains that the cause of death was a subarachnoid hemorrhage, a brain aneurysm.

"She died in her sleep, peacefully." That's how the woman on the phone put it.

By the time the electric mops are flopping all over the windshield, Pearl and Ruby learn that their mom's personal possessions (some letters, cards, and a few framed pictures) will be mailed to the Cherry Lane address, that she'd donated her body to science. In the three minutes it took to roll to the end of the car wash, it was done: there would be no remains to collect, no funeral home to visit, no pretty dress or floppy bonnet to pick out to replace their mother's baggy white prison uniform.

"Wow," Ruby says as they pull up to one of the self-serve coin-operated vacuums. "It's just all so unbelievable, right?"

"I hate thinking she died in there all alone," Pearl says. "Nobody should have to die alone."

Ruby nods. Sitting there in the driver's seat, she studies Pearl's profile. The bulk around Pearl's neck is less pronounced, but the sadness on her face is plain to see.

"Remember how much we used to love going to the car wash with her?" Ruby asks. "We must have thought it was like some ride at Six Flags or something. We used to get so excited."

Pearl nods and manages a small smile, then looks back at her phone and starts typing.

"What are you doing?" Ruby asks.

"I'm looking up subarachnoid hemorrhages," Pearl says.

"What good will that do?"

Pearl ignores the question and instead reads out loud the explanation she finds online.

"It says it occurs when a blood vessel just outside the brain ruptures. The area of the skull surrounding the brain rapidly fills with blood. A patient with a subarachnoid hemorrhage may have a sudden intense headache, neck pain, and nausea or vomiting. The sudden buildup of pressure outside the brain may cause rapid loss of consciousness or death."

"In that note to you, she said secrets aren't good for your health," Ruby says. "Remember? Mom said all they do is fester."

Silently, they both sit there thinking about that, wondering what other secrets their mother held on to, what secrets had suddenly died with her.

PART 4

Thick and Thin

Chapter 38

The conference room at Austin Weight Loss Specialists is filled with familiar faces. As Dr. Lisa Field wraps up her opening remarks, Pearl scans the various framed motivational quotes hanging on the walls, trying to determine which one is her favorite:

> You will find that it is necessary to let things go; simply for the reason that they are heavy. —C. JoyBell C.
>
> Growth and comfort do not coexist. —Ginni Rometty
>
> Courage is the power to let go of the familiar. —Raymond Lindquist
>
> You never change your life until you step out of your comfort zone; change begins at the end of your comfort zone. —Roy T. Bennett
>
> Dreams are the seeds of change. Nothing grows without a seed…and nothing ever changes without a dream. —Debby Boone

"So remember, everyone," Dr. Field says, bringing Pearl's attention back to front and center. "What's said in the group…" and then everyone in unison says, "…stays in the group."

For Pearl, there's something that feels a bit cultish about repeating mantras en masse like this, but this sense of belonging she's starting to feel far outweighs any of the initial skepticism she felt back in March. So she rolls with it, merging her voice with all the rest, like a singer in a church choir.

"Okay, so with that, I would like to turn the microphone over to someone we haven't heard from in a couple weeks. Pearl Crenshaw, we missed you, and we would like to know if you feel comfortable giving us a bit of an update on how you're doing?"

With a dozen pairs of eyes watching her approach the podium, Pearl makes her way to the mic. Being front and center isn't really her jam, but over the past several weeks, she's heard from just about everyone else, so she knows it's her turn.

"Hi, y'all?" she says, taken aback by the sound of her own amped-up voice.

"Hi, Pearl," the group says.

"So…um….my sleeve was two months and four days ago. Dr. George did it. And…um…as of about twenty minutes ago when I checked the scale right outside those doors, I'm officially down eighty-eight pounds since March thirteenth, the day of my surgery."

And that's all it takes. With the mere mention of her weight loss, the room erupts into a thunderous standing ovation. As she absorbs all the approval and support from every which way, she is overcome with emotion. When Pearl went in for her surgery, she had no way of knowing the full depth and breadth of the loss she was about to experience. More than anything, it pains her to know that her mom won't be around to witness these incremental accomplishments, much less her tuck-in weight (whatever that turns out to be), but as isolating as that feels, right at this very moment, standing among these fellow weight-loss warriors, she knows she's not alone, so she continues on, offering her testimony.

"I'm not gonna lie," Pearl says, interrupting the clapping. "This hasn't been an easy time for me. A few weeks ago, I lost my mom."

Hearing this, the group offers a collective round of sympathy, including a kindhearted "We love you, Pearl!" shout-out from the back of the room.

"Thanks," Pearl says, continuing. "Anyway, it's been really weird to not have my old coping strategies to fall back on in times of stress. The old me would've cozied up with a bag of cheesy combos from P. Terry's Burger Stand or something. Bite by bite, the old me would've tried to keep filling up all the lonely, empty spaces inside."

She pauses, trying to keep the trickle of tears from turning into an all-out sob. But as she looks around, she sees she's connecting. Based on the number of teary eyes, she can tell these people understand all too well exactly what she means. They've all come from more or less the same place, and these morbidly obese compatriots practically salute as Pearl stands there trying to compose herself.

"Pearl," Dr. Field says, redirecting. "Can you tell us about what new coping strategies you've discovered in this short time?"

Pearl nods, reflects on all the strange newness of her life in general.

"I…I don't know," she stammers. "I mean, other than where I live and where I work, it feels like not one thing about my life is the same. Like all of you, since my surgery, I've had to radically modify so many old habits, and once you realize you can basically live off liquid for an entire month and survive, you have this boost of confidence that makes making big changes somehow easier. I have the proof now that curly fries aren't going to solve my problems." There is a swell of laughter with this remark. "And I don't need to hide foods like some kind of obsessive food junkie anymore." She winces as she realizes she used the same word to describe herself that she and Ruby use to describe Skip. "With every change like this, my confidence seems to grow, and more and more, I'm trusting the process and trusting my body."

The group nods as she continues.

"I'm not kidding. Since my surgery, I've already done so many new things. I've gone swimming, and I've been to a couple of yoga classes, and even though I need a kickboard and despite the fact that I'm far from being a human pretzel, I'm at least moving my body in new ways, right? And with my CPAP, which I affectionately refer to as Mr. Winky, I'm getting the best sleep of my life, and although I still have a long way to go, I'm even amazed by simple stuff like how much less winded I am climbing a flight of stairs at work. So if I'm talking about coping and how overeating was my old way of dealing with life, I guess my new coping strategy is more about living life, doing stuff. I don't know. Does that make any sense?"

The group nods and claps their affirmation. They so get it—each and every one of them.

"And it's funny because I remember when I was filling out my bariatric intake form, which seems like so long ago now, but that question about what your post-op goals are…well, I listed four or five different things, but now that I'm on the other side of the surgery, it's like I keep adding to the list. Like one of my new goals is to be able to cross my legs, you know?"

"Woo-hoo!" someone shouts from the second row. The enthusiasm from the group is so palpable, and from the pulpit, Pearl continues to preach, evangelizing in ways both big and small.

"I want to fly on a commercial airplane. I want to be able to use the freaking bathroom on it, too. And I want to be able to park in the middle of a row rather than on the end. At a restaurant, I want to sit in a cozy booth instead of at a giant table in the middle of the room." Now her fellow meeting members are clapping loudly. "And when I came in here this evening and sat down and started looking around at all the motivational messages on the walls," she says, pointing toward her right, "this one really hit me: 'Dreams are the seeds of change. Nothing grows without a seed...and nothing ever changes without a dream.' So, Dr. Field," she says, shifting her focus, "I feel like that was a really long-winded way to answer your question."

Chapter 39

Ruby and Henry are both two beers into a spectacular sunset at the Oasis on Lake Travis. Despite the crowds, they've managed to score a semi-quiet table on one of the tiered decks. An old Pat Green song offers the perfect background mood music for this iconic central Texas tradition of watching day give way to night on this particular expanse of the Colorado River.

"I don't know what I'm gonna call it," Ruby says, referring to the launch of her new brand management consulting business. "But it feels right to stick around and sort of re-pot myself here in Austin."

"There are plenty of worse places you could be, that's for sure," Henry says, pointing off toward the west at the burnt-orange swath of sky. "For selfish reasons, I have to confess, I'm really glad you got an offer on your condo."

Ruby's face reddens, and she knows it's the warmth she feels for Henry, radiating from the inside out. Every time they're together, she feels him putting off the same kind of heat, and like a moth to the flame, she finds herself more and more drawn to it.

"I'm taking it as a God wink," Ruby says. "I told myself that if it sells, especially if it sells for ten percent above asking price, I would just assume this is where I'm meant to be—for now anyway."

Henry nods and dunks another chip into the bowl of guacamole they're sharing. "Well, it seems like this is going to be good for you and Pearl."

"I think so," Ruby says. "I've got this whole different lens I'm starting to see her through now, and of course my mom, too. God, I was just such a bitch for so long."

"Don't you think you're being a little hard on yourself?" Henry says, sipping his beer.

"It's nice that you say that, but no," Ruby says affirmatively. "I'm way clear that I should've been nicer. I mean, I'm not gonna beat myself up over it or anything, because we don't know what we don't know, right? Like, for instance, I never knew how much Pearl blamed herself for my dad dying. When I trace it back, I think that was the very beginning of her weight problems. She just started stuffing her guilt, hiding it. And then there I was, always angry with her for being so lazy and gluttonous. For a while, I actually couldn't believe that she and I were related, because we reacted so differently to the stressors in our lives. But after everything she's shared with me since Mom died, now I know why: we had such fundamentally different experiences, even under the same roof. And Pearl's experiences were far worse than mine. I'm still sorting it all out, but for the first time, I'm able to make a connection between this angry energy I have and the reasons for it." She pauses to take a drink. "Some fun date, huh?"

Henry laughs. "I think you're more self-aware than you give yourself credit for," he says.

"Well, it's a good thing I've always been a runner. Can't imagine what kind of lunatic I'd be by now if I weren't."

"Well, as a doctor, I can tell you there are plenty of healthy ways to relieve stress," Henry says suggestively. "And I think I can help you work through some of your pent-up hostility."

Ruby smiles, loving his wry sense of humor.

"Come on," he says, reaching for her hand. "Let's go hit that dance floor."

Chapter 40

Now that Ramsay Reynolds and Eva are husband and wife, the Wednesday lunches Pearl used to set aside for the elder Mr. Reynolds have gone by the wayside. Although Ramsay still shows up at Glenwood Manor like clockwork, each Wednesday at noon, Pearl no longer waits for him. She does, however, take notice of which days the disgustingly beautiful Eva tags along, which, much to Pearl's chagrin, is almost always. But on this particular Wednesday in June, as Pearl is very intentionally walking past their table, merely waving to them on her way out-side to the patio, Ramsay actually gets up from his seat and approaches her.

"Pearl, you look so wonderful!" Ramsay gushes.

"Thank you so much," Pearl says, taking full note that this compliment from Ramsay is the first time someone who knows nothing about her surgery has noticed her weight loss. "I'm very much in progress," she says. "Still have lots to lose, but I'm already feeling better."

"Well, keep doing whatever it is you're doing, Pearl," he says. "Because it looks really good on you."

Never has a man as handsome as Ramsay Reynolds been this generous with praise for Pearl. And it's so foreign to her that she almost doesn't know how to receive it, has no idea what to say. So instead, she smiles and nods somewhat bashfully.

"I hope I didn't embarrass you by saying that," he adds, reading her mind. "It's just, I couldn't help but notice."

"I'm glad," Pearl says, blushing. "Thank you, Ramsay. I mean, it's nice of you to say so."

Perry is waiting for her at their regular table out back on the terrace.

"You're late," he says, unfolding his paper napkin in his lap. "I thought you might have tried sneaking Ramsay Reynolds off to the broom closet or something."

"Ha ha ha," Pearl lilts. "You know I have a strict policy against making out with married men."

"Well, there's no harm in fantasizing about it," he says, winking. "For you or for me."

As Pearl lowers herself into the chair, Perry watches.

"Look at you," he says. "It's not even the end of June, and already you're disappearing. What's the total?"

"Counting the all the weight I've lost before and after my

surgery, ninety-two pounds," Pearl says, beaming. "Ramsay was just telling me how fabulous I look."

"Well, I couldn't agree more. Cheers," Perry says, holding up a cup of water. "You should be very proud. It took me a year and a half to drop eighty-seven pounds."

"Right, but you didn't have as much to lose, either," Pearl explains. "The heavier you are, the faster the weight comes off. Oh, and thanks for bringing lunch," Pearl says. "Seriously, Perry. It's such a treat the way you surprise me with some wildly good homemade food every Wednesday."

"Well, with your thimble-sized portions, it's not much trouble. Tell me what you think of this. It's baked ricotta with lemon and thyme on a small bed of shaved brussels sprouts."

Pearl takes a bite and falls in love.

"Oh my gosh," she says, savoring the flavors and the texture. "This may be my new favorite."

"You say that every week," Perry chides.

"I know, but it's true. I used to eat such crappy food, tons of it, but I'm more experimental now," she says, taking another modest bite. "My mom would be so proud of my ever-expanding palate."

"I agree," Perry says. "It does seem counterintuitive that the more your palate grows, the smaller you get."

"There's no accounting for good taste, I suppose," Pearl says, beaming.

"Well, speaking of good taste, it seems Ruby's made a nice

choice with Henry, but now that you're coming out of your shell, Pearl, have you started to consider your own love life?"

"What love life?" Pearl asks sarcastically.

"The hot, sexy love life you are going to create for yourself. Duh?"

"Well, as you know, my one true love has forsaken me for another," Pearl says, motioning toward the cafeteria.

"Oh, come on," Perry insists. "There are plenty of other fish in the sea. Ramsay is just a pretty speckled trout in a school of thousands. You just need to start casting some lines. There are dating sites where you can pretty much order off a menu, you know?"

"That's not my style."

"How do you know it's not your style if you've never tried it?" Perry asks.

"Look, I'm not totally opposed to dating sites. I mean, I get that they serve a purpose, and who knows? Maybe one day, you can help me create a profile or something, but I want my love life to be more organic than that, more spontaneous or something. Like yours or Ruby's."

"Well, look at you!" Perry says, folding his arms across his chest.

"What?"

"You did it," he says.

"Did what?"

"You put it out there in the universe. By saying what you want out loud, you're attracting it."

"Is this more of your ancient Chinese philosophy?" Pearls asks, wiping her mouth.

"It's the law of attraction, Pearl. Like attracts like. Positive thoughts sally forth from your body as magnetic energy, then return in the form of whatever it was you were thinking about."

"What if I want to attract, say, a twenty-percent pay raise?" Pearl asks, winking. "Or what if I want to attract insurance coverage for the plastic surgery I'll need to get rid of all the leftover skin I'll have once I lose all my weight?

"Now you're talking," Perry says. "Although, don't look at me for that last one," he adds, holding his hands up. "I have no decision-making authority with regard to our corporate coverage."

"Or, I know, what if I want to attract taking the rest of the day off?"

"Oh my God," Perry says, excusing himself from the table. "I've created a monster!"

Chapter 41

The hardest part about having a garage sale is the setup. For a week and a half, Ruby and Pearl have been thinning out every closet and cabinet in the entire house. With Ruby's condo selling, she needs a place to store her stuff—all of which they agree is nicer than most of the contents of their house on Cherry Lane. Now that they've both absorbed the sad fact that their mother is never coming home, the house they grew up in is more theirs than ever before, legally and otherwise. And it's with this new sense of ownership that Ruby and Pearl are deciding which items from their past they want to keep, and the contents of the kitchen alone offer endless debate.

"What about this?" Ruby asks, holding up one of Birdie's dented old tin pitchers.

"Keep that," Pearl says emphatically.

"Why?" Ruby says, mystified.

"It's rustic," Pearl says. "Joanna Gaines would never put that in a garage sale. I can use it as a vase or something and put it on a bedside table in the guest room."

"Well, in order to do that, you would first need to have a designated guest room. Remember, this is a crap-culling operation here, Pearl."

"Oh my gosh, remember these?" Pearl says, holding up a zip-lock gallon bag full of refrigerator magnets. She opens them up and pours them onto the island for closer inspection.

"Wow, blast from the past," Ruby says, studying the wild assortment of shapes and sizes: wallet-sized grade-school pictures tucked into tiny clear plastic frames, miniature ceramic Lone Star flags, summer events calendars for 2001 and 2002 at Barrow Creek Country Club, some red, white, and blue SMU Mustangs, Keep Austin Weird, a vintage Ann Richards for governor, Birdie's Catering, ThunderCloud Subs, several pictures of Ruby and Pearl with their dad and mom, ironically not a single image of Skip in the entire pile. "Truly amazing," Ruby says. "Who knew the early history of our lives could be reduced to fridge magnets?" she adds, opening another drawer.

"We're keeping these," Pearl says.

"Okay, come with me," Ruby says. "I have an idea."

In Pearl's bedroom, Ruby throws herself into the sinkhole at the center of her sister's queen-size bed. "This can't be healthy," she says. "You need a better mattress."

Pearl doesn't disagree, but unless she sells the house and takes her half of the proceeds to start buying new things, she doesn't have the budget for something as extravagant or expensive as a new mattress.

"I've needed one for a long time but just haven't gotten around to it," Pearl says sheepishly.

"Well, lucky for you, we're moving my furniture in here, so I am giving you the bed that was in my spare room in Dallas."

"The Sleep Number?" Pearl says enthusiastically.

"Yep," Ruby says. "Plus, it's adjustable. Perfect for binge-watching *Fixer Upper*, right?"

"Oh my gosh, thanks, but won't you need that bed whenever…"

They've agreed to make no sudden moves. Until Pearl has lost her weight and until Ruby's business is off and running, for the time being, they've agreed to cohabit. With this much space in what is still one of the most coveted neighborhoods in Austin, it just makes sense to stay put—at least for now. And although neither one of them has admitted it to the other, they both take more comfort than they expected in the time they've been sharing living together under one roof.

"I sold my house at ten percent above asking, remember?" Ruby says. "I'm not worried about replacing a mattress, Pearl."

"It's kind of fun shedding all these knickknacks and sprucing things up, you know? Feels like we're on our own episode of *Fixer Upper* and we're about to reconfigure the whole space."

Ruby lies there, looking up at the ceiling, taking note of the way the white paint above has yellowed over the years.

"Yep, this whole place could stand some rehab," Ruby says. "Don't you think it would be best to fix it up and sell it? I mean, with the real estate in this area, we would get ten times what Mom and Dad paid for it. I'm just saying, with everything that happened here, don't you want a fresh start? You could take the cash and buy something brand new."

"Or not," Pearl says.

"What's or not? I mean why not?" Ruby asks, propping herself up on her elbow.

"I mean, if I work hard, I could just try to keep putting my own touches on it and give it some new life."

"Right, but isn't the whole point of you losing weight about putting the old Pearl behind you and starting over?"

"The point of me losing weight is so I can keep living. It was so I didn't end up stuck in that bed, unable to help myself. Whether I live in this same old house or a new one has nothing to do with my weight. I can be happy anywhere as long as I'm comfortable in my own skin."

Ruby mulls this over then asks Pearl something she's never asked her before.

"So are you?"

"Am I what?"

"Comfortable in your own skin?"

Pearl glances toward the mirror, and studies her reflection. She wiggles her toes, recalling a time when she couldn't even see them.

"Yes. As a matter of fact, I finally feel good about who I am and how I look." She bends over to inspect her feet up close because, well, she can.

"What are you doing down there?" Ruby asks, cocking her head.

"I'm just hanging out, staring at my ankles. Is that weird?"

"Um, mildly?" Ruby says, trying to understand. "Everything okay?"

"Completely. I've just never noticed how good I look from the knee down. Yep, I have to say I'm definitely comfortable in my own skin, and check out my ankles—they're fire, right?"

Chapter 42

They didn't mean to pick the hottest day of the year to have their garage sale, but despite the 104-degree August heat, by the time the last shopper drives away with one of their mom's old rugs and a stash of wooden spoons, Ruby and Pearl have made nearly four thousand dollars. They sold sofas, side tables, lamps, a huge box of Birdie's old catering tablecloths, a toaster oven, two sets of Skip's old golf clubs, two decades' worth of comforters, dishes, and more.

Dog-tired and covered in dried salty sweat, they sit in the shade on the back patio, trying out some of Ruby's furniture.

"I can't believe how much better the porch looks with a table that's not all falling apart," Pearl says, sipping some water.

"Well, don't get too cozy," Ruby says. "We're only just getting started. Henry's on his way with a couple of guys to help us unload the rest of the stuff from my condo. Come on," she adds, catching her second wind. "Let's go do the fun part."

By late that evening, there isn't a single room in the house that looks or feels the same. The kitchen isn't nearly as cluttered, and Ruby's newer barstools replaced the ones they sat on growing up. In the living room, tufted leather sofas elevate the entire space, and they've updated the mantel, swapping an old wood-framed watercolor of some indeterminate hill country meadow for the blown-up childhood photo of Ruby and Pearl straddling their banana-seat bikes circa 1995. It's the same picture that hung in their mother's prison cell, and it serves as a silent yin-and-yang reminder to both of them of some of their happier childhood memories as well as the price their mom paid to avenge Skip's abusive behavior. Although neither of them can fully reckon with the senseless, tragic ending to Birdie's second marriage, at least Ruby now knows their mom wasn't as naïve as she once thought.

"I'm pouring a deep glass of chardonnay," Ruby says. "Care for a little splash?"

"Only about that much," Pearl says, using her index finger and thumb to show about an inch. "I'm not supposed to imbibe for nine more months."

"Well, a sip or two won't hurt," Ruby says, handing Pearl a glass. "So you excited to sleep in your new bed tonight?"

"Definitely," Pearl says, giving the spiffy kitchen another once-over.

"We've accomplished quite a lot, huh?" Ruby says.

"Uh-huh," Pearls says, nodding. "You know how good it feels when you clean out your purse and you get rid of all the wadded-up receipts and gum wrappers and spent ChapSticks?" Pearl asks, pacing between the kitchen and the living room.

"Yep," Ruby says. "A tidy purse sort of makes you feel like everything is right with the world."

"Exactly," Pearl says. "And that's how this feels to me. The house—it feels organized and fresh."

"Long overdue," Ruby says, taking a seat on the sofa.

"You say that, but think about it—everything in its due time, right? I mean, in what alternate universe would you have been moving your personal possessions back into this house? And if Mom hadn't died, we wouldn't even feel right about selling so many of her things to make space for your newer stuff, right?"

"I suppose so."

"My point is, even now, I sometimes catch myself wondering why in the world didn't I sell Mom's watches sooner? Like, why didn't I try to lose weight any sooner? Why didn't I tell you the truth during one of my visits to Dallas? I just wonder how much closer we might have been all these years and how much it might have made a difference in your relationship with Mom."

"Well, like you said, we can't go rewriting history, Pearl. Things played out the way they played out. So instead of looking back, let's look at how far we've come, especially how far you've come. I mean, on the bright side, you've finally said goodbye to that poor, worn-out saggy mattress, and we're going to sock away the profits from today's garage sale for your new tuck-in wardrobe. So cheers to us being where we are now."

"Right," Pearl says. "Cheers to us and to all life's better-late-than-nevers."

"Speaking of which, what do you say we get up early tomorrow and drive to Waco and hit the Magnolia Market at the Silos?" Ruby asks, draining her glass. "We can go source some Chip and JoJo accessories for the house."

"Oh my gosh!" Pearl says enthusiastically. "Best. Idea. Ever! You know I've never been, right?"

"Me either," Ruby says. "But hey, there's a first time for everything."

Chapter 43

From their house on Cherry Lane, it's roughly one hundred miles to the entrance of Magnolia Market at the Silos. And just as it appears on the website, this expansive outdoor shopping complex located in downtown Waco really is the Shangri-la of shiplap, the Disneyland of down-home farmhouse décor. Anchored architecturally by two 120-foot silos, the grounds are just as inviting as a newly revealed Chip and Joanna Gaines fixer-upper.

"Okay, just pinch me," Pearl says as they walk through the entrance.

"As much as you like their show, I can't believe you haven't been here yet," Ruby says, scanning the rambling warehouse space.

For Pearl, who is walking around with her mouth agape, the Magnolia Market is total sensory overload. Any direction she looks, for as far as she can see, it's all stuff she wishes she could cram into her sister's Lexus and haul back to Austin.

"You know, farmhouse may not be my personal vibe for décor," Ruby says, sniffing a candle. "But I have to hand it to them, their branding is on point."

From the Magnolia scent collection featuring candles of every shape and size, including hundreds of hand-dipped beeswax tapers draped over clotheslines, to rows of galvanized stock tanks filled to capacity with dried flowers and wreaths, to the home accents featuring homespun fabrics, Magnolia blankets and throw pillows, accent lighting, wall art, and more, the market is brimming with the items Joanna Gaines uses to stage her *Fixer Upper* renovations. Virtually everything with a Magnolia tag looks simultaneously farm fresh and gently frayed. And being there is almost like walking onto a set of one of their episodes, right down to the apparel section, where Pearl has already sourced a mustard Magnolia Seed & Supply ball cap, the same one Joanna wears when she's checking on one of Chip's demos.

"How do I look?" Pearl asks, trying it on for size.

"Like a total groupie," Ruby says, reaching for a Magnolia canvas gardener's apron. "Here, what about this?" Ruby suggests, handing one to Pearl. "This is something you need."

Pearl pauses to admire, but hesitates to try it on. With two strings that tie at the waist, she doubts they will reach, but with Ruby standing there watching and waiting, arms folded, reluctantly, she gives it a try.

"Oh my gosh," Pearl says, beaming. "Look, Ruby, it fits! I mean, it's a little snug, but I'll grow into it, right?"

"What do you mean grow into it?" Ruby asks, quizzically. "It already fits, and if the apron fits, girl, you better buy it."

Standing side by side in the three-way mirror modeling their Magnolia gardening gear, it hits Pearl that this is the first time they've tried on anything together since they were in middle school, and it thrills her to no end that they are actually wearing the same exact item. *So what if it's one size fits all?* she thinks. Wearing these matching aprons, she and Ruby are the same size, equal in a way that Pearl has never quite felt before.

"My treat," she says to Ruby. "I'm buying these for us."

For a couple of hours, it's like this—two sisters, doing normal sister stuff like comparative candle sniffing and hunting for housewares. They roam every square foot of the space, leaving no display untouched, no essential oils unsampled, until Ruby, weighed down with bags, says the words that threaten to test Pearl's weight loss resolve in the cruelest of ways.

"Let's go hit the bakery," Ruby insists, donning her sunglasses. "I need to see what those cupcakes are all about."

"You know I can't have sugar," Pearl says, following her sister to the Silos Baking Co. entrance.

"Right," Ruby says. "But I can," she adds, opening the door. "It wouldn't be the full experience if we didn't at least buy one cupcake. Am I right?"

Pearl cannot deny this indisputable fact. She just wishes, for a moment, that she still had the capacity to gobble up a baker's dozen. The smell of the bakery alone, with all its buttercream goodness, is something Pearl wishes she could bottle up and chug. And as they peruse the racks of perfectly frosted cupcakes and pastries, Pearl admires the sheer artistry of it all and settles on one firm conclusion—it's all too pretty to eat.

That is what she tells herself while Ruby pays for a single small Silobration signature cupcake. Outside, they sit at a two-top in the shade, Pearl nursing more water and Ruby sipping a lemonade.

"Well, I volunteer to eat all but one bite of this and verify whether it tastes as good as it looks," Ruby teases.

"That's so big of you," Pearl says, studying the thick, chocolate-sprinkled swirl on top. She watches as Ruby digs in.

"Oh my gosh, not gonna lie," Ruby says, licking frosting from the corners of her mouth. "It really is a Silobration."

Watching this, Pearl does a gut check and is surprised by how not tempted she really is. Since childhood, food has always been a source of comfort, a way to keep stuffing her real emotions. But sitting with her sister at this dainty table for two, surrounded by shopping bags, wearing her favorite new ball cap, and still digesting the half of a Quest protein bar she ate earlier, Pearl realizes something beautiful: she's actually plenty full. And as she dips her finger into the frosting, allowing herself one tiny taste, she is absolutely aware that this feeling of fullness, even more than the cupcake, is the real celebration.

PART 5
Light

Chapter 44

Back at her one-year post-op weigh-in, Pearl was astounded to learn that she'd lost 250 pounds—an eighth of a ton. She'd left that weigh-in amazed that, at 281 pounds, she was nearly fully half of her former number.

Now, six months later, as she steps on the scale for her eighteen-month postsurgical weigh-in, with Ruby and Henry and pretty much the entire staff of Austin Weight Loss Specialists hovering behind her, the number on the scale literally shocks her so much she gasps: 182 pounds.

"Oh my gosh, how is this even possible?" Pearl says, crying tears of joy.

Ruby is the first to squeal with pride.

"I'm so blown away by you, Pearl! You did it! You really did it," she says, hugging her sister.

"Now I really know I've done something huge," Pearl says, noticing the tears freely flowing down Ruby's face. "If you're crying, I know I've done something big!"

"Everyone, you're looking at the new poster child for bariatric surgery," Henry says, giving Pearl a high five. "I'm not kidding, Pearl. What you've managed to do in just eighteen months is beyond amazing."

"I can't wait to go to group and share this update," Pearl says, beaming.

"Okay, everybody stand back," Ruby instructs. "Let's give the diva some space and let me get a picture of Pearl hitting her tuck-in weight."

They form a small horseshoe around her as Ruby takes out her phone. At this point, so many months later, all of them struggle to remember the 531-pound version of Pearl. Now, with her feet planted firmly, confidently, on the scale, wearing her stylish boyfriend jeans and the crisp white button-front oxford, Pearl looks positively radiant.

"Okay, girl! Tuck that shirt in and say protein!" Ruby says, positioning the camera.

Pearl tugs at the loose denim, tucks in the front tail of her top, and smiles.

The cheers fill the lobby, and from where Pearl is, she can see through the glass reception window to a few of the new, still-heavy patients waiting for their initial consultations, and even more than the tucking in of her shirt, seeing those people, still very much at the beginning of their journeys, makes it easier for Pearl to see how far she's really come.

"Say I did it!" Ruby says, tapping the photo button.

"I did it," Pearl says, hands on hips she can now easily feel. "I really did it."

Chapter 45

Along with Perry and Ruby and the gift card she still hasn't used from the whole team at Glenwood Manor, plus some of the proceeds from their garage sale, Pearl struts into the Nordstrom at the Domain like a woman on a mission. Today is going to be the biggest shopping spree of her life. Perry and Ruby are basically there to help carry her bags and help her pick out some basics for her near-empty closet.

"First, if I may suggest, we need to work our way over to foundations," Perry says with all the authority of a stylish gay man. "It doesn't matter what's on top until we smooth out everything underneath," he adds, winking.

"All this extra skin is the suckiest part of my whole weight loss," Pearl says. "I hate having these stupid bat wings. They make me look ancient. And no matter what, my thighs and sagging tummy are still going to leave me with some limited wardrobe options."

"That's why God made Spanx, Pearl," Ruby says, hopping onto the escalator.

"Maybe one day, I'll have the surgery to remove all this skin and a boob job to replace my shriveled-up raisin tits."

"No, no, no," Perry says, shaking his index finger. "No negative self-talk, remember? There's no reason for negative self-talk when you've just lost three hundred and forty-nine pounds. Hello? Can you please try to keep this in perspective? You look absolutely radiant!"

"Plus," Ruby adds, "Henry says that skin surgery is highly vascular and, in some ways, more dangerous than the endoscopic bariatric procedure. If I were you, I wouldn't be in too big of a hurry for any of that."

Pearl rolls her eyes. "Thanks, Dr. Ruby. I'll keep that in mind," Pearl says facetiously.

"What happened to you being comfortable in your own skin?" Ruby asks. "It's time for you to start rocking those ankles."

"True that," Pearl says, scanning the sea of options in the Intimates Department. "I see myself stocking up on Spanx for sure."

"They don't call it shapewear for nothin,'" Perry says, selecting a nude and a black pair of something called the Higher Power panties. "Here, these are a must," he adds, handing them to Pearl.

"Um, I don't mean to sound too concerned, but how do you know so much about women's underwear, Perry?" Pearl asks with an evil grin.

"Wouldn't you love to know," Perry says, unfazed. "Come on, girls. Let's work our way over to activewear."

Within half an hour, they have amassed too many selections to fit into a single dressing room, so the sales associate brings over a rolling wardrobe rack to park next to Perry and Ruby, who are sitting just outside the changing area in a couple of cozy chairs, ready to watch Pearl play dress-up.

"Come out when you have something fabulous to show us," Ruby says.

"Oh my gosh," Pearl says from beyond the slatted door. "This is so overwhelming. I'm not used to having so many choices."

"And isn't that just a wonderful metaphor for life?" Perry says while scrolling his phone and winking at Ruby.

When Pearl emerges wearing a simple, elegant three-quarter-sleeve plum tunic dress, which falls over her slimmer torso and features a side slit that shows just the right amount of calf and, of course, ankle, Perry and Ruby are slack-jawed.

"What do we think of this?" Pearl asks, reading their faces.

"Shut up!" Ruby says.

"That. Is. Beyond," Perry says, echoing Ruby's awe.

"I kind of like it," Pearl says, staring into the three-way mirror.

"You have to get that," Ruby says. "It's so flattering, Pearl!"

"Wear it on Wednesdays when Ramsay comes with Eva, and tell him to eat his heart out," Perry says.

The thought of that, however ridiculous, is somewhat

gratifying, and Pearl considers where she might wear something so dressy.

"I just, I don't know," she says, taking in a side view. "It's really weird because I've never had a style. When what you've had to wear your whole adult life can only be described as 'tent,' it's all a little confusing."

"So that's why you try lots of things on and see which outfits give you the biggest smile," Ruby explains.

"Sometimes, we have to kiss some toads before we find our prince, Pearl. Trust me, this applies to romance and fashion. Just keep trying things on: you'll know when you've found the perfect fit."

For the next hour or so, Pearl continues her fashion show, trying on dresses, skirts, tops, and trousers and separating what she loves from what she merely likes until finally, she steps out in a stunning black, long-sleeved, off-the-shoulder dress.

"Can you help me zip it up?" she asks Ruby.

"Happily," Ruby says, jumping to her feet.

With Pearl holding her long brown hair off to the side, Ruby tugs on the zipper. Together, looking into the mirror, there is an unspoken moment between them where they both know it's impossible to distinguish which one of them is the fairest of them all.

"You look beautiful," Ruby says.

Pearl shrugs her shoulders, admiring the concavity of her newly visible collarbone.

"Look, Ruby," she says, pointing at her bony protrusion. "What's this called again?"

"Your clavicle, silly!"

"Oh right, I forgot," Pearl says before spinning around to show off. "Hey, Perry, look at this," she says, still shrugging and smashing her boobs together.

"What? The girls?" he says, not understanding.

"No, forget about tits! Look at my amazing clavicle," she says, pointing at it. "Y'all, I have an actual clavicle! Forget about my ankles! I swear, this is my new favorite body part. Yes, I am definitely buying this dress."

Chapter 46

By October, Pearl has stopped going for the regular weigh-ins at Austin Weight Loss Specialists. She has reached a healthy, happy weight where she is no longer obsessing about the number on the scale and instead is able to focus on eating and exercising in ways that feel right to her, and she is certainly doing something right, as all her fun new clothes fit.

She is also no longer officially a patient of Dr. Henry George, but she is soon to become something even better—his sister-in-law.

Despite all the many changes in her life, the one constant that Pearl has come to rely on is her postsurgical therapy group. It's the one place where she knows she'll be surrounded by supportive others who fully understand everything she's been through and everything that's yet to come.

Tonight, as Dr. Field is sharing the agenda for an upcoming

conference, Pearl notices someone new in the room. He's tall, with thick salt-and-pepper hair, and he's still fairly heavy, but based on the extra room inside his Patagonia fleece vest, Pearl call tell he's probably at least a couple of months post-op. Without even trying, she catches his eye, and he smiles before taking his seat at the end of her row. Pearl looks over both shoulders to be sure the smile was meant for her.

"So I can't stress enough how informative and affirming this conference is," Dr. Field says from behind the podium at the front of the room. "I'm excited to report that this year, the city of Las Vegas is hosting Obesity Week November first through fifth, and for those of you who don't know, Obesity Week is the world's largest obesity-centric expo, with the most comprehensive bench-to-bedside and continuum of care content. Now, I've got brochures circulating around the room, and I'll be sure to leave some here on the table as well, so be sure to grab one. For those of you who do plan to attend, you're in for a very information-packed week. There are always world-renowned experts on hand to share breakthroughs and innovations for both the treatment and the prevention of obesity. Think of it as one giant TED Talk focused exclusively on the kinds of things we discuss in this room each and every week. And I would be remiss if I didn't take this opportunity to put a plug in for our own Pearl Crenshaw, who has been selected by the Obesity Society board of managers to be one of this year's featured speakers. So how about you join me in a round of applause as we invite Pearl to start us off with a little teaser about what she plans to share in Vegas."

The room erupts as Pearl makes her way to the front. Wearing cropped trousers and a long, fitted jacket with stylish block-heel sling-backs, there isn't anything about Pearl Crenshaw that looks one bit the same. Even her new haircut, a shoulder-length bob, reflects the head-to-toe, new and improved version of herself. But what's more striking than her weight loss, the hair, or her signature Rouge Allure Pirate red lips is the confidence radiating from her as she approaches the microphone.

"Hi, y'all," she says, smiling, no longer nervous about sharing her story. "My name is Pearl Crenshaw, and as many of you know, nineteen months ago, the very first time I walked into this building, when I stepped on the scale on the other side of those double doors, I weighed five hundred and thirty-one pounds. Suffice it to say, it wasn't my best look."

The group laughs, and Pearl notices the new guy sitting up in his chair, craning his neck to see her.

"Anyway, how I got that big is a really long story, the details of which many of you already know, so I won't bore you with those tonight. Instead, I want to talk about the three hundred and forty-nine pounds I've lost since then."

Again, the group erupts in applause. This time, it's a standing ovation, including some passionate attagirls and whistles.

"Thank you. Really. Thanks so much. I couldn't have done this without your support," Pearl says as the group sits back down. "So what I want to talk about isn't my weight, or your weight, or some number on the scale but rather the weight of the burdens we carry and our often-unhealthy coping strategies. It's taken me a long time to connect what was eating at me to what I was eating. I know most you can relate to this. The pounds I put on over the course of my life were in direct proportion to the personal problems I was too afraid to face. At five hundred and thirty-one pounds, it was plain to see that I simply didn't value myself enough, didn't love myself the way I should. But one of the traps of obesity is that if we don't prevent it, it can become a kind of self-perpetuating maze, and once we enter, it can be very difficult to find our way back out again.

"When I was five hundred and thirty-one pounds, I just couldn't visualize another version of myself. But I knew I was at that tipping point. I knew I was so big that if I got much bigger, I probably wouldn't live much longer. I was a breath away from needing one of those tripod canes or a scooter to even make it from the parking lot to my desk at work, and I just didn't want to tip the scales against my favor by gaining one more pound. Some piece of me was desperate to get out from under the weight of it all so that I would no longer be defined by the sum total of all the pain and pounds I'd collected over the years. And you know, people who know nothing about obesity or bariatric surgery think a gastric bypass or a sleeve is like a one and done or some easy way out, but it's not. We all know this is something we've committed to for life and that there's damn sure nothing easy about it, either.

It's funny how life works out, right? I mean, you're looking at a girl who's never even flown on a plane, because if I'd even tried, I would have been required to pay for two seats instead of one. Two years ago, the idea of me flying anywhere seemed about as likely as me being on the cover of the *Sports Illustrated* swimsuit edition. And yet here I am. There are three hundred and forty-nine pounds fewer of me now, and in a few more weeks, I'm going to be taking my maiden voyage on Southwest Airlines to speak about my dramatic weight loss, which happens to be a subject that, up until my surgery, didn't look like I knew much about.

"My goals for the trip are threefold. First, I want to speak with passion and conviction about the many ways in which child abuse and trauma are manifested in the form of morbid obesity. Second, I hope to be able to serve as a walking, talking example of the dramatic, positive benefits of bariatric surgery and why more employers should be covering the costs to treat the disease of obesity. And last but definitely not least, I want to pee in the bathroom on the plane."

She pauses and smiles, lets the group giggle a little while before she continues.

"So for those of you who do plan to attend, let's talk after tonight's meeting, and maybe we can try to be on the same flight."

"Okay, thank you, Pearl," Dr. Field says, resuming her post. "Next up, I want to invite our newest member of the group to come introduce himself and say a few words. Please join me in a warm welcome for Sam Spencer."

In a hearty show of enthusiasm and support, the group, including Pearl, puts their hands together while the fleece-vested new guy makes his way to the mic.

"Hi there, everybody," he says somewhat bashfully. "Like Dr. Field said, my name is Sam Spencer. I'm one of these rare people who was actually born and raised right here in Austin. I'm forty years old, and I've had a weight problem for most of my life. As a contractor, the older I got, the more I realized I had to do something drastic, or I would never be able to keep working. You see, I do fixer-uppers, mostly residential, and it is fairly physical work. If I didn't do something to turn things around, I was going to lose my business. So I finally took the plunge, and back around the first of September, I had a sleeve gastrectomy. I can't quite tell yet whether it's gonna turn out to be the best decision I ever made, but I'm already down forty-two pounds, so that counts for somethin', right? And since I'm up here, I just want to say, Pearl, I know we don't even know each other, but if I end up lookin' half as good as you in another eighteen months, you think you might give me your number?"

Chapter 47

For Pearl, the click of the metal seat belt across her lap could not sound any sweeter. By November, Henry and Ruby are buckled up next to her on the flight to Vegas. It's Pearl's first airplane ride, and in midair, they clap for her as she comes strolling out of the tiny bathroom grinning from ear to ear. She fits. For the first time, Pearl fits into everything—even the potty on the plane. She hasn't even stepped foot in a casino yet, but already she feels like she's winning.

The next day, as she takes the stage in the Mandalay Bay auditorium, Ruby and Henry are cheering for her again. Thanks to Ruby's handiwork with her cell phone camera and all those pictures she took of her incredible shrinking sister, as Pearl speaks to the crowd about the weight of it all, a photographic montage featuring the Pearl before and the Pearl after fill the jumbo screen behind her, giving everyone in the audience a visual appreciation of her dramatic metamorphosis.

"Numbers don't lie," she says to a crowd of easily seven hundred. "When I was at my heaviest, I was living my life in denial…"

From the stage, she can't see Ruby's tears of pure joy. Pearl's testimony is filled with so many never-before-heard candid and self-reflective details. Like different flowers from the same garden, in so many ways, the speech and the time-lapse images over all these months reveal her sister in full bloom. And listening to the hidden truths about their past fills Ruby with gratitude. As she crumples the spent, soggy tissue in her hand, it strikes her that their shared yet separate life stories are the same ones that led them both to this very auditorium, to this very moment, and it's all so deliciously disorienting. Up until now, Ruby always viewed Pearl as being so very different from herself. But right now, it's as if she's looking into a funhouse mirror—where the image is just slightly distorted but the essence of it is plain to see. From the gut-wrenching junk food details about Pearl's endless hunger for love and acceptance to the shame of dark secrets she was too afraid to tell, with every anecdote, Ruby sees something in Pearl she's never noticed before—her own reflection. And there's something in Pearl's story that the rest of the crowd must recognize in themselves, too, because at the end of her speech, there's a standing ovation. And Henry squeezes Ruby's hand as they rise together, cheering for Pearl.

Afterward, Sam Spencer, weighing sixteen pounds less than when she last saw him, approaches Pearl from the crowd.

"Hey, beautiful lady, remember me?" he says.

Although on the inside, she is feeling that old familiar Ramsay Reynolds giddiness, Pearl plays it cool.

"Oh my gosh, Sam, I didn't know you were coming."

"I couldn't resist the lineup," he says.

Biting her Rouge Allure–tinted lip, Pearl pauses, trying to fully process that he is indeed hitting on her.

"So I'm not supposed to have cocktails for another nine months or so, but would you care to go have something else to drink?"

"Absolutely," Pearl says.

"Great! What sounds good? Coffee? Tea?"

Reflecting on all her many options, she pauses to savor this moment and the multitude of choices she never had before.

"Anything but kombucha," she says, smiling.

"Kom-what?" Sam looks at her quizzically.

Pearl laughs and takes his arm. "It's nothing," she adds, radiating confidence. "Let's go find some good old-fashioned iced tea, and you can tell me about your latest fixer-upper."

Together, arm in arm, they make their way through the crowded convention hall and out toward the sunny, wide-open reception center, where they find a comfortable booth to share.

Epilogue

It's springtime before Birdie's ashes make their way back to Cherry Lane. Although there was never any ceremony, in their own separate ways, Pearl and Ruby are still reckoning with her loss by finding fresh ways to honor her memory. Their mom's old rose garden now includes a raised bed where, together, they're growing their own herbs and vegetables. And right down to the shiplap walls, Birdie's kitchen now looks like Chip and JoJo had their way with it.

For weeks, they've wrestled with what to do with her ashes, but during one of their now routine sister strolls along Lady Bird Lake, with the first Texas bluebonnets of the season just starting to emerge, Ruby and Pearl make up their minds.

"Don't forget the helmets," Ruby says, filling up their water bottles at the kitchen sink. "Pearl, are you ready yet?" she asks, placing them on the counter next to their parents' urns.

"I'm coming," Pearls says, tugging on her bike shorts. "Is it just me, or are these supposed to feel like you're wearing an entire box of maxi pads?"

"Believe me, after a few miles, the bike shorts will be your best friend."

Before they go, the stark incongruity of seeing what's left of their parents sitting side by side in the kitchen for the very last time makes them pause.

"Ready?" Ruby says finally.

"Let's do this," Pearl replies. "I'll take Dad. You still need to make up for some lost time with Mom," she adds, winking.

In the garage, their old childhood Schwinns have been replaced with new and improved Electra Townies, complete with baskets and bells. Carefully, they strap the urns into their wicker containers, and for the first time in twenty years, Ruby and Pearl venture out, pedaling up Cherry Lane together.

As they wind along the bike lanes through West Austin, the overcast sky begins to clear. Just like old times, Ruby leads the way, but for once in her life, Pearl has no trouble keeping up. When they reach the hike and bike trail at Lady Bird Lake, it's a sea of central Texas Saturday morning humanity. On the banks of the river, a tai chi class is in full flow, and they both giggle when they notice the *sifu* is wearing a cowboy hat. With all Austin's weirdness on full display, two women on Townies with urns in their baskets won't turn a single head. Of this much, they are certain.

For a mile or so, they cruise tandem over crushed granite, gliding by runners, walkers, purebreds, and rescues. Neither one of them knows exactly where they plan to stop, but as the trail splits off, they veer toward the left, toward a secluded spot near the water.

Together, they dismount, walking over the wild rye grass, until they are standing at the bank of the river. With their bikes safely propped under a Mexican plum tree, they stand there for a little while taking in the scenery.

"So tranquil," Pearl says.

"Daddy always said Texas was as close as he would ever get to heaven. You remember that?"

Pearl nods and smiles. Considering the tragedies from their childhood, she is grateful some fond memories remain intact.

"Seems like a nice spot to set Miss Birdie free," Pearl says.

On the surface, all the lily pads seem suspended, and Ruby and Pearl stare at them for a moment, noticing their own warbled reflections in the gently rippling current.

"Shall we?" Ruby asks, unbuckling her helmet.

Having never disposed of ashes before, neither one of them gives much thought to ceremony until they're each holding what's left of Teddy and Elizabeth "Birdie" Crenshaw. Although they don't say it out loud, the heft of what little remains of them weighs heavily on their hearts. Silently, Ruby and Pearl do what they came to do. Together, they release the powdery contents into the river, surprised how quickly the ashes dissolve—just like old wounds.

"Look," Pearl says, pointing to a pair of birds landing on a nearby floating log.

"White-winged dove," Ruby says. "A sign of peace. What a coincidence."

"I'm not sure there's any such thing," Pearl says.

With lighter loads, they pedal back toward Tarrytown— back to their old house for a new beginning. There is less than a mile to go before they get to the top of Cherry Lane, and at the light on Exposition, they pause side by side, straddling their bikes. Pearl squeezes the last drops of water out of her bottle while Ruby reties her shoes.

When the light turns green, before Ruby has a chance to look up, Pearl hops back on the saddle and takes off.

"Last one home is a rotten egg," she yells, flicking the bell on her handlebars.

Ruby is no longer the fastest girl this side of the lake, but she gives Pearl a good long head start anyway. And minutes later, when Pearl gets to the top of Cherry Lane, Ruby watches from behind as her little sister, with a big new life ahead of her, coasts all the way home.

A Letter from the Author's Sister

When we were little girls growing up in the suburbs of Dallas, Texas, my sister, Wendy, and I used to ride our bikes to school. It was only a couple of miles or so away from our house, but for me, the long slog up the steep pitch of Ridgewood Drive was always a struggle. I can't recall a time in my childhood when I wasn't "chubby" or "husky" or "big boned." I was "that" kid—the "fat girl"—the one who was always picked last at Red Rover and the one who was always dead last pedaling up our block. I remember my bike was red and orange with flames painted on the sides, and it had one of those banana seats. It looked like a bike for a faster kid, and I'm sure that's what I was trying to manifest when our parents let me pick it out at the bike shop. But despite how racy my bike looked, I was the sweaty slowpoke with glasses sliding halfway down my nose, always trying to keep up with my sister and all the rest of the neighborhood kids.

Wendy had always been more athletic than me, and no matter how far ahead she was, when she looked back and saw me struggling, she would make an instant U-turn and get behind me and say anything she could think of to try to motivate me to pedal faster. She used to say, "Tiff, come on, pump your legs harder. There is a lion chasing us!" The lions we were forever trying to outrun were, of course, make-believe, but my sister's fierce loyalty and love for me has always been real. The love between my sister and me is complicated, nuanced, and perhaps the most intimate of all relationships I've ever had. And as I reflect on this beautiful story she wrote, what I love about Pearl and Ruby is how very "real" these two flawed characters are. My sister was my earliest critic and my greatest admirer—and I am the same for her. When Wendy asked me to read the scene she wrote with Pearl and Ruby riding their bikes to school, it brought back the lions and all of the silly, simple, and sometimes stupid ways we, as sisters, have done whatever we could think of (even if it meant embellishing the truth) for the sake of saving each other.

Pearl's vulnerability is important because by showing us her darkest thoughts and her untamed yearnings, we begin to understand and have empathy for people like her. For Pearl, her scary past was always chasing her down. Like me, the heavier she became, the more isolated she became. She kept her past trauma a secret the same way she tried to hide her escalating food addiction. Pearl is me. And Pearl is like so many young, overweight people who are just trying to make it. What I love about this story is how Pearl takes control. She takes the initiative to strive for a healthier weight and begins to reckon with the way her disordered eating served as a self-destructive coping strategy. Once she starts taking these steps to love herself, her world gets bigger. Instead of all her self-limiting thoughts, Pearl finally gains a sense of self-confidence.

People come in all shapes and sizes. Pearl is important because she is a rare example in fiction of an unlikely heroine—one with a debilitating, life-threatening weight problem who saves herself. In the end, she is making peace with her past, with her sister, and with her body. And I love that she wasn't trying to attain some specific number on the scale but rather a personal level of comfort in her own skin—her "tuck-in" weight. For Pearl, her "tuck-in" weight wasn't about some societal ideal. It was about her personal freedom—freedom to do things like walk without getting winded, cross her legs, travel, buckle her seat belt, and yes—freedom to get back on the bike again.

I relate to this so much because I look at Pearl and I see me—the me I was, the me I sought to become, and the me I'm still trying to figure out. Of course, my sister, Wendy, has loved me through each of these seasons. And what I can tell you is that the flawed but fierce sister bond between Pearl and Ruby is a beautiful example of art imitating life.

Reading Group Guide

1. Why does Pearl reach her limit and decide to make changes when she reaches 531 pounds?

2. Many people in Pearl's life assume that if she *just* tried one thing or another, she would be able to drop her weight. Why are acquaintances, and even strangers, so comfortable giving her unsolicited advice? What changes besides the surgery actually help Pearl?

3. At her heaviest, Pearl feels incredibly dehumanized in public spaces. How does our diet-obsessed culture moralize weight and work against positive health outcomes for everyone?

4. Pearl's childhood trauma manifests visibly in her weight. How did Ruby's manifest?

5. One thing Pearl and Ruby agree on is that Birdie gave Skip

too many second chances. What do you think was the biggest factor that kept Birdie in that marriage? Why did she snap so completely on the night of the murder?

6. When thinking about their negative experiences as children, Ruby blames their mother and Pearl blames herself. What connection do you see between the person each sister blames and her coping mechanisms?

7. Toasting Pearl, Perry says, "We are all only one decision away from a totally different life." What was the last decision you made that really changed your life?

8. Compare Pearl's and Ruby's support systems at the beginning of the book and the end. How did developing those resources change their trajectories?

9. Renovating Birdie's house helps Pearl and Ruby bond and also brings them ownership over their lives. How does your environment shape your mindset? Thinking about where you live now, what one small renovation would make it feel more like home?

10. After their garage sale, Pearl and Ruby discuss the idea of "long overdue" changes. What conclusion do they come to? How would you apply that mindset to changes in your own life?

A Conversation
with the Author

**What was the inspiration for _The Sisters We Were?_ What was
the first thing you did when you started writing the book?**

When the initial idea for this story began to germinate, my
sister and I had just reconciled after a long period of estrange-
ment. The polarity of our personalities and coping strategies had
me reflecting on sisterhood in general. I've always been fascinated
by the elasticity of sibling relationships—how they expand and
contract over time. My own sister's dramatic weight loss was sort
of symbolic of this. So naturally, she was the first person I con-
sulted with my concept for this book. At the time, I was living
in Middleburg, Virginia. My sister was visiting from Texas, and
we were on a five-mile walk together along the bucolic banks of
Goose Creek. That power walk on Crenshaw Road was the first
time we had done something so physical and sweaty together
since high school. It felt triumphant—both of us moving at the

same pace. Once I had her blessing, I created the characters of Pearl and Ruby Crenshaw, and the story emerged from there.

Though much less visible to the world, Ruby's anger is as toxic as Pearl's obesity. How did you approach healing each sister as you wrote? Was one more difficult than the other?

Healing is very much a process, and both sisters come at this in their own unique way. I liked the idea of using Pearl's very visible health crisis as a catalyst for the sisters to begin to heal the wounds we can't see. Through humility, empathy, and, ultimately, honesty, we get to see their sister bond restored and renewed. I wanted the protagonist to be Pearl because the world needs more big, unassuming heroines. Since my own personality is a bit more like Ruby's, it was somewhat harder for me to show her development because it forced me to look at myself in ways I would rather not.

At the outset of the book, Pearl dreads asking Ruby for help because she's received such unhelpful advice from her sister in the past. What change allowed Ruby to see the help that Pearl actually needed and to rebuild her compassion for her sister?

Going home to the house on Cherry Lane for reasons she would rather not share with Pearl makes Ruby vulnerable. It's this vulnerability, both of them being unsure and afraid, that forces them to, once again, cling to each other. Initially, the level of disrepair in the house serves as a metaphor for Pearl's own dysfunction—but all of that is just symptomatic of what's really going on. Not until hidden truths are revealed is their sisterly intimacy reestablished. Ruby's compassion for Pearl grows as she begins to face the reality that their shared childhood secrets have taken such a physical toll on Pearl's health.

Pearl and Henry both correlate childhood trauma with adult obesity. What resources do you think could reduce that correlation?

Secrets are heavy. As victims of childhood sexual abuse, my sister and I understand the insidious nature of shame and how it can manifest in our lives and in our bodies. This story explores that topic and how, in the absence of their biological father and mother, Pearl and Ruby Crenshaw were left to cope as best they could. As a writer, I'm very intrigued by the wide variance that exists between how people respond to adversity. For Pearl, her disordered eating spiraled out of control, and her weight increasingly insulated her from facing her deepest wounds. There are several themes in this story, but certainly chief among them is the notion that truth really can set us free. In order for Pearl to let go of the stuff that weighed her down, she had to reckon with it.

Pearl's *decision* to have bariatric surgery (not the surgery itself) triggers the snowball of positive changes we see throughout the book. Can you talk about why it was so important for those changes to be mindset-driven?

For Pearl, it took waiting until the stakes were extremely high, almost do or die, before she made up her mind to have such life-altering surgery. Because her weight had become such a disability, the very prospect of bariatric surgery forces Pearl to weigh her sense of worth. The grueling process she goes through to get to the surgery and beyond are glimpses of a young woman declaring her value. She decides she is, in fact, worth the effort. With each courageous step into the unknown, this is affirmed for her, and we see her life change well beyond the physical transformation. Pearl's decision to have bariatric surgery was never about making a change so that others might love her more, but rather it's about Pearl finally learning to love herself.

The Austin setting really comes alive as Ruby and Pearl dare each other to try new things. What drew you to set the story there?

As a native Texan and someone who grew up in Austin and Dallas, it was a natural canvas for me. Write what we know, right?

Who are your biggest inspirations as a writer?

I can't possibly name them all, but for a long time, my favorite novel has been Zora Neale Hurston's *Their Eyes Were Watching God*—so short but so mighty. Beyond that, I savor the work of writers like Ann Patchett, Maria Semple, Barbara Kingsolver, Kiese Laymon, Wally Lamb, Dave Eggers, Junot Díaz, John Green, Kate Elizabeth Russell, and Susan Choi.

Acknowledgments

At the time this novel is being published, the Centers for Disease Control estimates that nearly 43 percent of Americans are considered obese. With such prevalence, this means I'm certainly not the only one who loves or who has loved someone struggling with this king of life-threatening disease. In fact, it means that it's likely nearly half of the people reading this book may very well be struggling with this issue themselves. And yet, in our culture there remains an anti-fat bias that is, in many ways, more destructive than fat itself. Long before I signed a publishing agreement with Sourcebooks, I had submitted a version of this manuscript to several literary agents seeking representation. One agent read my story and wrote back saying she could not possibly sell my story because she believed "readers would find a 531-pound protagonist to be distasteful." When I read those words, they sent me right back to fifth grade, when I was consoling my sobbing little sister after yet another mean-mouthed kid on the bus called her "fatty four-eyes." After my fiercely loyal literary agent, Marly Rusoff, sold my book to Sourcebooks, I vowed that this story, once published, would be dedicated to anyone who has ever been ridiculed, ostracized, or persecuted because of their size or the way they look.

We all have different coping strategies, different body types, and different backgrounds—and I thank God for that, because otherwise writers would have no material.

A special thanks goes out to the many cherished people who have helped me share *The Sisters We Were* with each of you. My editors, Shana Drehs and Emily Heckman, pushed me to take seemingly endless critical looks at my own work and keep revising. I'm blessed to have Amy, Andrea, Bridget, Cindy, Courtney, Diana, Eleanor, Laura, Lisa, Michelle, Terri, Toni, and Wendy "Red" as some of my many dedicated beta readers and trusted confidants whose encouragement and wisdom informed my writing.

Most importantly, I want to thank my family—Tiffany, Cory, LeighAnn, Karen, Faith, Bill, Bob, and Robert. My son, Truman, and my daughter, Harper, grew up witnessing the long hours I spent crafting stories, and they remain my greatest labors of love. My parents, Ted and Sondra Willis, left this world too soon to see this published, but I take great comfort knowing they never doubted it would be. Through it all, my loving husband, Nevan Baldwin, paved the way for me to focus on my passions. I'm forever grateful for his keen ear and soft spot for storytelling.

This tale of two sisters is filled with equal parts tragedy and triumph, and I hope it inspires you to let go of whatever excess baggage you've been carrying around—emotional or physical. It's about the sometimes-long slog we take getting comfortable in our own skin and tolerance for the brokenness we so easily see in others but often refuse to see in ourselves.

About the Author

© Harper Leigh

The Sisters We Were is Wendy Willis Baldwin's debut novel. Together, she and her sister host the *Life After Fat Pants* podcast. A native of Texas, Baldwin now lives on a farm in New Hampshire with her husband, her dogs, and thousands of honeybees.